CHALLENGER
DEEP

CHALLENGER
DEEP

NEAL SHUSTERMAN

WALKER
BOOKS

First published in Great Britain 2020 by Walker Books Ltd
87 Vauxhall Walk, London SE11 5HJ

Published by arrangement with HarperCollins Children's Books,
a division of HarperCollins Publishers

2 4 6 8 10 9 7 5 3 1

Text © 2015 Neal Shusterman
Interior illustrations © 2015 Brendan Shusterman
Cover design by Jon Gray

This book has been typeset in Garamond and Piexe Frito

Printed and bound by CPI Group (UK) Ltd, Croydon CR0 4YY

British Library Cataloguing in Publication Data:
a catalogue record for this book is available from the British Library

ISBN 978-1-4063-9611-9

www.walker.co.uk

For Dr. Robert Woods

There are two things you know. One: You were there. Two: You couldn't have been there.

Holding these two incompatible truths together takes skill at juggling. Of course juggling requires a third ball to keep the rhythm smooth. That third ball is time – which bounces much more wildly than any of us would like to believe.

The time is 5 a.m. You know this, because there's a battery-powered clock on your bedroom wall that ticks so loudly you sometimes have to smother it with a pillow. And yet, while it's five in the morning here, it's also five in the evening somewhere in China – proving that incompatible truths make perfect sense when seen with global perspective. You've learned, however, that sending your thoughts to China is not always a good thing.

Your sister sleeps in the next room, and in the room beyond that, your parents. Your dad is snoring. Soon your mom will nudge him enough to make him roll over and the snoring will cease, maybe until dawn. All of this is normal, and there's great comfort in that.

Across the street a neighbor's sprinklers come on, hissing loud enough to drown out the ticking of the clock. You can smell the sprinkler mist through the open window – mildly chlorinated, heavily fluoridated. Isn't it nice to know that the neighborhood lawns will have healthy teeth?

The hiss of the sprinklers is not the sound of snakes.

And the painted dolphins on your sister's wall cannot plot deadly schemes.

And a scarecrow's eyes do not see.

Even so, there are nights where you can't sleep, because these things you juggle take all of your concentration. You fear that one ball might drop, and then what? You don't dare imagine beyond that moment. Because waiting in that moment is the Captain. He's patient. And he waits. Always.

Even before there was a ship, there was the Captain.

This journey began with him, you suspect it will end with him, and everything between is the powdery meal of windmills that might be giants grinding bones to make their bread.

Tread lightly, or you'll wake them.

2 Forever Down There

"There's no telling how far down it goes," the captain says, the left side of his mustache twitching like the tail of a rat. "Fall into that unknowable abyss, and you'll be counting the days before you reach bottom."

"But the trench has been measured," I dare to point out. "People have been down there before. I happen to know that it's 6.8 miles deep."

"Know?" he mocks. "How can a shivering, malnourished pup such as you know anything beyond the wetness of his own nose?" Then he laughs at his own assessment of me. The captain is full of weatherworn wrinkles from a lifetime at sea – although his dark, tangled beard hides many of them. When he laughs, the wrinkles stretch tight, and you can see the muscles and sinews of his neck. "Aye, it be true that those who have ventured the waters of the trench speak of having seen the bottom, but they lie. They lie like a rug, and get beat twice as often – but just so it scares the dust out of 'em."

I've stopped trying to decipher the things the captain says, but they still weigh on me. As if maybe I'm missing something. Something important and deceptively obvious that I'll only understand when it's too late to matter.

"It's forever down there," the captain says. "Let no one tell you any different."

3 Better for This

I have this dream. I am lying on a table in an overlit kitchen where all the appliances are sparkling white. Not so much new as pretending to be new. Plastic with chrome accents, but mostly plastic.

I cannot move. Or I don't want to move. Or I'm afraid to move. Each time I have the dream, it's a little bit different. There are people around me, only they aren't people, they're monsters in disguise. They have gone into my mind and have ripped images from it, turning the images into masks that look like people I love – but I know it's just a lie.

They laugh and speak of things that mean nothing to me, and I am frozen there among all the false faces, at the very center of attention. They admire me, but only in the way you admire something you know will soon be gone.

"I think you took it out too soon," says a monster wearing my mother's face. "It hasn't been in long enough."

"Only one way to find out," says the monster disguised as my father. I sense laughter all around — not from their mouths, because the mouths of their masks don't move. The laughter is in their thoughts, which they project at me like poison-tipped darts shot from their cutout eyes.

"You'll be better for this," says one of the other monsters. Then their stomachs rumble as loud as a crumbling mountain as they reach toward me and tear their main course to bits with their claws.

4 How They Get You

I can't remember when this journey began. It's like I've always been here, except that I couldn't have been, because there was a before, just last week or last month or last year. I'm pretty certain that I'm still fifteen, though. Even if I've been on board this wooden relic of a ship for years, I'm still fifteen. Time is different here. It doesn't move forward; it sort of moves sideways, like a crab.

I don't know many of the other crewmen. Or maybe I just

don't remember them from one moment to the next, because they all have a nameless quality about them. There are the older ones, who seem to have made their lives at sea. These are the ship's officers, if you can call them that. They are Halloween pirates, like the captain, with fake blackened teeth, trick-or-treating on hell's doorstep. I'd laugh at them if I didn't believe with all my heart that they'd gouge my eyes out with their plastic hooks.

Then there are the younger ones like me: kids whose crimes cast them out of warm homes, or cold homes, or no homes, by a parental conspiracy that sees all with unblinking Big-Brother eyes.

My fellow crewmates, both boys and girls, go about their busywork and don't speak to me other than to say things like, "You're in my way," or "Keep your hands off my stuff." As if any of us has stuff worth guarding. Sometimes I try to help them with whatever they're doing, but they turn away, or push me away, resentful that I've even offered.

I keep imagining I see my little sister on board, even though I know she's not. Aren't I supposed to be helping her with math? In my mind I see her waiting for me and waiting for me, but I don't know where she is. All I know is that I never show up. How could I do that to her?

Everyone on board is under constant scrutiny by the captain, who is somehow familiar, and somehow not. He seems to know everything about me, although I know nothing about him.

"It's my business to have my fingers curled around the heart of *your* business," he told me.

The captain has an eye patch and a parrot. The parrot has an eye patch and a security badge around his neck.

"I shouldn't be here," I appeal to the captain, wondering if I've told him this before. "I have midterms and papers due and dirty clothes I never picked up from my bedroom floor, and I have friends, lots of friends."

The captain's jaw is fixed and he offers no response, but the parrot says, "You'll have friends, lots of friends here too, here too!"

Then one of the other kids whispers in my ear, "Don't tell the parrot anything. That's how they get you."

5 I Am the Compass

The things I feel cannot be put into words, or if they can, the words are in no language anyone can understand. My emotions are talking in tongues. Joy spins into anger spins into fear then into amused irony, like leaping from a plane, arms wide, knowing beyond a shadow of a doubt that you can fly, then discovering you can't, and not only don't you have a parachute, but you don't have any clothes on, and the people below all have binoculars and are laughing as you plummet to a highly embarrassing doom.

The navigator tells me not to worry about it. He points to the parchment pad on which I often draw to pass the time. "Fix your feelings in line and color," he tells me. "Color, collar, holler, dollar – true riches lie in the way your drawings grab me, scream at me, force me to see. My maps show us the path, but your visions show us the *way*. You are the compass, Caden Bosch. You are the compass!"

"If I'm a compass, then I'm a pretty useless one," I tell him. "I can't find north."

"Of course you can," he says. "It's just that in these waters, north is constantly chasing its own tail."

It makes me think of a friend I once had, who thought that north was whatever direction he was facing. Now I think that maybe he was right.

The navigator requested me as a roommate when my old roommate, who I barely even remember, disappeared without explanation. We share a cabin that's too small for one, much less two. "You are the most decent among the indecents here," he tells me. "Your heart hasn't taken on the chill of the sea. Plus, you have talent. Talent, talons, tally, envy – your talent will turn the ship green with envy – mark my words!"

He's a kid who's been on many voyages before. And he's farsighted. That is to say, when he looks at you he's not seeing you, but instead sees something behind you in a dimension several times removed from our own. Mostly he doesn't look at people. He's too busy creating navigational charts. At least that's what he calls them. They're full of numbers and words and arrows and lines that connect the dots of stars into constellations I've never seen before.

"The heavens are different out here," he says. "You have to

see fresh patterns in the stars. Patterns, Saturns, Saturday, Sunday, sundial. It's all about measuring the passing day. Do you get it?"

"No."

"Shore to boat, boat to goat. That's the answer, I'm saying. The goat. It eats everything, digesting the world, making it a part of its own DNA, and spewing it out, claiming its territory. Territory, heredity, heresy, hearsay – hear what I say. The sign of the goat holds the answer to our destination. It all has a purpose. Seek the goat."

The navigator is brilliant. So brilliant that my head hurts just being in his presence.

"Why am I here?" I ask him. "If everything has a purpose, what is my purpose on this ship?"

He goes back to his charts, writing words and adding fresh arrows on top of what is already there, layering his thoughts so thick, only he can decipher them. "Purpose, porpoise, dolphin, doorframe, doorway. You are the doorway to the salvation of the world."

"Me? Are you sure?"

"Just as sure as we're on this train."

6 So Disruptive

Doorway, doorframe, dolphins dancing on the walls of my sister's room as I stand in her doorway. There are seven dolphins. I know because I painted them for her, each representing one of

Kurosawa's *Seven Samurai*, since I wanted her to still appreciate them when she's older.

The dolphins glare at me tonight, and although a lack of opposable thumbs makes swordplay unlikely, I find them far more threatening than usual.

My father is tucking Mackenzie into bed. It's late for her, but not for me. I've just turned fifteen; she's about to turn eleven. It will be hours until I sleep. *If* I sleep. I may not. Not tonight.

My mother is on the phone with Grandma downstairs. I hear her talking about weather and termites. Our house is being chewed to bits. "... but tenting is so disruptive," I hear my mom say. "There must be a better way."

Dad kisses Mackenzie good night, then turns and sees me standing there, not quite in, but not quite out of the room.

"What is it, Caden?"

"Nothing, it's just ... never mind."

He stands up and my sister rolls away to face her wall of dolphins, making it clear she is ready for dreamland. "If something's wrong, you can tell me," Dad says. "You know that, don't you?"

I speak quietly so that Mackenzie can't hear. "Well, it's just that ... there's this kid at school."

"Yes?"

"Of course I can't be sure..."

"Yes?"

"Well ... I think he wants to kill me."

7 Charitable Abyss

There's this donation bucket at the mall. A big yellow funnel collecting for some children's charity that's really unpleasant to think about. "Limbless Children of Foreign Wars," or something like that. You're supposed to put your coin in a slot and let it go. It spins round and round the big yellow funnel for like a minute, making a rhythmic whirring sound that gets tighter and tighter, more intense, more desperate as it spirals closer to the hole. It keeps spinning faster – all that kinetic energy forced down the neck of the funnel until it's blaring like an alarm – then it falls silent as it drops into the black abyss of the funnel.

I'm that coin on its way down, screaming in the neck of the funnel, with nothing but my own kinetic energy and centrifugal force keeping me from dropping into darkness.

8 Reality Check

"What do you mean he wants to kill you?" My dad steps out into the upstairs hallway and closes the door to my sister's room. Dim light comes at a cautious angle from the bathroom farther down the hall. "Caden, this is serious. If there's a boy at school threatening you, you have to tell me what's going on."

He stands there waiting, and I wish I hadn't opened my mouth. Mom is still on the phone downstairs talking to Grandma, and I start to wonder if it really is Grandma, or if Mom is just pretending – talking to someone else, maybe about me, and maybe using code words. But why would she do that? That's nuts. No, she's just talking to Grandma. About termites.

"Have you reported this kid to your teachers?"

"No."

"What has he done? Has he openly threatened you?"

"No."

Dad takes a deep breath. "Okay, then if he hasn't actually come out and threatened you, maybe it's not as bad as you think. Does this kid bring some sort of weapon to school?"

"No. Well, maybe. Yeah – yeah, I think he maybe has a knife."

"You've seen it?"

"No, I just know. He's the type of kid who'd have a knife, y'know?"

Dad takes another deep breath and scratches his thinning hair. "Tell me exactly what this boy has said to you. Try to remember everything."

I dig down and try to find the words to explain, but I can't. "It's not what he said, it's what he *hasn't* said."

My dad's an accountant: very left-brained, very linear, so it doesn't surprise me when he says, "I don't follow."

I turn and fiddle with a family picture on the wall, making it crooked. That bothers me, so I quickly make it straight again. "Never mind," I say. "It's not important." I try to escape down the stairs, because I really want to hear the conversation Mom is having, but Dad gently grabs my arm. It's enough to keep me from leaving.

"Just wait," he says. "Let me get this straight. This kid that's got you all worried – he's in a class with you, and there's something about his behavior that you find threatening."

"Actually, I don't have any classes with him."

"So how do you know him?"

"I don't. But I pass him in the hallway sometimes."

My dad looks down, doing some mental calculations, then looks back up at me again. "Caden ... if you don't know him, and he's never threatened you, and all he's ever done is pass you in the hallway, what makes you think he wants to hurt you? He probably doesn't even know you."

"Yeah, you're right, I'm just stressed."

"You're probably overreacting."

"Right, overreacting." Now that I've said it out loud, I can see how silly I've been sounding. I mean, this kid doesn't even know I exist. I don't even know his name.

"High school can be unsettling," Dad says. "A lot of stuff can make you anxious. I'm sorry you've been carrying around something like that. What a thing to be thinking about! But sometimes everyone needs a reality check, right?"

"Right."

"So, you feel better now?"

"Yeah, I feel better. Thanks."

But he keeps studying me as I walk away, like maybe he knows I'm lying. My parents have been noticing how anxious I've been lately. My dad thinks I should take up a sport to release my nervous energy. My mom thinks I should do yoga.

The sea stretches in all directions. Before us, behind us, to starboard, to port, and down, down, down. Our ship is a galleon, weathered from a million voyages going back to ages even darker than this.

"She's the finest vessel of her kind," the captain once told me. "Put your faith in her and she won't steer you wrong."

Which is good, because there's never anyone at the tiller.

"Does she have a name?" I once asked the captain.

"To name her is to sink her," he told me. "That which we name takes greater weight than the sea it displaces. Ask any shipwreck."

Above the arch of the main hatch is a sign burned in wood that reads *You are not the first and you will not be the last*, and I marvel at how it makes me feel both insignificant and singled out at the same time.

"Does it speak to you?" the parrot asks, perched above the hatch, watching me, always watching me.

"Not really," I tell him.

"Well, if it does," instructs the parrot, "write down everything it says."

I visit the White Plastic Kitchen almost every night. The particulars change each time, just enough that I can't predict the outcome of the dream. If it was the same, at least I would know what to expect – and if I knew, I'd be able to brace myself for the worst of it.

Tonight I'm hiding. Scarce few places to hide in the kitchen. I'm wedged in a state-of-the-art refrigerator. I shiver, and I think about the captain. How he called me a shivering pup. Someone opens the door; a mask I don't remember. She shakes her head.

"Poor thing, you must be cold." She pours some coffee from a full carafe, but instead of offering me some, she reaches right through my navel and retrieves the milk from somewhere behind me in the refrigerator.

11 Nothing Awful Is without Its Beautiful Side

Beneath the main deck are the crew's quarters. The crew deck is much larger than the ship appears on the outside. Impossibly so. There's a long hallway that goes on and on and never seems to end.

Between the slats of wood that make up the hull and decks of the ship is foul-smelling black pitch to keep the water out. Nowhere is that smell more pungent than down below. It's sharp and organic, as if whatever life-forms that were distilled by time into the tar haven't entirely finished decomposing. It smells of concentrated sweat and body odor, and the stuff that collects beneath your toenails.

"The smell of life," the captain said proudly when I once asked him about the stench. "Life in transformation, perhaps, but life, nonetheless. It's like the briny reek of a tide pool, boy — pungent and putrid but at the same time refreshing. A wave will pound that shore, sending spray up your nostrils, and do you curse it? No! For it reminds you how much you love the sea. That summery smell of beach that brings you to the most serene place in your soul is nothing more than a gentle wafting of marine putrefaction." Then he had taken a deep satisfying breath of it to prove his point. "Indeed, nothing awful is without its beautiful side."

12 Spree

When my friends and I were younger and we were at the mall bored out of our minds, we used to play this game. We called it Psycho Shopping Spree. We would single out someone, or a couple, or sometimes a whole family – although for the purposes of the game, it was always better to single out a person shopping alone. We would then make up a story about the chosen shopper's secret purpose. Usually that purpose involved an ax and/or chain saw, and a basement and/or attic. One time we settled on this little old woman hobbling through the mall with such pinch-faced purpose, we decided she was the perfect serial killer of the day. The story was, she would buy all this stuff at the mall – far too much to carry, and she would have it delivered. Then she would capture the delivery man, and kill him with the very object he delivered. She had a whole collection of newly purchased murder weapons and dead UPS men in her basement and/or attic.

So we followed her for like twenty minutes, thinking this was hilarious … until she went into a cutlery store, and we watched her purchase a nice new butcher knife. Then it became even more hilarious.

When she left the store, though, I made eye contact with her – mainly because I dared myself to. I know it was entirely in my imagination, but there was this cruel and malevolent look in her eyes that I will never forget.

Lately I've been seeing her eyes everywhere.

I stand in the middle of the living room, curling my toes into our plush but soullessly beige carpet.

"What are you doing?" Mackenzie asks me as she comes home from school, hurling her backpack onto the sofa. "Why are you just standing there?"

"I'm listening," I tell her.

"Listening to what?"

"Listening for the termites."

"You can hear termites?" The thought horrifies her.

"Maybe."

She fiddles nervously with the big blue buttons on her yellow fleece coat, as if she can button out the termites like the cold. Then she tentatively puts her ear to the wall, I suppose figuring it would be easier to hear them that way than by standing in the middle of a silent room. She listens for a few moments, then says, a little uneasily, "I don't hear anything."

"Don't worry," I tell her in my most comforting voice, "termites are just termites." And although there couldn't be a more neutral statement, it defuses any insectious worries I might have given her. Satisfied, she goes into the kitchen for a snack.

I don't move. I can't hear the termites but I can feel them. The more I think about them, the more I feel, and it's distracting. I'm very distracted today. Not by the things I can see, but the things that I can't. The things in the walls, and the many things beneath my feet, which I have always had a weird fascination for. That fascination has infested me today like the wood-eating bugs that slowly lay waste to our house.

I tell myself that this is a good distraction, because it keeps me from spiraling into thoughts of nasty things that may or may not be happening at school. It's a helpful distraction, so for a while I indulge it.

I close my eyes and feel, pushing my thoughts through the soles of my feet.

My feet are on safe, solid ground, but that's just an illusion. We own our house, right? But not really, because the bank holds the mortgage. So what do we own? The land? Wrong again, because although we have a deed to the land our house sits on, we don't own the mineral rights. And what are minerals? Everything that's in the ground. Basically, if it's valuable, or might be valuable someday, we don't own it. We own it only if it's worthless.

So what is beneath my feet, really, beyond the lie that it belongs to us? When I concentrate, I can feel what's down there. Beneath the carpet is a concrete slab that rests on earth that was compacted twenty years ago by heavy machinery. Beneath that is lost life that no one will ever find. There could be remnants of civilizations destroyed by wars or by beasts or by immune systems that failed a sudden bacterial pop quiz. I feel the bones and shells of prehistoric creatures. Then I send my thoughts even deeper to the bedrock, where pockets of gas bubble and brew from earth's intestinal distress as it tries to digest its long and often sad history of life. The place where all God's creatures are eventually distilled through the rock into black gunk that we then suck out of the ground and burn in our cars, turning those once living things into greenhouse gases, which I guess is better than spending eternity as sludge.

Deeper still, I can feel the cold of the earth replaced by heat until there are caverns of red-hot, then white-hot magma, swirling under unthinkable pressure. The outer core, then the inner core, to the very center of gravity, and then gravity reverses. The heat and pressure begin to decrease. Molten rock turns solid again. I push through the granite, the sludge, the bones, the dirt, the worms, and the termites, until I'm bursting through into some rice paddy in China, proving that there's no such thing as down, because eventually down is up.

I open my eyes, almost surprised to find myself in my living room, and it occurs to me that there is a perfect plumb line from my home to somewhere in China, and I wonder if pushing my thoughts down that line the way I just did could be a dangerous thing. Could my thoughts be magnified in the heat and pressure of the earth and come out the other side as an earthquake?

And I know it's just a tweaky stray thought, yet the next morning, and the morning after that, and every morning from that moment forward, I check the news in secret terror to see if there was an earthquake in China.

Although I have been told by various frightened crewmen not to venture into the unknown corners of the ship, I can't help myself. Something compels me to seek out things that are better left alone. And how can one be on a great galleon and not check it out?

Rather than heading on deck for roll call one morning, I get up early enough to explore. I begin to make my way down the long, dimly lit corridor of the crew deck. I take my parchment pad, and draw quick impressions.

"Excuse me," I say to a crew member I haven't seen before, lurking in the shadows of her cabin. She has wide eyes, runny mascara, and wears a pearl choker that looks like it might actually be choking her. "Where does this hallway go?"

She looks at me with suspicion. "It doesn't go anywhere, it stays right here." Then she ducks back in and slams her door. I hold her image in my mind, and on my pad I sketch her face as it looked when she retreated into shadows.

I continue to walk, keeping track of my distance down the unending hallway by counting the ladders. One, two, three. I get to the tenth ladder, but the corridor just continues ahead of me. Finally I give up and climb ladder ten, only to find myself coming out onto the deck through the midship hatch, and I realize that every one of those ladders, regardless of where it is on the crew deck, exits up through that same hatch. I've walked that corridor for twenty minutes, yet have gotten nowhere.

Sitting on the railing above me is the parrot, as if he's been waiting there just to mock me.

"You can't get there from here," he says. "Don't you know? Don't you know?"

15 No Passage of Space

My job on the ship is as a "stabilizer." I can't recall when I was assigned this task, but I do remember the captain explaining it to me.

"You shall sense as the ship heels side to side on the sea, and position yourself opposite of the roll, starboard to port, port to starboard," the captain had said.

In other words, just like a vast majority of the crewmen, my job is to run side to side across the deck and back again to counteract the rolling motion of the sea. It's completely pointless.

"How could our weight possibly make a difference on a ship this size?" I once asked him.

He glared at me with his bloodshot eye. "Would you prefer to be ballast then?"

That had shut me up. I'd seen the "ballast." Sailors crammed into the cargo hold like sardines, in order to lower the ship's center of gravity. If there's no task for you on this ship, you become ballast. I should have known better than to complain.

"As we near our destination," the captain once told me, "I will be selecting a special team for our great mission. Do your job with hearty sweat and vigor, and you may earn your nearly worthless hide a place on that team."

Although I'm not sure I want that, it may be better than shuffling pointlessly around the deck. I had once asked the captain how far we were from the Marianas Trench, because each day the sea is exactly the same. We seem no closer, and no farther from anything.

"'Tis the nature of a liquid horizon to feel no passage of space," the captain said. "But we will know as we near the trench, because there will be signs and dark portents."

I won't dare ask the captain what those dark portents might be.

16 Swabby

When the sea is calm, and I don't have to run from side to side, I sometimes hang out on deck with Carlyle. Carlyle is the ship's swabby — a guy with bright red hair in a short peach fuzz, and a smile friendlier than anyone else's on the ship. He's not a kid, he's older, like the ship's officers, but he's not really one of them. He seems to make his own hours and his own rules, with little interference from the captain, and is the only one on the ship who makes any sense.

"I'm a swabby by choice," he told me once. "I do it because it's needed. And because you're all such slobs."

Today I catch sight of rats scurrying away from the water of his mop, disappearing into dark corners of the deck.

"Blasted things," Carlyle says, dipping his mop into a bucket of cloudy water and washing the deck. "We'll never get rid of them."

"There are always rats on old ships," I tell him.

He raises an eyebrow. "Rats? Is that what you think they are?" Although he doesn't offer me an alternate theory. The truth is, they scuttle so quickly, and hide so deep in shadows, I can't be sure what they are. It makes me nervous, so I change the subject.

"Tell me something about the captain I don't know."

"He's your captain. Anything worth knowing you already must know."

But even the way he says it, I can tell he is an insider in a way that few others are. I figure if I'm going to get any answers, though, I need to be specific with my questions.

"Tell me how he lost his eye."

Carlyle sighs, looks around to make sure we're unobserved, and begins to whisper.

"It is my understanding that the parrot lost his eye before the captain. The way I've heard it told, the parrot sold his eye to a witch to make a magic potion that would turn him into an eagle. But the witch double-crossed him, drank it herself, and flew away. The parrot, who didn't want to be the only one with an eye patch, clawed out the captain's eye as well."

"That's not true," I say with a grin.

Carlyle keeps his expression solemn as he splashes soapy water on the deck. "It's as true as it needs to be." The tar between the planks seems to retreat from his deluge.

The navigator says a view from the crow's nest will bring me "comfort, clarity, charity, chastity."

If it's a multiple choice test, I choose both "A" and "B," although considering the crew, I may just blacken in choice "D" with my number two pencil.

The crow's nest is a small circular tub, high up on the mainmast. It's only large enough to hold one, maybe two crewmen on lookout. I conclude it would be a good place to be alone with my thoughts, but I should already know that my thoughts are never alone.

It's early evening as I climb the frayed ratlines that drape the ship like shrouds. The last hint of dusk slowly vanishes from the horizon, and in the sun's absence, the strange stars are coaxed to shine.

The rope lattice of the ratlines narrows as I near the crow's nest, making the climb feel increasingly treacherous. Finally I pull myself over into the small wooden tub that hugs the mast – only to find it's not small at all. Like the crew's quarterdeck, it may look small from the outside, but once inside, the circular space appears to be a hundred feet in diameter. There are members of the crew reclining in velvet chairs, sipping neon-bright martinis with faraway eyes, and listening to a live band that plays smooth jazz.

"Party of one? Right this way," says a hostess, and she leads me to my own velvet chair, which looks out at moonlight shimmering on water.

"Are you a jumper?" asks a pale man sitting in the next chair, drinking something blue and possibly radioactive. "Or are you just here to watch?"

"I'm here to clear my head."

"Have one of these," he says, pointing to his radioactive drink. "Until you find your own cocktail you can share mine. Everyone here must find their cocktail or you'll be whipped soundly and sent off to bed. That's how all nursery rhymes end here. Even the ones that don't rhyme."

I look around at the dozen or so people enjoying themselves in vaguely psychedelic stupors. "I don't understand how this can all fit in the crow's nest."

"Elasticity is a fundamental principle of perception," my companion says. "But as rubber bands break when left too long in the sun, I suspect that the crow's nest will, in time, realize we've abused its fine elastic nature and it will break, too, shrinking back down to its appropriate size. At that time, anyone caught inside will be crushed; their blood, bones, and various insides squeezed through the knotholes of the wood like so much Play-Doh." Then he raises his glass. "I'd pay to see that!"

A few yards away, a crewman in a blue jumpsuit climbs to the lip of the crow's nest, spreads his arms wide, and leaps toward certain death. I stand, and look over the edge, but he's vanished. All those gathered applaud politely, and the band begins to play "Orange-Colored Sky," although the twilight sky is bruise-purple.

31

"Why is everyone just sitting here?" I shout. "Didn't you all see what just happened?"

My drinking companion shrugs. "Jumpers do what jumpers do. It's our job to applaud their pluck and celebrate their lives." He casually glances over the side. "It's so far down you never see them splat, though." Then he gulps the rest of his drink. "I'd pay to see that!"

18 Mystery Ashtray

There is no one at school who wishes me harm.

I tell myself this each morning after checking the news for Chinese earthquakes. I tell myself as I hurry between classes. I tell myself on the occasions that I pass the kid who wants to kill me, and yet doesn't seem to know I exist.

"You're overreacting," my father had said. Which might be true – but that implies there was something to actually react to. In better moments I want to beat the crap out of myself for being so stupid as to think the kid had it in for me. So what does it say about me if beating the crap out of myself is one of my better moments?

"You need to be more centered," my mother would say. She's all into meditation and raw vegan food, I suppose as a way to cope with how much she hates cleaning meat out of people's teeth for a living.

Centering, however, is easier said than done. This I learned from a ceramics class I once took. The teacher made throwing a pot look easy, but the thing is, it takes lots of precision and skill. You slam the ball of clay down in the absolute center of the pottery wheel, and with steady hands you push your thumb into the middle of it, spreading it wider a fraction of an inch at a time. But every single time I tried to do it, I only got so far before my pot warped out of balance, and every attempt to fix it just made it worse, until the lip shredded, the sides collapsed, and I was left with what the teacher called "a mystery ashtray," which got hurled back into the clay bucket.

So what happens when your universe begins to get off balance, and you don't have any experience with bringing it back to center? All you can do is fight a losing battle, waiting for those walls to collapse, and your life to become one huge mystery ashtray.

19 Deconstructing Xargon

My friends Max and Shelby and I get together after school some Fridays. We believe we're designing a computer RPG game, but we've been doing it for two years and it never seems any closer to completion. Mainly because as each of us gets better and wiser in our particular areas of expertise, we have to toss everything and start over, deeming the old material to be childish and unprofessional.

Max is the driving force. He's the one who will stay at my

house long past the time my parents have patience for him because, even though he's the computer whiz of our trio, his own computer is a piece of garbage that crashes if you whisper the word *graphics* within a three-foot radius.

Shelby is our concept queen. "I think I've figured out the story problems," she says this particular afternoon. Like she says just about every time we're working on this. "I think I need to limit the characters' bio-integrated weaponry. Otherwise every battle is a bloodbath, and that's boring."

"Who says bloodbaths are boring?" Max asks. "I like bloodbaths."

Shelby looks to me for support, but she's looking in the wrong place.

"Actually, I like them, too," I tell her. "I think it's a guy thing."

She glares at me and throws me a few pages of new character descriptions.

"Just draw up the characters and give them enough armor so not every blow is a mortal one. Especially Xargon. I've got big plans for him."

I flip open my sketch pad. "Didn't we promise to stop doing this if we ever started to sound like nerds? I think today's conversation is the official marker of that moment."

"Oh please! That moment came last year," Shelby points out. "If you're so immature that you're afraid of being labeled by morons, then check out and we'll find another artist."

I've always liked the way Shelby tells a person exactly what she thinks. Not that there was or would ever be anything romantic between us. I think that ship sank in dry dock for both of us. We like each other too much to become awkwardly involved. Besides, our three-way friendship allows us benefits. Like the benefit of finding out from Shelby stuff about the girls Max and I like, and being able to tell Shelby whatever she needs to know about any guy she likes. It all works too well to ever mess with.

"Listen," Shelby says, "we don't live this stuff, it's just a hobby. We indulge a few days a month. I, for one, do not feel socially stifled by this."

"Yeah," says Max. "That's because you've got plenty of other things to stifle you."

She hits him hard enough to send the wireless mouse flying from his hand across the room.

"Hey," I yell. "If that breaks, my parents will make me pay for it. They're big on personal responsibility."

Shelby looks at me coolly, almost glaring. "I don't see you drawing."

"Maybe I'm waiting for inspiration to occur." But inspired or not, I take a deep breath, and read her character descriptions. Then look at the blank page of my sketch pad.

It was a problem with empty space that led me to art. I see an empty box, and I have to fill it. I see a blank page, and I can't leave it like that. Blank pages scream at me to be filled with crap from my brain.

It started with doodles. Then the doodles grew into sketches, the sketches grew into pieces, and the pieces are now "works." Or "oeuvres," if you're really pretentious, like some of the kids in my art class who wear berets, like somehow their brains are so creative, they need a covering more unique than anyone else's. My own "oeuvres" are mostly comic book art. Manga and stuff, but not always. Lately my art has been getting more and more abstract, as if the lines are pulling my hand rather than the other way around. There's an anxiety to it now when I begin. An urgent need to see where the lines are taking me.

I work as diligently as I can on the sketches of Shelby's characters, but am impatient about it. The moment I have one colored pencil in my hand, I'm itching to drop it and grab another one. I see the lines I'm drawing, but not the whole. I love drawing characters, but today it's like the joy is running a few yards ahead of my thoughts and I can't catch up.

I show her my sketch of Xargon, her new and improved bloodbath-proof battle-team leader.

"Sloppy," she says. "If you're not gonna take this seriously—"

"It's the best I can do today, all right? Some days I feel it, some days I don't." And then I add, "Maybe it's your sketchy character descriptions making my artwork sketchy."

"Just try harder," she says. "You used to be so … concrete."

I shrug. "So? Everyone's style evolves. Look at Picasso."

"Fine. When Picasso designs a computer game, I'll let you know."

And while our meetings are always about butting heads, which is half the fun of it, today feels different because deep down I know Shelby is right. My artwork isn't evolving, it's deconstructing, and I don't know why.

The captain calls me in for a meeting in spite of the fact that I have tried to keep a low profile.

"You're in trouble now," the navigator tells me as I leave our cabin. "Trouble, Hubble, hobble, gobble – he's been known to gobble down crewmen whole."

It makes me think of my dream in the White Plastic Kitchen – but the captain isn't in that dream.

The captain's "ready room" is aft, at the very back of the ship. He says it's so he can reflect on where he's been. Right now he's not reflecting. He's not in his ready room at all. Only the parrot is there, sitting on a perch between the captain's cluttered desk and a globe that has all the landmasses wrong.

"Good of you to come, good of you to come!" says the parrot. "Sit, sit."

I sit down and wait. The parrot sidesteps from one end of his perch to the other, and back again.

"So, why am I here?" I ask him.

"Exactly," says the parrot. "*WHY* are you here? Or should I ask 'Why are *YOU* here?' Or 'Why are you *HERE*?'"

I begin to lose my patience. "Is the captain coming, because if he's not—"

"The captain didn't call for you," the parrot says. "I did, I did." Then he bobs his head, to indicate a piece of paper on the desk. "Please fill out the questionnaire."

"With what?" I ask. "There's no pen."

The parrot hops down to the desk, kicks around some of the mess, and when he finds no pen, he gnaws off a blue-green feather from his back. It falls to the desk like an old-fashioned quill.

"Very clever," I tell him, "but there's no ink."

"Touch it to the pitch between the planks," the parrot says. I reach to the nearest wall and touch the tip of the quill to the darkness residing between two slats of wood, and something darker than ink sucks into the hollow of the quill. The sight of it makes me shiver. As I fill out the questionnaire, I make sure not to let any of the stuff touch my skin.

"Does everyone have to do this?" I ask.

"Everyone."

"Do I have to answer every question?"

"Every question."

"Why does any of this matter?"

"It matters."

When I'm done, we just look at each other. It occurs to me that parrots always appear to have a pleasant smile, kind of like dolphins, so you never truly know what they're thinking. A dolphin might be thinking of ripping your heart out, or poking you to death with its bottlenose, the way it might do to a shark, but since it's always smiling, you think it's your friend. It makes me think about the dolphins I painted on my sister's bedroom wall. Does she know they may want to kill her? Have they already?

"Getting along with the crew, the crew?" the parrot asks.

I shrug. "I guess."

"Tell me something I can use against them."

"Why would I do that?"

The parrot whistles out a sigh. "My, my, so uncooperative today." When he realizes he won't get anything out of me, he hops back onto his perch. "We're done for the day, for the day," he says. "Off to dinner now. Couscous and mahi mahi."

21 Crew Member Questionnaire

Please rate the following statements from one to five using the scale below:

1 strongly agree *2 totally agree* *3 agree emphatically*
4 in absolute agreement *5 how did you know?*

I sometimes worry that the ship might sink.	①	②	③	④	⑤
My fellow crewmen are hiding biological weapons.	①	②	③	④	⑤
Energy drinks allow me to fly.	①	②	③	④	⑤
I am God, and God does not fill out questionnaires.	①	②	⓪	④	⑤
I enjoy the company of brightly colored birds.	①	②	③	④	⑤
Death tends to leave me hungry.	①	②	③	④	⑤
My shoes are too tight, and my heart two sizes too small.	①	②	③	④	⑤
I believe all the answers lie at the bottom of the sea.	①	②	③	④	⑤
I often find myself surrounded by soulless zombies.	①	②	③	④	⑤
Sometimes I hear voices from the Home Shopping Network.	①	②	③	④	⑤
I can breathe underwater.	①	②	③	④	⑤
I have visions of parallel and/or perpendicular universes.	①	②	③	④	⑤
I need more caffeine. Now.	①	②	③	④	⑤
I smell dead people.	①	②	③	④	⑤

22 The Mattress Didn't Save Him

My family and I go to Las Vegas for two days while they tent our house for termites. I draw in my sketch pad for the whole drive, and get carsick. One step short of vomiting. Which, I suppose, makes me like everyone else in Vegas.

Our hotel is a thirty-story pyramid with diagonal elevators. Las Vegans are very proud of their elevators. The glass ones, the mirrored ones, the ones with chandeliers that quiver and tinkle like each rise and fall is a tremor. The hotels are all in competition to see who can get their guests from their rooms to the casino faster. One hotel even has slot machines in the elevators for the people who can't wait that long.

I'm nervous for no reason that I can figure. "You need to eat," Mom tells me. I eat, and it doesn't go away. "You need a nap," Dad tells me, like I'm a toddler, but it's not that either, and they both know it. "You need to get over this social anxiety, Caden," they tell me more than once. The thing is, I never had social anxiety before – I was always pretty confident and outgoing. They don't know – I don't even know yet – that this is the start of something bigger. It's just the dark tip of a much larger, much deeper, much blacker pyramid.

My parents spend half a day gambling until they've decided they've lost enough money. Then they argue and blame each other.

"You don't know how to play blackjack!"

"I told you, I prefer roulette!"

Everyone needs someone to blame. Married couples blame each other. It's easier that way. The whole thing is aggravated by the fact that Mom broke the left heel of her favorite red shoes, and had to limp back to the hotel, because walking barefoot on the streets of Las Vegas is not an option. Walking on coals would be less painful.

While our parents console themselves with spa treatments, I go out with my sister and walk along the strip, watching the Bellagio fountain show. I'm kind of bothered to be with Mackenzie right now, because she happens to be sucking on her favorite candy – a blue Ring Pop. It makes her look much younger than almost-eleven, and makes me feel like I'm a baby-sitter. It's also embarrassing to be around someone whose entire mouth has turned blue.

As we walk, I collect business cards for escort services from sleazy guys handing them out to anyone who will take them. Not that I intend to call the numbers on the cards, but it's something to collect. Like baseball cards. Except these have pictures of girls in underwear. Worth an entire major league team.

I know that one of these buildings on the strip used to be the MGM Grand, which had a deadly fire a long time ago. It was such bad karma, the company sold it to some other hotel chain, and built a new hotel – a massive green Oz-like gambling cathedral. But the old hotel is now camouflaged by a different name. A lot of people died in that fire. One guy jumped out of a high window on a mattress to escape the flames. The mattress didn't save him.

Now I get to thinking about our hotel, and what would happen if it caught on fire. How would you get out of a flaming glass pyramid where the windows don't open? My thoughts start spinning. What if one of these scummy guys on the street decides he's tired of handing out dirty business cards, and decides that a little arson is in order. And when I look at one of them — really look at him, I see it in his face, and I know that he's the one. I've gotten a powerful premonition, almost like a voice, telling me I can't go back to our hotel. Because he's watching me. Because maybe they all are. Maybe all those sleazy card-hander-outers are working together. And I can't go back to our hotel, because if I do, it will be true. So I convince my sister, who's whining that her feet hurt, to keep on walking, but I don't tell her why. I suddenly feel like it's all up to me to protect her from the creeps.

"Let's check out Caesars Palace," I tell Mackenzie. "It's supposed to be real cool."

As we walk in, I begin to feel a little safer. There are huge stone centurions with spears, wearing armor, guarding the entrance. I know they're just for decoration, but they make me feel safe from all the scheming, scuzzy fire-starters.

Inside, among the shops that push perfume, diamonds, leather, and mink, there's an alcove where one more stone sculpture stands. It's a perfect marble replica of Michelangelo's *David*. Everything in Las Vegas is a perfect replica. The Eiffel Tower, the Statue of Liberty, half the city of Venice. The real world made fake for your amusement.

"Ew, what's with the naked guy?" Mackenzie asks.

"Don't be dumb, it's *David*."

"Oh," she says, and mercifully doesn't ask "David who?" Instead, she asks, "What's that in his hand?"

"A slingshot."

"It doesn't look like a slingshot."

"It's a biblical slingshot," I tell her. "The one he used to kill Goliath."

"Oh," Mackenzie says. "Can we go now?"

"In a second." I can't leave yet, because I'm struck by David's stone eyes. His body seems relaxed, like the kingdom is already his, but the expression on his face … it's full of worry, and concern he's trying to hide. I begin to wonder if David was like me. Seeing monsters everywhere and realizing there aren't enough slingshots in the world to get rid of them.

23 Eight-Point-Five Seconds

My parents are a little drunk on that first evening of our Las Vegas extravaganza.

Their fight over who was responsible for the day's gambling losses is over. They decide to rise above it all. Literally.

See, every hotel in Las Vegas has a gimmick, and the biggest gimmick of all is the Stratosphere Tower, which claims to have 113 floors, although I think they're measuring floors in Las-Vegas-inches, which stretch and contract to fit whatever lie you're trying to sell. Still, it's pretty impressive, this circular glass crown atop a sleek concrete spire. The elevator attendant claims they have the fastest elevators in Western civilization. Las Vegans and their elevators.

The four-story circular crown has a revolving restaurant and a lounge with live music. People sit in red velvet chairs and drink neon-bright drinks that appear to be radioactive. The tower also has amusement park rides. One ride drops you 108 stories on a cable at near free fall without so much as a mattress to keep you company on your way down. A camera goes down with you, though, videotaping your simulated death, so you can take it home and relive those 8.5 seconds in the comfort of your living room.

"Are you up for it?" my father asks. "There's no line."

I think he's kidding at first, but by the sparkle in his eye, I can tell that he's not. My father rarely gets drunk, but when he does, he becomes the poster child for bad choices.

"No thanks," I tell him, and try to get away, but he grabs me, and says it's a family event. He's got discount coupons. Two for one. Four for two. Such a deal.

"Loosen up, Caden," he says. "Give yourself over to the universe."

My father did not live through the sixties, but alcohol turns him from a registered Republican to a hippie wandering Woodstock.

"What are you afraid of?" he asks. "It's perfectly safe."

In front of us someone all trussed up in a harness and blue

jumpsuit leaps into the void, and disappears down the side of the tower never to be seen again. People applaud, and my fingers begin to feel numb.

"Anyone ever go splat?" some pale bozo with a neon drink asks the people running the ride, and then he laughs with his bozo friends. "I'd pay to see that!"

"Either we go as a family, or none of us goes," Dad says, which gets my sister working on me, complaining that I always ruin her life. My mother just giggles, because margaritas turn her into a twelve-year-old in a forty-year-old body.

"C'mon, Caden," Dad says. "Live in the moment, man. It'll be something you'll remember for the rest of your life."

Right. All 8.5 seconds of it.

I stop protesting because it's three against one. Then when I look in my father's eyes, I see it. The same thing I saw in the card-carrying creep who I know wants to burn down our hotel. Who is my father, really? What if he's part of some secret society? What if everything about my life has been a sham, like Venice-on-the-strip, and it's all been about bringing me here, luring me to jump to my death? Who are these people? And although a part of me knows how ridiculous my thoughts sound, there's another part of me that gives a foothold to my awful "What if?" It's the same part of me that secretly checks under my bed and in closets after watching a scary movie.

Before I know what's happening, we're dressed in the blue outfits, and for the first time it hits me why they're called jumpsuits and we're standing out on a gantry like a team of astronauts, and my sister goes first because she wants to prove she's the bravest girl on planet earth, and then my mother's hooked to the cable, and she jumps, her giggle turning into a plunging screech, and my father's waiting behind me, making sure I go before him, because he knows I'll take the elevator down if given the chance.

"It'll be fun, you'll see."

But there's no fun to be had, because that living cloud in the corner of my mind that looks under the bed is now a ground fog spreading over my brain like the angel of death over the firstborn of Egypt.

People watch with mild interest through the glass wall of the Stratosphere crown – well-dressed people eating escargot and drinking radiation as their restaurant slowly revolves – and I realize I'm part of the evening's entertainment. Like at the circus, everyone secretly wants to see someone go splat.

And my terror isn't just butterflies. It isn't just the adrenaline anticipation at the peak of a roller coaster's first drop. I know for a fact – for a FACT – that they're only pretending to attach my cable. That my life is about to end in a high velocity explosion of pain. The truth is in all of their eyes. The pain of knowing is killing me more than killing me would kill me, so I jump just to end it.

Screaming, screaming, and screaming down the side of a tower and into a bottomless black pit so real, I will always, always believe it's true – and yet 8.5 seconds later, I slow down, and am caught by a team at the base of the tower. I'm so

"Time is happening"

surprised that I am still alive, I can't stop shaking, and my one victory from this awful night is that my dad, who jumps after me, pukes on the way down – but not even that can take away the hellish black-hole feeling that I'm still standing on the ledge of something unthinkable.

24 Don't Think You Own It

I awaken from a nightmare I can't remember to the violent pitching of the ship. The lantern hanging from the low-slung ceiling of our cabin swings wildly, casting wavering shadows that rise and flow just as uneasily as the waves. The entire ship creaks in painful complaint, and the perspiring boards of the hull stretch and contract, straining against the miserable black tar that holds them together. The tar itself seems to moan with the effort.

The navigator peers down from his bunk above mine, not seeming to care that the ship is about to be shredded into driftwood by the enraged sea.

"Bad dream?" he asks.

"Yeah," I squeak.

"Were you in the kitchen?"

That catches me by surprise. I never told him about it. "You know about that place?"

"We all go to the White Plastic Kitchen sometimes," the navigator says. "Don't think you own it, because you don't."

I make my way to the bathroom, which is down the hallway. My feet feel like they're chained to the ground. My arms feel as if they're chained to the wall. That on top of the motion of the ship makes my bathroom journey a fifteen-minute ordeal.

When I'm finally back in my bed the navigator drops down a torn piece of paper with lines and arrows curving this way and that.

"Way out, stay out, stay home, way home," he says. "Take that with you the next time you're in the kitchen, is what I'm saying. It maps the way out."

"I can't take a piece of paper into a dream," I point out.

"Well, then," he says, insulted. "You're screwed."

"Draw me," the parrot says, eyeing my sketch pad. "Draw me." I don't dare refuse.

"Strike a pose," I tell him. He preens on the railing, raising his beak majestically, fluffing his feathers. I take my time. When I'm done, I present it to him. It's a picture of a steaming turd.

He looks at it for a few moments, then says, "It looks more like my brother. After he was eaten by a croc, of course."

That actually makes me smile. So I do a second sketch that does look like the parrot, eye patch and all.

The captain, however, has been watching, and when the parrot flaps off very self-satisfied, he confiscates my pencil and pad. But at least he doesn't have my drawing hand cut off. Rumor has it that the crewmen with peg legs got that way because they were caught playing soccer on deck.

"You were not given permission to have talent," the captain tells me. "It may offend the other crewmen who have none."

And although talent comes whether you ask permission or not, I bow my head and ask, "Please, sir ... may I be allowed the talent to draw?"

"I will consider it." He looks at the portrait of the parrot, wrinkles his nose, and throws it overboard. Then he looks at the picture of the steaming turd and says, "A very good likeness." Then he throws that one overboard, too.

In the morning, the bartender calls me up to the crow's nest to make me my cocktail. There are no jumpers today so the crowd is thin.

"This cocktail shall be yours and yours alone." He holds a long beat of eye contact with me, until I nod an acceptance. Satisfied, he grabs bottles and potions from the shelf, his hands moving so fast you'd think he had more than two. He shakes it all up in a rusty martini shaker.

"What's in it?" I ask.

He looks at me like I'm an imbecile for asking. Or maybe an imbecile to think I'll get an answer. "Garbage, and spice, and all things not nice," he says.

"Specifically?"

"Cartilage of cow," he tells me, "and spine of black beetle."

"Beetles have no spines," I point out. "They're invertebrates."

"Exactly. That's why it's so rare."

The parrot arrives, flapping up from far below, and sits on the cash register. Seeing the register reminds me that I can't pay, and I tell the bartender so.

"Not a problem," the bartender says. "We'll bill your insurance."

He pours the concoction into a crystal champagne flute and hands it to me. The brew bubbles red and yellow, but the two colors do not blend. My cocktail is a lava lamp.

"Drink up, drink up," says the parrot. He turns his head slightly and watches me with his good eye.

I take a sip. It's bitter but not entirely unpleasant. A faint flavor of banana and almond. "Bottoms up," I say, then I down it in a single gulp, leaving the empty glass on the bar.

The parrot bobs his head in deep satisfaction.

"Excellent! You'll visit the crow's nest twice a day."

"What if I don't want to visit the crow's nest?" I ask him.

He winks at me. "Then the crow's nest will visit you."

27 Hand-Sanitized Masses

Our family took a trip to New York a long time ago. Since all the convenient hotels were either booked or required multiple pounds of flesh in payment, we ended up off the beaten tourist path.

Our hotel was somewhere in the left armpit of a fat guy in Queens. It was an area of Queens with the unfortunate name of "Flushing." New York's founding fathers, like most New Yorkers, had a keen sense of irony.

Long story short, as a New Yorker might say, we had to take the subway everywhere, which was always an adventure. I believe one time we ended up in Staten Island, and there isn't even a subway line that goes there. We kept running out of money on our MetroCards, which vomited digital cash every time you went through a turnstile, and Dad lamented the golden age of the brass subway token, when you could count your journeys in the palm of your hand.

My mother was very clear about THE RULES OF THE SUBWAY, which involved lots of Purell, and never making eye contact with people.

During that week I became a student of the crowd, studying the unwashed and un-hand-sanitized masses. In the streets, for instance, I discovered that New Yorkers never look up at the awe-inspiring buildings towering above them. They move fast and efficiently through dense mobs, as if they have a Teflon coat, very rarely bumping into one another. And in the subway, where everyone must stand still as the train rattles from station to station, not only don't people make eye contact, but they exist in their own extremely tight universe, as if wearing an invisible space suit. It's kind of like driving on the freeway, except that your personal space is only half an inch from your clothes, if that. I marveled that people could live so close – that you could literally be surrounded by thousands who were only inches away – and yet be completely isolated. I found it hard to imagine. It's not hard for me to imagine anymore.

28 Skippy Rainbow

Our house is now termite-free, and the wonders of Sin City are memories best suppressed. But home feels no more comfortable. I have this urge to pace. Back and forth, back and forth. It's pointless. When I'm not pacing, I'm drawing; when I'm not drawing, I'm thinking – which just leads me back to pacing and drawing again. Maybe I'm being affected by the pesticide residual.

I sit at the dining room table. Before me is a spread of colored pencils, oil pastels, charcoal. Today I work in colored pencil, but I hold them so hard and press so powerfully, the pencils keep breaking. Not just the points, but the pencils themselves. I toss the ruined ones over my shoulder, not allowing for delays.

"You're like a mad scientist," my mother observes.

I hear her about ten seconds after she says it. It's too late to respond, so I don't. I'm too busy to respond anyway. There's this thing in my head that I have to purge onto the page before it changes the shape of my brain. Before the colorful lines cut into it like a cheese wire. My drawings have lost all sense of form. They are scribbles and suggestions, random, and yet not. I wonder if others will see the things in them that I see. These images have to mean something, don't they? Why else would they be so intense? Why would that silent voice inside be so adamant about getting them out?

The magenta pencil breaks. I toss it and pick up vermilion.

"I don't like it," says Mackenzie, passing with a spoonful of peanut butter that she licks like a lollipop. "It's creepy."

"I only draw what's called for," I tell her. Then I get a flash of impulsive inspiration; I reach over, dig my thumb into her spoon, and smudge an ocher arc across the page.

"Mom!" yells Mackenzie. "Caden's drawing with my peanut butter!"

To which Mom replies, "Serves you right. You shouldn't be eating peanut butter before dinner."

Still, Mom spares a glance from the kitchen at me and my project. I feel her wave of worry like a patio heater – faint and ineffective, but constant.

29 Some of My Best Friends Are Cirque-ish

I sit with my friends for lunch. And yet I don't. That is to say, I'm among them, but I don't feel *with* them. Used to be I could easily fit in with whatever friends I was hanging out with. Some people need a clique to make them feel safe. They have this little protective bubble of friends that they rarely venture away from. I was never like that. I could always flow freely from table to table, group to group. The athletes, the brainiacs, the hipsters, the band kids, the skaters. I was always well liked and well accepted by all, and I always managed to fit in like a chameleon. How strange, then, that now I find myself in a clique of one, even when I'm with a group.

My friends scarf down their lunches, and laugh about something I didn't hear. It's not like I'm intentionally zoning out, but somehow I can't land myself in the conversation. Their laughter feels so far away it's as if there's cotton in my ears. It's been happening more and more. It's like they're not even talking English – they're speaking that weird fake language the clowns speak in Cirque du Soleil. My friends are all conversing in Cirque-ish. Usually I'll play along. I'll join in the laughter so I can stay camouflaged and appear to be in step with those around me.

But today I'm not in the mood to pretend. My buddy Taylor, who is slightly more observant than the others, notices my absence, and raps me gently on the arm.

"Hey, earth to Caden Bosch – where are you, man?"

"In orbit around Uranus," I tell him, which makes everyone laugh, and it starts a whole round of rude puns that all sound Cirque-ish, because I've already checked out again.

30 The Movements of Flies

While we crewmen do our business, pacing back and forth on deck with no seeming point to the endeavor, the captain stands above us at the helm. Like a preacher, he pontificates his own peculiar brand of wisdom.

"Count your blessings," the captain says. "And if you count less than ten, cut off the remaining fingers."

I watch the parrot checking in with the crew members one at a time, landing on their shoulders, or perching atop their heads for a few moments before flying off to the next. I wonder what he's up to.

"Burn all your bridges," the captain says. "Preferably before you cross them."

The navigator sits on a leaky barrel of yuck that was once full of food, but its stench testifies to the fact that the food-stuffs have decayed into something other. He creates a new navigational chart based on the movements of flies swarming around the barrel. "Their motions are more truthful than the stars," he tells me, "because common flies have compound eyes."

"Why does that make a difference?" I dare to ask.

He looks at me as if the answer is obvious. "Compound eyes confound lies."

I can see why he and the captain get along so well.

The parrot lands on my shoulder as I do my endless shuffle across the deck. "Crewman Bosch! Hold fast, hold fast!" He then peers into my ear with his unpatched eye, bobbing his head as he does. "It's still there," he says. "Good for you! Good for you!"

I assume he's talking about my brain.

He flies off to check in the ear of another sailor. His low whistle betrays disappointment at what he finds – or fails to find – between the boy's ears.

"There is nothing to fear but fear itself," the captain announces from the helm, "and the occasional man-eating monster."

31 Is That All They're Worth?

Although the pesticide residue is gone from our house, I can't stop thinking about termites. If antibacterial soap creates super germs like they say, what if toxic tenting creates super insects? I sit with my sketch book in this New Age kind of rocking chair we have in the living room – a piece of furniture left over from when Mackenzie and I were babies, and Mom breast-fed us. I'm sure I must have some old sense memory, because when I sit in the chair and rock, I usually feel a little more relaxed and content – although, thankfully, the memory of breast milk has been lost in the tunnels of time.

Today, however, I'm not feeling relaxed at all. I can't stop thinking about squirming things evolving. I begin drawing what's in my head, as if maybe by drawing it, it will exorcise the super bugs from my brain.

After a while I look up to see Mom standing there, watching me. I have no idea how long she's been there. And when I look down again, I see that the page is still blank. I haven't drawn anything at all. I even flip the page back to see if maybe the drawing is on a previous page, but no. The bugs are still in my head, and won't come out.

She must see something unsettling in my face because she says, "A penny for your thoughts?"

I don't feel like sharing my thoughts, so instead I challenge the question. "Really? Is that all they're worth? A penny?"

She sighs. "It's just an expression, Caden."

"Well, find out when the expression was thought up, and then adjust for inflation."

She shakes her head. "Only you would go there, Caden." Then she leaves me to stew in thoughts I refuse to sell.

32 Less Than Nothing

I read somewhere that they're going to be doing away with pennies entirely one of these days, because I guess thoughts are all they're good for. Bank accounts will be rounded to the nearest nickel. Fountains will reject copper. Purchases will be required by law to end in either zero or five. Nothing in between will be allowed. Except that there *is* something in between, even if everyone denies it.

It's like all those subway tokens that became obsolete when New York started using magnetic cards instead. No one knew what to do with those tokens. It was like this dragon's hoard of worthless brass that not even Smaug's underachieving brother would want – and with real estate being so expensive in the city, the cost of storing them was probably astronomical. I'll bet they just hired the Mafia to dump them into the East River, along with the body of whatever city planner thought MetroCards was a good idea.

If pennies become worthless, does that devalue our thoughts to less than nothing? It makes me sad to think about it; billions of copper bits spinning down the yellow funnel into oblivion. I wonder where they'll go. All those thoughts have to end up somewhere.

I decide to try out for the track team, to keep my mind from being idle, and to reconnect with my fellow human beings. My father is overjoyed. I know he's secretly marking this as a turning point for me. The end of my anxious days. I think he wants it so badly, he doesn't seem to notice that I'm still anxious – but him thinking that I'm okay makes me feel like I am, too. Forget solar energy – if you could harness denial, it would power the world for generations.

"You've always been a fast runner," he says, "and with those long legs, I'll bet you could be a hurdler."

My dad was on his high school tennis team. We have pictures of him in ridiculous Adidas shorts that leave nothing to the imagination, and a headband holding back long hair, most of which has since washed down the drain.

"The coach wants us to walk or run everywhere," I tell my parents. Now I walk to and from school each day. My feet develop calluses and sores. My ankles hurt all the time.

"It's a good kind of hurt," my father tells me, then he quotes some sports guru, saying, "Pain is weakness leaving the body."

We go out to buy new, expensive running shoes and better socks. My parents say they'll try to make it to my first meet, even if they have to take off from work. This would all be fine, if it weren't for one thing. I'm not actually on the track team.

I didn't lie about it – not at first. I really did go out for track, but I only went to practice for three days. As much as I tried, I just wasn't feeling it. Lately there's this subway-like bubble of isolation around me, and when I'm in a place filled with camaraderie, like on a team, it's only worse. *Don't be a quitter* my father always told me. That's how I was raised, but is it quitting when you never really joined?

So now I walk after school, instead of run. It used to be that walking was just a way to get from place to place, but lately it seems to be both the means and the ends. It's like that urge to fill an empty space with drawings. I see a vacant sidewalk, and I have to fill it. For hours at a time I walk. The calluses and aching ankles are all from walking. And I see things. Not so much see, but feel. Patterns of connection between the people I pass. Between the birds that swoop from the trees. There is meaning out there, if only I can find it.

I walk for two hours in the rain one day, my hoodie soaked, my body chilled to the bone.

"I should have a talk with that coach of yours," my mom says, fixing me some hot tea. "He shouldn't make you run in this kind of downpour."

"Mom, don't," I tell her. "I'm not a baby! Everyone on track does it, and I don't want to be singled out!"

I wonder exactly when it was that lying became so easy.

"Caden, I have fer you a challenge," the captain says, "to prove whether or not you have the mettle for the mission." He puts his large hand on my shoulder and squeezes so tightly that it hurts, then he points to the front of the ship.

"See there? The bowsprit?" He indicates the mast-like pole that pokes out at the front of the ship, like Pinocchio's nose after the second or third lie. "The sun has aged it and the sea has weathered it. It's high time the bowsprit was polished." Then he puts a rag in one hand and a tin of wood polish in the other. "Get to it, boy. If you succeed without perishing, you shall be a part of the inner circle."

"I'm fine in the outer circle," I tell him.

"You misunderstand," the captain says sternly. "This isn't a choice."

Then, gauging my continued reluctance, he snarls, "You've been to the crow's nest, haven't you? You've been partaking of its odious libations. I can see it in your eyes!"

I glance to the parrot on his shoulder, and the parrot shakes his head, making it clear I should keep my mouth shut.

"Don't lie to me, boy!"

And so I don't. Instead I say, "If you want this done right, sir, I'll need more polish and a bigger rag."

He glares at me a moment more, then bursts out laughing, and orders another crewman to provide me with better supplies.

Luckily it's a calm day at sea. The bow rises and falls just slightly as it rides the waves. I'm given no rope, no way to secure myself. I am to shimmy out to the very tip of the pole with no protection but my balance to keep me from plunging into the sea, where I would be taken down beneath the ship, and shredded by its barnacle-encrusted hull.

Rag in one hand, polish in the other, I straddle the pole, pressing my thighs together to keep myself from falling into the bottomless blue. The only way to do this is to start at the far end and shimmy my way back – because once the wood is polished I know it will be too slick to cling to, so I carefully make my way to the front and begin, doing my best to forget about the waters passing beneath me. My arms ache from the work, my legs ache from holding on. It feels like it takes forever, but finally I am back where I started at the bow.

I carefully turn myself around so I'm facing the ship, and the captain grins broadly. "Competently done!" he says. "Now come off there before the sea or something in it devours your semi-worthless hide." Then he leaves, satisfied that I've been sufficiently tormented.

Perhaps it's that I get a little cocky at my success, or perhaps the sea is spiteful that it hasn't claimed me – but as I climb back to the bow, the ship lurches on a sudden swell. I slip and I slide off the pole.

It should be the end of my miserable life, but someone catches me, holding me as I dangle by a single arm above doom.

I look up to see who has saved my life. The hand that grips me is brown, but not brown like flesh. It's ashen, and the fingers rough and hard. My gaze tracks up the arm until I see that I am being held by the ship's figurehead – a wooden maiden carved into the bow, beneath the bowsprit pole. I don't know whether to be more thankful or terrified – but terror dissolves as I realize how beautiful she is. The wooden waves of her hair dissolve into the timbers of the ship. Her perfect torso tapers into the bow, as if the rest of the ship is just a part of her body. And her face – it's not so much familiar as it is reminiscent of girls I've seen in secret fantasies. Girls who make me blush when I think about them.

She studies me as I dangle, her eyes as dark as mahogany.

"I should drop you," she says, "for looking at me like an object."

"But you *are* an object," I point out, and realize it's the wrong thing to say, unless I want to die.

"Perhaps so," she says, "but I don't appreciate being treated like one."

"Will you save me? Please?" I ask, ashamed to be begging, but feeling I have no other choice.

"I'm considering it," she says.

Her grip is firm and strong, and I know that as long as she's still considering, she won't let me fall.

"There are things going on behind my back, aren't there?" she asks – and since she's the figurehead of the ship, the answer is, of course, "Yes."

"Do they speak ill of me? The captain and his pet? The crewmen and their demons that hide in crevices."

"They don't speak of you at all," I tell her. "At least not since I arrived."

That doesn't please her. "Out of sight must truly be out of mind," she says with the sticky bitterness of oak sap. Then she studies me a few moments more. "I will save you," she says, "if you promise to tell me all the things that go on behind my back."

"Agreed."

"Very well." She squeezes my hand tighter, and I know it will be badly bruised, but I don't care. "Visit me, then, to vary my days." And then she smirks. "And maybe one of these days, I'll allow you to polish *me*, instead of just that pole."

Then she swings me side to side, building momentum, and finally heaves me back onto the bow, where I land hard on the deck.

I look around. No one is nearby. Everyone on deck is occupied in their own particular obsession. I resolve to keep this encounter a secret. Perhaps the wooden maiden will be an ally when I need one.

35 The Unusual Suspects

The mission team has been chosen. The captain gathers a half dozen of us in the map room – a sort of library beside his ready room, filled with scrolls of maps, some of which already show signs that the navigator has had his way with them. There are six seats, three on either side of a pockmarked table. On my side is the navigator, and the scream-faced girl with the pearl choker. Across from us is another girl with hair as blue as a Tahitian bay, an older kid with a hard-luck face God forgot to give cheekbones, and the obligatory fat kid.

At the head of the table stands the captain. There's no seat for him. That's intentional. He towers over us. The light from a flickering lamp behind the captain casts his shadow across the table – a shifting blob, that almost, but not quite, mimics his actions. The parrot sits perched on some scrolls, his talons digging into the parchment.

Carlyle, the swabby, is also there. He sits on a chair in the corner, whittling on his mop handle, like he's turning it into a very thin totem pole. He observes but says nothing at first.

"We bob above many things unseen," the captain begins. "Mountains of mystery lie low in the lightless, bone-crushing depths... But as you all know, it be not the mountains that obsess us, but the valleys."

Then his single seeing eye looks to me. I know he's making eye contact with all of us as he speaks but I can't help but feel that he's singling me out as he waxes pirate poetic.

"Aye, the valleys and trenches. And one in particular. The Marianas Trench ... and that place in its icy depths called Challenger Deep."

The parrot flaps to his shoulder. "Been watching you, we have," the parrot says. Today he sounds like Yoda.

"Indeed we have been scrutinizing your ways," adds the captain, "and fiercely reckon that you be the ones to play a crucial part in this mission."

I roll my eyes at his strained pirate-ese. I wouldn't doubt he spells everything with triple *rrr*'s.

All is silent for a moment, and from the corner, Carlyle, without looking up from his whittling, says, "Of course, I'm just a fly on the wall, but this would all go much more smoothly if the six of you shared your opinions."

"Speak," orders the parrot. "All must speak of what you know of the place we seek."

The captain says nothing. He seems a bit irritated that his authority has been undermined by the parrot and the swabby.

He crosses his arms in a display of power, and waits for one of us to say something.

"Well, I'll go first," says the girl with the pearl choker. "It's a deep, dark, terrible place, and there are monsters that I really don't want to talk about ..." and then she proceeds to tell us about monsters none of us cares to hear about – until she's interrupted by the obligatory fat kid.

"No," he says. "The worst monsters aren't *in* the trench, they guard it. The monsters come before you get there."

Choker-girl, who insisted she didn't want to talk about them, obviously wanted to, because she's miffed that she's been cut off. Now everyone's attention turns to the fat kid.

"Go on," says the captain. "Everyone's here to listen."

"Well ... the monsters keep people away by killing anyone who gets close. And if one doesn't get you, another one will."

"Very good," says the captain. "Well-spoken! You know your lore."

"Lore-master," says the parrot. "Make him Lore-master."

"A clear choice," the captain agrees. "You shall be our designated expert on lore."

The fat kid panics. "But I don't know stuff – I only heard you talking once."

"Then learn." The captain reaches to a shelf I didn't know was there a moment ago, grabs a volume the size of an unabridged dictionary, and slams it down on the table in front of the poor kid.

"Thanks for sharing," says Carlyle from the corner, flicking a bit of wood from his knife to the ground.

The captain turns his gaze to the girl with blue hair, waiting for her contribution. She looks off to the side as she speaks, as if her lack of eye contact is the ultimate rebellion against authority. "There must be sunken treasure or, like, whatever," she says. "Otherwise, why would you want to go there?"

"Aye," says the captain. "All treasures lost at sea seek the world's lowest point. Gold and diamonds and emeralds and rubies taken by the jealous sea are dragged by its watery tentacles along the seafloor and dropped into the unknowable depths of Challenger Deep. A king's ransom without the nuisance of a kidnapped king."

"Kidnap, sand trap, sandstorm, life-form," says the navigator. "Life-forms never seen by the human eye lie in wait for a challenger."

"So who is the challenger?" asks the kid with a dearth of cheekbones.

The captain turns his gaze to him. "Since you asked the question, you will prophesize answers." Then he turns to the parrot. "Bring him the bones."

The parrot flies across the room and returns with a small leather sack in his beak.

"We shall call you the prophet and you shall interpret the bones for us," the captain says.

"These," says the parrot, "are the bones of my father."

"Whom we devoured one fine Christmas," the captain adds, "when no one would be the turkey."

I swallow and think of the White Plastic Kitchen. Then the

captain looks at me and I realize that everyone's spoken but me. I consider what everyone else has said and I can feel my anger building. The captain with his single bloodshot eye; the parrot, his head bobbing in anticipation of whatever nonsense I would add to this foolishness.

"The Marianas Trench," I say. "Nearly seven miles deep – the deepest place on earth – and southwest of the island of Guam, which isn't even on your globe."

The captain's eye opens wider so it appears to have no lids. "Go on."

"It was first explored by Jacques Piccard and Lieutenant Don Walsh in 1960 in a submersible called the *Trieste*. They didn't find any monsters or treasures. And if there are treasures, you'll never get to them. Not without a heavy-duty diving bell – a bathyscaphe made of steel that's at least six inches thick. But as this is a preindustrial ship, I don't think that's going to happen, because you don't have that kind of technology, do you? So this is a waste of everyone's time."

The captain folds his arms. "How very anachronistic of you," he says. "And you believe this because…?"

"Because I did a report on it," I tell him. "In fact, I got an A."

"I think not." Then he calls to Carlyle. "Swabby," he says. "This crewman has just earned an F. I order that it be branded on his forehead."

The prophet snickers, the lore-master groans, and everyone else waits to see whether or not it's an idle threat.

"You are all dismissed," the captain says. "All except for our insolent F."

The others shuffle out, the navigator giving me a sympathetic gaze. Carlyle hurries out and returns in seconds with a branding iron, red-hot and smoking, as if it had been waiting just outside. Two of the nameless ship's officers hold me against the bulkhead, and although I fight, I can't get free.

"Sorry about this," says Carlyle, holding the red-hot brand, the heat of which I can feel two feet away.

The parrot flies off, not wanting to watch, and the captain, before he gives the order to do the deed, leans close to me. I can smell his breath. It reeks of bits of old meat pickled in rum. "This not be the world you think it to be," he says.

"Then what world is it?" I ask, refusing to give in to my fear.

"Don't you know? 'Tis a world of laughter, a world of tears." Then he lifts up his eye patch, revealing a nasty hole that has been plugged with a peach pit. "But mostly, it's a world of tears."

And he signals for Carlyle to give me an F on my report.

36 Without Her We're Lost

In the aftermath of my branding, the captain becomes gentle. Apologetic even, although he never actually apologizes. He sits by my bedside dabbing water on the wound. Carlyle and the parrot stop in once in a while, but only for a moment. Once they see the captain there, they retreat.

"This is all the parrot's fault," the captain tells me. "And Carlyle's. The two of them put ideas in your head, and get you all riled up when I'm not around."

"You're always around," I remind him. He ignores me, and dabs my forehead again.

"Those damn trips to the crow's nest aren't helping you either. Away with the spirits – to the devil with your potion. Mark my words, those unholy concoctions will rot you from the inside out."

I don't tell him that it was the parrot who insisted I get myself a cocktail.

"You go up there because you want to fit in," he says. "I know about these things. Best thing to do is pour it overboard when no one's looking."

"I'll keep that in mind," I tell him. I think of the lonely maiden decorating the bow; how she asked me to be her eyes and ears on the ship. I figure if the captain is ever going to be open to questions, now would be the time, when he feels guilty for my raging F.

"When I was on the bowsprit, I saw the ship's figurehead. It's very beautiful."

The captain nods. "A work of art to be sure."

"Sailors used to believe they protect ships. Is that what you believe?"

The captain looks at me curiously, but not quite suspiciously. "Did she tell you that?"

"She's a piece of wood," I say quickly. "How could she tell me anything?"

"Right." The captain fiddles with his beard, then says, "She protects us from the challenges we will face before we reach our destination. The monsters toward which we sail."

"She has power over them?"

The captain chooses his words carefully. "She watches. She sees things no one else sees, and her visions echo in the hollows of the ship, strengthening it against the onslaught. She is good luck, but more than that, her gaze can charm all nature of aquatic beast."

"I'm glad we have protection," I tell him. I know not to push any further, because then he might get suspicious about my questioning.

"Without her we're lost," the captain says, then gets up. "I expect you at roll call in the morning. No complaints." Then he strides out, tossing the wet rag to the navigator, who clearly has no interest in nursing my wound.

37 Third Eye Blind

My headache is like a brand on my forehead. It makes it hard to focus on my schoolwork – hard to do anything. The aching comes and it goes, and with each return, it's a little bit worse. The more I think the more my head hurts, and lately my brain has been in constant overdrive. I keep taking showers to cool it down, like the way they pour water on an overheating machine. I usually feel better after the third or fourth shower.

After today's multiple showers, I go downstairs and ask my mom for aspirin.

"You take too much aspirin," my mom tells me, and hands me a bottle of Tylenol.

"Tylenol sucks," I tell her.

"It brings down fevers."

"I don't have a fever. My forehead is growing a freaking eye."

She looks at me, gauging my seriousness, and it bugs me. "I'm kidding."

"I know," she says, turning away. "I was just looking at the way you wrinkle your forehead. That's why you get those headaches."

"So, can I have aspirin?"

"How about Advil?"

"Fine," I say. It usually works all right, although it makes me moody as hell when it starts to wear off.

I go to the bathroom with a Mountain Dew and take three pills, feeling too rebellious to take the recommended dose of two. In the mirror I can see the wrinkles on my forehead that my mother was talking about. I try to relax, but I can't. My reflection looks worried. Am I worried? That's not quite what I'm feeling today — but lately my emotions are so liquid, they flow into one another without my noticing. Now I realize that I *am* worried. I'm worried about being worried.

38 Ah, Here's the Proboscis

I have this dream. I'm dangling from the ceiling. My feet are a few inches from the ground. Then, as I look down, I see I have no feet. My body tapers into a squirming, wormlike bit of flesh, as if I'm a larval version of myself, suspended above the dark ground. Suspended by what, though? I realize that I'm caught in something that's like a net but more organic. A web, sticky and dense. I shudder to think what kind of creature could spin a web like that.

I can move my arms but it takes such an incredible force of will to move a single inch, it doesn't feel worth the effort. I think there are others in here with me, but they're all out of view, behind me, just past the edge of my peripheral vision.

It's dark around me, but dark isn't the word for it, more like lightless. As if the concept of light and dark have not yet been born, leaving everything a persistent shade of somber gray, and I wonder if this is what the void was like before there was anything. Not even the White Plastic Kitchen exists in this dream.

The parrot comes out of the lightlessness, strutting toward me, but he's the size of a man. It's frighteningly intimidating to see a bird that big. A feathered dinosaur with a beak that could snap my head off with a single bite. He looks me over with that grin that never goes away, and seems to approve of my helpless situation.

"How are you feeling?" he asks.

"Like I'm waiting for something to suck out my blood," I try to say but all that comes out is, "Waiting."

The parrot looks past me, over my shoulder. I try to turn my head, but can't move enough to see what he's looking at.

"Ah, here's the proboscis!" he says.

"What's that?" I ask, realizing too late that it's a word I'd rather not have defined.

"Its stinger. The sting is the only pain you'll feel. Then you'll drift off as easily as falling asleep."

And sure enough, I feel the sting, potent and painful. I can't tell exactly where the unseen creature stings me. Is it in my back? In my thigh? In my neck? Then I realize that it's everywhere at once.

"There, that wasn't so bad, was it?"

Even before my terror can blossom, the venom takes effect and in an instant, I don't care. About anything. I hang there in absolute peace as I am slowly devoured.

A science exam, which, for once, I did not study for. It occurs to me that I don't have to take this test, because I know more than the teacher. I know so much more. I know things that aren't in the book. I know the inner workings of all things biological down to the cellular level. Because I've figured things out. I KNOW how the universe works. I'm practically bursting with the knowledge. How can a single person have so much crammed in their brain and not have their head explode? Now I know the reason for the headaches. This knowledge is nothing specific that I can describe. Words are completely ineffective. I can draw it, though. I *have* been drawing it. But I must be careful who I let know the things I know. Not everyone wants the information spread.

"You will have forty minutes for this test. I suggest you use your time wisely."

I snicker. There's something about what he said that strikes me as funny, but I can't say why.

The moment I receive my Scantron and flip over the exam, I realize the words on the paper aren't the real exam at all. The true test is something deeper. The fact that I'm having trouble focusing on the printed questions is a clear indication that I must look for more meaningful answers.

I begin to fill in the little circles with my number two pencil, and the world goes away. Time goes away. I find patterns that are hidden within the grid. The answer key to everything, and suddenly it's—

"Pencils down! Time is up. Pass your answer sheets forward."

I do not remember forty minutes passing. I look at both sides of my Scantron to see wild constellations that don't exist in the heavens, and yet are more true than the stars we can see. All that remains is for someone to connect the dots.

40 Hell Asail

The girl with blue hair is made Mistress of the Treasury and is given a trunkful of manifests from sunken ships. Her job is to go through them and find evidence of lost treasure, based on what was listed as the ship's cargo. It might not be so bad, except that all the pages are shredded into confetti, and must be pieced back together. She labors at this day in and day out.

The pudgy kid, who everyone now calls the lore-master, struggles to learn what he can from the massive volume the captain inflicted upon him. Unfortunately, the entire book is written in runes from some language that I suspect is either dead or never actually existed.

"This is hell on earth," the lore-master declares to me in his frustration, and the parrot, who seems to hear things before they're even spoken, points out that since land is nowhere to be seen, it would best be described as "hell asail."

The choker-girl is in charge of morale – odd because she's always so dismal.

"We're all gonna die, and it's going to be painful," she's said several times, although she always finds a different way of saying basically the same thing. So much for morale.

The boy with the bag of bones has become skilled at telling fortunes. He holds the little leather pouch of the remains of the parrot's father, ready to roll-and-read whenever the captain asks.

Bone-boy confides in me that he makes up most of his readings – but he's vague enough that it all can be interpreted to be true by someone who really wants it to be.

"How do you know I won't give away your secret?" I ask him.

He smiles and says, "Because I can just as easily prophesize that you'll get thrown overboard by a crewman destined to be rich and famous."

Which, of course, would make any member of the crew want to hurl me into the sea. I have to admit it, this guy is no idiot.

The navigator continues to do what he's done since I met him. He creates his navigational charts, searching for meaning and direction to guide us to the trench and back again.

"The captain has special plans for you," the navigator tells me. "I think you'll like them." And somehow, in four steps he conjures "special plans" to "swollen glands," and begins to feel his throat in a troubled way.

"You, my insolent F, shall be our artist in residence," the captain tells me. Just the mention of the brand reminds me that the pain in my forehead never quite goes away. Mercifully there are no mirrors on board, so I can't actually see it, only feel it. "Your purpose shall be to document our journey in images."

"The captain is partial to images over words," the navigator whispers to me, "because he can't read."

41 Nothing of Interest

I know I should hate the captain with all my heart, and yet I don't. I can't explain why. The reason must go as deep as the trench we sail toward – it must hide in a place that no light can reach except for the light you bring with you, and right now I feel pretty much in the dark.

I peer off the side of the ship, pondering the depths, wondering what unknowable mysteries lie beneath us. When I look at the roiling sea long enough, I see things in the randomness of the waves. There are eyes everywhere in those waters scrutinizing me, judging me.

The parrot is watching, too. He struts along the railing toward me. *"Look into the abyss and the abyss looks into you,"* the parrot says. "Let's hope the abyss finds nothing of interest."

In spite of the captain's disdain of the crow's nest, I still make the climb twice a day to have my cocktail, and commune with my fellow crewmen – although few of them are social once their potion is in hand.

Today the sea is a roller coaster, doing everything short of corkscrews and loops, and the ship's rolling motion is always worst in the crow's nest, which pitches to and fro atop the mainmast like the weighted tip of a metronome. Even as I try to hold my drink steady, it sloshes within the glass, spilling a little bit on the ground, where it flows into the dark spaces between the planks and disappears.

"It's alive, you know," says the master-at-arms – a seasoned crewman in charge of the cannon, with unpleasant tattoos up and down his arms. "It's alive, and waits to be fed." I then realize that the voice isn't coming from his mouth, but from one of the skulls inked on his arm. The one with dice for eyes.

"What's alive?" I ask the tattoo. "The ship?"

The skull shakes its head. "The dark sludge that holds the ship together."

"It's just caulking," I tell it, and that makes all the other skulls begin to laugh.

"Keep telling yourself that," says the dice-eyed skull, "but when you wake up with a few less toes, you'll know it's been tasting you."

42 Spirit of Battle

I climb out to the bowsprit in the middle of the night, avoiding the crewmen on watch. Once there, I intentionally slide off the well-polished pole, and the maiden – the ship's figurehead – catches me, as I knew she would. At first she holds me by my wrists, but then she pulls me close, embracing me with her wooden arms. Although there's nothing but her arms keeping me from plunging into the depths, somehow I feel safer here than I do on board.

The sea is calm tonight. Only the occasional swell sprays us with a light, salty mist. As she holds me I whisper to her the things I've learned.

"The captain believes that you are good luck," I tell her. "That your gaze will charm the sea monsters."

"Good luck?" she scoffs. "How lucky am I if I must pose forever on this bow and take all the abuse the sea doles out upon me? And as for sea monsters, nothing will charm them but a full belly – of that you can be sure."

"I'm just telling you what he said."

We hit a swell and the ship rides high, and then dips low. She holds me so tightly that I don't have to hold on anymore. I reach out my hand and run it gently across her flowing teak-wood hair.

"Do you have a name?" I ask.

"Calliope. Named for the muse of poetry. I've never met her, but I've heard she's beautiful."

"So are you."

"Careful," she says with the faintest of grins, "false flattery might make me lose my grip, and then where would you be?"

"All wet," I say, grinning right back at her.

"Do *you* have a name?" she asks.

"Caden."

She considers it. "A goodly name," she says.

"It means Spirit of Battle," I tell her.

"In what language?"

"I have no idea."

She laughs, I laugh. The ocean seems to laugh, but not in a mocking way.

"Keep me warm, Caden," she whispers, her voice like the tender creak of a sapling branch. "I have no warmth of my own – only what the sun brings me, and the sun is halfway around the world. Keep me warm."

I close my eyes, and radiate body heat. It's so nice being there, I don't even mind the splinters.

43 It's All Kabuki

"Do you know why you've been called in here?" the school counselor asks. Her name is Ms. Sassel. Kids like to say it because it sounds like something else.

I shrug. "To talk to you?"

She sighs, realizing this is going to be one of *those* conversations. "Yes, but do you know *why* you're here to talk to me?"

I hold my silence, knowing the less I say the more control I have over the situation. The fact that I can't stop my knees from bouncing undermines any sense of control, though.

"You're here because of your science exam."

"Oh, that." I break eye contact, then realize you must never break eye contact with the school counselor, or she'll find something deeply psychological in your downward glance. I force eye contact again.

She opens a file. I have a file in the counselor's office?

Who else has a copy of my file? Who gets to put things in and take things out? Is it in any way related to my permanent record? What *is* a permanent record? When does it stop following you? Will I have to spend my life looking over my shoulder for my permanent record?

Out of the file, Ms. Sassel (I like saying it, too) pulls out the Scantron from my science test, which has more than the usual number of circles filled in. "It's a very creative ... interpretation of an exam," she says.

"Thank you."

"Could you tell me why you did it?"

There is really only one answer a person can give in a situation like this. "It seemed like a good idea at the time."

She knew I would say that. I know she knew, and she knows I know she knew. This is all like a formal ritualistic performance for both of us. Like Japanese Kabuki theater. I actually feel for her having to go through this with me.

"Mr. Guthrie isn't the only teacher who has expressed concern for you, Caden," she says as kindly as she can. "You're missing classes; your attention hasn't been on your work. Historically that's not like you."

Historically? I'm being studied like history? Are they filling out Scantrons about me somewhere? Are they giving letter grades on the subject of *me*, or is it pass/fail?

"We're concerned, and we just want to help you, if you'll let us."

Now it's my turn to sigh. I have no patience for Kabuki.

"Let's get to the point. You think I'm on drugs."

"I didn't say that."

"Then neither did I."

She closes my file and puts it aside, perhaps a gesture to imply our conversation has just become informal and off the record. I don't buy it. She leans a little closer, but her desk is like a wasteland between us.

"Caden, all I know is that something is wrong. It could be lots of things, and, yes, drugs is one of those things, but only one. I'd like to hear from you what's going on, if you'd like to tell me."

What's going on? I'm in the back car of a roller coaster at the top of the climb, with the front rows already giving themselves over to gravity. I can hear those front riders screaming and know my own scream is only seconds away. I'm at the moment you hear the landing gear of a plane grind loudly into place, in that instant before your rational mind tells you it's just the landing gear. I'm leaping off a cliff only to discover I can fly ... and then realizing there's nowhere to land. Ever. That's what's going on.

"So you're not going to say anything?" Ms. Sassel asks.

I put my hands firmly on my knees, pushing down to stop them from bouncing, and I keep serious eye contact. "Look, I had a bad day, and I took it out on the test. I know it was stupid, but Mr. Guthrie drops the lowest grade anyway, so it won't even affect my grade."

She leans back, a little bit smug, but trying to hide it. "Did that occur to you before or after you turned in the test?"

I've never been a poker player, but now I bluff with the best of them. "C'mon, do you really think I would have done it if I thought it would affect my grade? Historically, I'm not that stupid."

Ms. Sassel only half buys it, but she's a good enough counselor to know that pushing me will only be counterproductive.

"Fair enough," she says.

But I know there's nothing fair about it.

44 Boss Key

The need to walk fills me more and more. I pace my room when I should be doing my homework. I pace the living room when I should be watching TV.

Normal afternoon shows have been replaced by a live report of a kid somewhere in Kansas who fell into an old abandoned well. There are interviews with the kid's tearful parents, firefighters, rescue workers, and experts on wells – because there are experts on everything these days. They keep cutting to an aerial helicopter view as if they're watching a car chase, but the kid in the well isn't going anywhere.

Through all of this I pace, drawn to the drama, unable to keep still.

"Caden, if you want to watch, sit down," my mother says, patting the seat on the sofa beside her.

"I've been sitting in school all day," I tell her. "That's the last thing I want to do."

I go upstairs to get out of her hair, and lie on my bed for

a whole ten seconds before getting up to go to the bathroom, even though I don't really have to go, then back downstairs to get a drink even though I'm not thirsty, then back upstairs.

"Stop it, Caden!" Mackenzie says when I pass her room for like the tenth time. "You're freaking me out."

Mackenzie is currently addicted to a video game that she won't stop playing until she beats it, forty or fifty game-hours from now. I've already beaten it, although I doubt I'd have the patience to play it now.

"Can you help me?" she asks. I look at the screen. There's a large treasure chest in a caged room that appears to have no way in or out. The chest is sparkling gold and red. That's how you know it's not just any treasure chest. Sometimes you bust your ass to get to one, only to find there's nothing inside but a stinking rupee. But the red and gold chests – they hold the real treasures.

"The boss key is in there," Mackenzie says. "It took me an hour to find the key to unlock that chest, and now I can't get to it." Funny that you need a key to unlock a chest that just gives you a bigger, better key.

She continues to run around the outside of the caged room, as if maybe the iron bars won't be there the next time around.

"Look up," I tell her.

She does and sees the secret passageway right above her avatar's head. So easy when you know the answer.

"But how do I get up there?" she asks.

"Just reverse gravity."

"How do you do that?"

"Didn't you find the lever?"

She growls in frustration. "Show me!"

But I'm done, because my walking fever has reached a critical mass. "I can't do everything for you, Mackenzie. It's like math; I can help you, but I can't give you the answer."

She throws me her best glare. "Video games are *not* like math, and don't convince me they are, or I'll hate you!" Resigned, she searches for the antigravity lever, and I head out. Not just out of her room, but out of the house. Even though it's almost dark — even though it's just a few minutes to dinner, I have to walk. So while Mackenzie runs herself ragged in game temples, I wander through my neighborhood making random turns, maybe in search of my own boss key.

45 Ten Graves Deep

How unlucky does a kid have to be to fall into an abandoned well? You hear these stories all the time. Some kid's playing out in a field somewhere with his dog, and down he goes — fifty feet or more, vanishing into nowhere.

If the kid is lucky, and the dog isn't too stupid, people find out in time, and they get someone with no collarbones to go down the well and fish the kid out. Then the no-collarbones guy gets to spend the rest of his life feeling there was a reason he was born with no discernible shoulders, and the rescued kid gets to pass his genetic material on to future generations.

If the kid isn't lucky, then he dies down there, and the tale ends sadly.

What must it be like to suddenly be swallowed by the earth, finding oneself nearly ten graves deep? What thoughts go through a person's mind? "Man, this sucks" doesn't quite cover it.

There are times I feel like I'm the kid screaming at the bottom of the well, and my dog runs off to pee on trees instead of getting help.

46 Food Fight

"You're skin and bones," my mom tells me at dinner the next day.

"He needs more meat!" is my father's instant solution, attacking my mom's attempts to vegan-ize us. "Protein to build muscle."

Dad hasn't noticed I've just been moving the food around my plate. Since eating has always been a given for me, he treats it like breathing. He assumes it's happening. Mom, however, is the one who has to toss out my unfinished meals.

"I eat," I tell them. Which is true, I just don't eat very much anymore. Sometimes I don't have the patience, and other times I forget.

"Supplements," Dad says. "I'll get you some protein shakes."

"Protein shakes," I repeat. "Good."

My answer seems to satisfy them, but now both of them have been alerted to my eating patterns, and watch my plate like it's a time bomb.

Our ship has turned to copper. It happened overnight. All the wood, my bunk, the sparse furniture. It's all been turned into tarnished metal, the color of a worn-out penny.

"What's going on?" I ask, mostly to myself, but the navigator answers from across the room.

"You said the ship was too old-fashioned for the mission, and what you say makes a difference around here," he tells me. "Difference, inference, interference. You've interfered with the order of things is what I'm saying. You should have left it the way it was. I liked this place when it was wood."

I run my fingers along the wall. Instead of smooth plates – which you might expect on a metal ship – it's still made of grooved planks, but they seem to have changed at the molecular level, like wood that has petrified into copper. There are no bolts and rivets – the metal planks are still held together by dark pitch that seems to squirm in the crevices.

I leave my quarters and go up on deck to find that the entire ship has petrified into brown metal, shiny in some places but dull in most, already beginning to turn green in the corners, as copper will do. It's still the same ship, but now it's a copper galleon. All very steampunk without the steam, or the punk. I didn't know there was that much copper in the world.

The captain sees me and grins. "Look at what your thoughts have bought you," he says loudly, gesturing to the copper deck around him. He's no longer wearing a pirate's costume. Now his uniform looks more like something from a mock nineteenth-century navy. A blue, woolen coat with oversized brass buttons and gold-tasseled shoulders, plus an equally ridiculous hat.

I glance down to see that my clothes look sailorly as well, although just as worn and frayed as before. The slippers on my feet are scuffed patent leather. My striped shirt looks like a sun-faded barber pole.

"After careful consideration, we have modernized, as per your suggestion," the captain tells me, although there's nothing modern about it. "We even have a diving bell!" And he points to a perfect replica of the Liberty Bell sitting heavily on the deck. A porthole has been cut into its face and through it I see a lone sailor trapped inside. I hear his dull thuds on the metal as he pleads to get out.

"You see what you've done?" says the parrot from the captain's shoulder. "You see? You see?"

The eyes of the other sailors are on me, and I can't tell if their stares hold approval or disdain.

48 Really That Lonely

That first night of our copper transmutation, I venture out to see how Calliope has weathered the change. I slide down to her, and her arms embrace me with a different kind of firmness. A harsher kind of strength.

"You should not have handed the captain so many of your

thoughts," she says. "It's so cold now. *I'm* so cold."

It's true. She's much colder now. Smoother. Harder.

"Keep me warm, Caden. And I promise I'll never let you fall."

Since she faces the saline spray, her copper skin has already turned green, but she wears it majestically, nobly.

"You're like … the Statue of Liberty now," I tell her, but it doesn't comfort her.

"Am I really that lonely?" she asks.

"Lonely?"

"That poor shell of a woman must forever hold her torch aloft while the world does its business around her," Calliope says sadly. "Have you ever considered how lonely it is to be the girl on a pedestal?"

49 Don't You Want a Whopper?

I fill the empty neighborhood streets with my presence. It's a Saturday during spring break, so I have all the time in the world. I'm going to see a movie with my friends this afternoon, but I have the morning to walk.

Today I start a game. The signs I see will tell me what to do.

LEFT TURN ONLY!

I make a sharp left turn and cross the street.

DON'T WALK!

I cease walking and count to ten before moving again.

FIFTEEN MINUTE ZONE

I sit on the curb for fifteen minutes – challenging myself to keep still for that long.

The road signs become too repetitive, so I expand to other things. An advertisement on a bus stop says, *"Don't you want a Whopper?"* I don't, but I walk to the nearest Burger King and get one anyway. Can't remember if I eat it or not. I may have just left it there.

"Time to upgrade? Visit your neighborhood Verizon store today!"

The nearest one is pretty far away, but I make the trek, and have the clerk spend twenty minutes trying to sell me on a phone I have no intention of buying.

There are so many signs out there! I'm out until the sun sets. I never make it to the movies.

I can't recall when it stops being a game.

I can't recall when I begin to believe that the signs are giving me instructions.

50 Garage Widows

Not all spiders have perfect webs. Black widows don't. There are black widows in our garage, or at least there were before the house was tented. But even if they're gone, they'll be back faster than the termites. Black widows are easy to identify. A red hourglass design on their bellies. They're hard and shiny – they look almost like plastic Halloween spiders. They're not as deadly as people think. Without antivenom you

might lose a limb at worst. It would take three or four bites from different spiders to kill a full-grown human. The thing is, they're shy spiders. They don't bite easily; they'd rather just be left alone. Very reclusive. Ironically it's the brown recluse spider that's aggressive and will go after you. Their venom is pretty deadly.

I always know when there's a black widow in the garage because of the web. Black widow webs are messy. No pattern. Like whatever mechanism in their tiny brains that makes webs is broken. They lack the engineering skill to make picture-perfect, fly-catching nets. Or maybe they just can't be bothered. Maybe they embrace the randomness. Maybe the lines they draw have meaning to them that the rest of the arachnid world is blind to.

For this reason I have more than the usual amount of sympathy when I crush them with my shoe.

51 Not Entirely Me

"I can't contain myself," I tell Max as we work together in my living room on a school project.

"What's that supposed to mean? Are you happy or something?" He doesn't bother to look up from the PowerPoint that he's creating on my computer. I can't get comfortable in my chair. I wonder if I actually look happy, or is he just ridiculously unobservant?

"Ever have an out-of-body experience?" I ask.

"What are you on?"

"I asked you a simple question. Why is it so hard to answer?"

"It's not, you're just acting like a freak."

"Maybe I'm fine and everyone else is a freak. Have you considered that?"

"Whatever." Finally he looks at me. "Are you gonna work with me on this, or do I have to do it all myself? You're the artist – you should be doing the PowerPoint."

"Digital is not my medium," I tell him. Then for the first time I focus my attention on the screen. "What's the project again?"

"You're kidding, right?"

"Yeah, of course I am." But I'm not kidding and it troubles me that I'm not.

Max moves the mouse like it's a living thing. Maybe it is. He clicks and drags and drops. He's building a fictional earthquake scenario in Miami. A science project. Now I remember. After my last test, I know I should take this seriously, but my mind keeps flying elsewhere. We chose Miami because the city's skyscrapers are designed to withstand hurricanes, not earthquakes. In our PowerPoint, glass towers crumble. Mega-devastation. It should get us an A.

But it makes me think of the earthquake in China that I worry I could cause if I think about it too much.

"Would a seven point five do this much damage?" he asks. I watch his hand continue to move the mouse, but sometimes it feels like it's my hand, not his. I can feel my fingers clicking that mouse. It's unnerving.

"I'm not entirely *in* myself," I say. I meant to say it in my head, but it came out of my mouth.

"Just shut up with the freaky crap, okay?"

But I can't stop. I'm not sure if I want to. "I'm kind of like … all around me. I'm in the computer. I'm in the walls."

He looks at me, shaking his head.

"I'm even in you," I tell him. "In fact, I know what you're thinking, because I'm not entirely me anymore. I'm partially in your head."

"So what am I thinking?"

"Ice cream," I instantly say. "You want ice cream. Mint chip, to be exact."

"Wrong. I was thinking that Kaitlin Hick's rack would really bounce big-time in a seven-point-five earthquake."

"No, you're confused." I tell him. "That's what *I* was thinking. I just put it in your head."

Max leaves a few minutes later, kind of backing out of the front door, like there's a dog that might bite his behind if he turned his back on it. "I'll finish the project alone," he says. "No problem. I'll do it myself." And he's gone before I can even say good-bye.

52 Evidence of the Truth

Dad calls to me in that "we have to talk" kind of voice after a dinner that I had no appetite for. I have an urge to bolt, but I don't. I want to pace the family room, but I force myself to sit on the sofa. Still, my knees bounce like my feet are on miniature trampolines.

"I emailed the track coach to get a schedule of meets," he tells me. "He says there is no Caden Bosch on the team."

I knew this would happen eventually.

"Yeah, so?" I say.

My father gives an exasperated puff of air that could blow out birthday candles. "It's bad enough that you lied to us about this – but that's another conversation."

"Good, can I go now?"

"No. My question is why? And where do you go after school? What have you been doing?"

"That's three questions."

"Don't be cheeky."

I shrug. "I go walking," I say honestly.

"Walking where?"

"Just around."

"Every day? For hours?"

"Yeah. For hours." My sore feet are evidence of the truth, but it still doesn't give him what he needs.

He runs his fingers through his hair, imagining his hair actually gives him some resistance. "This isn't like you, Caden."

I stand up and find myself yelling. I don't even mean to, I just am. "SINCE WHEN IS WALKING A CRIME?"

"It's not just the walking. It's your behavior. Your *thinking*"

"What are you accusing me of?"

"Nothing! This is not an inquisition!"

"I didn't make the team, okay? I got cut and I didn't want to disappoint you, so now I go walking, all right? Are you happy?"

"That's not the point!"

But it's the only point he's getting. I head for the door.

"Where are you going?"

"For a walk. Unless I'm grounded for getting cut from the team." And I'm out the door before he can say anything more.

On the way to school a few years ago, Dad had an unusual freak-out moment. Unusual, because anytime my dad freaks out, it's as predictable as a tax table, but this was something new. Mackenzie was in the back, and I was riding shotgun. From the moment we left the driveway, Dad was jittery, like he had had too much coffee. I figured it was something to do with work, until he let out an unsettled sigh and said:

"Something's wrong."

I didn't say anything, I just waited for him to explain, because he never says anything provocative without explaining himself. Mackenzie, however, doesn't have patience to wait.

"What's wrong with what?" she asked.

"Nothing," Dad said. "I don't know." He was distracted enough to miss a yellow light, and had to slam on the brakes to keep from careening into the intersection as the light turned red. He looked at the cars around us nervously, and said, "I'm just having trouble driving today."

I started to worry that maybe he was having a heart attack or a stroke or something, but before I voiced my concerns, I noticed something at my feet right next to my backpack. It was metallic and oddly shaped, but was only odd because of its location. It was a common enough object, but you generally don't see such a thing lying on the floor. Only after I picked it up did I realize what it was.

"Dad?"

He glanced over to me, saw what I was holding, and all of his anxiety melted with a single short laugh of recognition. "Well, that would explain things, wouldn't it?"

Mackenzie leaned forward from her spot in the backseat. "What is it?"

I showed it to her. "The rearview mirror," I told her.

Dad pulled over to the side of the road to readjust himself mentally to the idea of driving without being able to instantly see behind him.

I remember looking at the adhesive pad on the windshield where the mirror should have been, and shaking my head like my father was clueless. "How could you not know it was gone?"

Dad shrugged. "Driving's automatic," he said. "You don't think about those things. All I knew was that I felt somehow ... impaired."

I didn't get it at the time, but that feeling – knowing something is wrong, but not being able to pinpoint what it is – is a feeling I've come to know intimately. The difference is, I've never been able to find something as easy and as obvious as a rearview mirror lying at my feet.

54 Due Diligence

I stare at my homework, unable to lift a finger to do it. It's as if my pen weighs a thousand tons. Or maybe it's electrified. That's it – it's electrified – and if I touch it, it will kill me. Or the paper will slice an artery. Paper cuts are the worst. I have legitimate reasons for not doing my work. Fear of death. But the biggest reason of all is that my mind doesn't want to go there. It's in other places.

"Dad?"

It's getting toward "that time of year," and my father sits at the kitchen table with his laptop, stressed and distracted by the new tax code, and some client's haphazard collection of receipts. "Yes, Caden?"

"There's this boy at school who wants to kill me."

He looks at me, into me, through me. I hate when he does that. He glances back to his laptop, takes a deep breath, and he closes it. I wonder if he's doing it to hide something from me. No, it couldn't be. What would he be hiding? That's crazy. But still...

"Is this the same kid as before?"

"No," I tell him. "It's someone different."

"Someone different."

"Yes."

"A different kid."

"Yes."

"And you think he wants to kill you."

"Kill me. Yes."

Dad takes off his glasses, and pinches the bridge of his nose. "Okay. Let's talk about this. Let's talk about these feelings you're having—"

"How do you know it's just a feeling? How do you know he

hasn't already done something. Something bad!"

Again he takes that deep breath. "What has he done, Caden?"

I start getting louder. I can't help myself. "It's not what he's done – it's what he's going to do! I can read it in him! I know! I know!"

"All right, just calm down."

"Are you even listening to me?"

Dad stands up, finally maybe taking this as seriously as he should. "Caden, your mother and I are worried."

"Well, that's good, right? You should be. Because he might be after you, too."

"Not about him," my father says. "About you. Do you understand?"

Mom comes in behind me, making me jump. My sister is with her.

My parents' eyes meet, and it's like mind reading. I can feel their thoughts shooting through me: Dad, to Mom, and back to Dad again. Mental Ping-Pong through my soul.

My mom turns to my sister. "Go upstairs."

"No, I wanna stay here." My sister puts on a face to match her whine, but Mom won't allow it.

"Don't argue with me. Just go!"

My sister slumps her shoulders and stomps up the stairs, exaggerating every footfall.

I'm alone with my parents now.

"What's wrong?" Mom asks.

"Remember what I told you? About a kid at school?" Dad

says, making it crystal clear that I can't tell either of them anything in confidence. I give her the details, and she weighs it a little differently than Dad.

"Well, maybe we need to look into this. Find out about this boy ourselves."

"See, that's what I'm saying. Look into it!" I feel the tiniest bit relieved.

Dad opens his mouth like he's going to speak, but closes it again, reconsidering his reaction. "Okay," he says. "I'm all for due diligence, but…"

He never finishes the "but." Instead he goes into the living room, kneeling by the bookshelf. "Where's last year's yearbook?" he asks. "Let's see this kid for ourselves."

And now that they believe me, I feel relieved. But not really. Because I know they *don't* believe me. They're just going through the motions, to placate me. To make me feel like they're on my side. But they're not. They're like Ms. Sassel and my teachers and the kids who look at me with evil intent. It's like these aren't my mother and father, they're just masks of my parents, and I don't know what's really underneath. I know I can't tell them anything anymore.

55 A Regular Infestation

What I had once thought were rats on the ship's deck are not rats at all. Although I think I'd prefer it if they were.

"They're a nuisance," Carlyle tells me, as he does his best to poke them out of corners and wash them from the deck. They run from his soapy water. They don't like being wet, or for that matter clean. "Just when you think you've got a handle on 'em, more of 'em show up on deck."

Some ships are infested with rodents. Others cockroaches. Ours has an infestation of free-range brains. The smallest are the size of a walnut, the largest are the size of a fist.

"The damn things escape from sailors' heads when they're asleep, or when they're not paying attention, and go feral." Carlyle pushes his mop toward a cowering batch of them, and they skitter away on purple little dendrite legs.

"When the day comes to do the dive," Carlyle tells me, "I gotta make sure there's not a single brain on deck to foul things up."

"If they're brains from the crew, why are they so small?" I ask.

Carlyle sighs sadly. "Either they didn't use 'em and they atrophied – or they used them too much, and they burned out." He shakes his head. "Such a waste."

He dips his mop into his bucket of soapy water and sloshes it into dark corners, flushing the hapless brains out from their hiding places, and washing them out of the ship's drainage holes into the sea.

He finds a small one clinging to the strands of his mop and he bangs the mop against the rail to dislodge it. "There's no end to them. But it's my job to get 'em off the ship before they breed."

"So … what happens to the brainless sailors?" I ask.

"Oh, the captain finds something to fill their heads with, and then sends them on their merry way."

But somehow it doesn't sound too merry to me.

56 The Stars Are Right

It's the middle of the night. I stand above Calliope at the tip of the bow, and I'm filled with a nasty kind of anticipation. Like the feeling you get five minutes before you realize you're going to throw up.

There's a storm on the horizon. Lightning illuminates the distant clouds in erratic bursts, but it's still too far away to hear the thunder. The sea is too rough for me to drop down into her arms tonight. She has to shout over the roar of the sea to be heard.

"The captain is not entirely wrong to think me magical," she confides. "I see things no one else does."

"Things in the sea?" I ask. "Things beneath the waves?"

"No. It's toward the horizon that I cast my eyes. I see the future in the stars that ride the horizon. Not just one future but all possible futures at once, and I don't know which one is true. It's a curse to see all that *might* happen but never know what *will.*"

"How can you see anything in the stars?" I ask her. "The stars are all wrong."

"No," she tells me. "The stars are right. It's everything else that's wrong."

Max and Shelby don't come over anymore for our game-creation sessions. Max doesn't come at all even though my house has been like a second home to him. He even avoids me in school.

Shelby, on the other hand, makes an effort at conversation in school, but I doubt her motives. If she really wanted to talk to me it wouldn't be so forced. What is she really up to? What is she saying to Max about me when I'm not there? I'm sure they've gotten another artist for their game. They'll blindside me with it any minute. Or maybe they won't tell me at all.

Shelby corners me for a conversation. She tries to make small talk. Shelby is more about talking than listening, which is usually fine, but lately I haven't been a good listener. Mostly I nod when I think it's appropriate, and if a response is required I usually say, "I'm sorry, what was that?"

But this time Shelby isn't taking any of it. She sits me down in the cafeteria, forcing me to look her in the eye.

"Caden, what's going on with you?"

"That seems to be the question of the month. Maybe it's what's going on with you."

Then she leans close and gets quiet. "Listen, I know about these things. My brother started getting drunk in tenth grade, and it just about destroyed him. I might have been like him, except that I saw what it did to him."

I pull away. "I don't drink, okay? Maybe a beer at a party once in a while, you know, but that's all. I don't get drunk."

"Well, whatever it is you're doing, you can tell me. I'll understand. Max will, too – he just doesn't know how to say it."

Suddenly all my words come out at Shelby in hard consonants. "I'm fine! I'm not *doing* anything. I don't smoke crack, I don't snort Ritalin or suck gas from whipped cream cans, and I don't shoot up Drano."

"Okay," says Shelby, not believing me in the least. "When you feel like talking about it, I'll be here."

58 Head-banger

There was this kid I knew back in the second grade. When he got mad, he would bang his head against the wall or the table – whatever was close by and bangable. The rest of us thought it was funny, so we tried to get him mad at every opportunity, just to see him do it. I was guilty of it, too. See, the teacher moved him around the room, hoping to find a spot where he would be okay. Eventually he got moved next to me. I remember this time I had grabbed his pencil while he was doing math, and pushed down on it, just hard enough to break the tip. He got mad, but not that mad. He glared at me and went to sharpen his pencil. When he got back I waited a minute, then tugged on his paper so his pencil left a streak across the page. He got mad, but not mad enough. So I waited a minute, then I kicked his desk hard enough to send his math book flying off the table and to the ground. The third time was the charm. He glared at me with crazy eyes and I remember saying to myself that I had really gone too far. Now he'd go nuts on me, and it would be my own fault. But instead he began to bang his head against his desk. Everyone was laughing and the teacher had to wrestle with him to get him to stop.

The thing is, we never saw him as a person, just as an object of comic relief. Then one day I saw him in the playground. He was playing all by himself. He seemed fairly content, and it occurred to me that his odd behavior had left him friendless. So friendless that he didn't know any better.

I had wanted to go over and play with him, but I was scared. I don't know of what. Maybe that his head-banging was contagious. Or his friendlessness. I wish I knew where he was today, so I could tell him I understand how it was. And how easy it is to suddenly find yourself alone in the playground.

59 Man on Fire

I have never ditched school. Leaving school without permission gets you detention or worse. I'm not that kind of kid. But what choice do I have now? The signs are there. Everywhere, all around me. I know it's going to happen. I know it will be bad. I don't know what it's going to be or what direction it's going to come from, but I know it will bring misery and tears and pain. Horrible. Horrible. There are a lot of them now. Kids with evil designs. I pass them in the hall. It started with one, but

it spread like a disease. Like a fungus. They send one another secret signals as they pass between classes. They're plotting – and since I know, I'm a target. The first of many. Or maybe it's not the kids. Maybe it's the teachers. There's no way to know for sure.

But I know things will calm down if I'm not in the middle of it. Whatever they're planning to do won't happen if I leave. I can save everyone if I leave.

The bell rings. I bolt from class. I don't even know what class it was. The teacher was speaking Cirque-ish today. Today, sounds and voices are muffled by a liquid fear so overwhelming I could drown in its waters and no one would ever know, sinking down to the depths of some bottomless trench.

My feet want to take me to my next class by force of habit, but there's a force more powerful compelling my feet now right out the front entrance of the school, my thoughts racing ahead of me like a man on fire.

"Hey!" yells a teacher, but it's an incompetent, impotent protest. I'm out of there, and no one can stop me.

I race across the street. Horns blare. They won't hit me. I bend the cars around my body with my mind. See how the tires squeal? That's me doing that.

There's a strip mall diagonal to the school. Restaurants, pet shop, doughnut place. I am free, but I am not. Because I can feel the acid cloud following me. Something bad. Something bad. Not at school – no, what was I thinking? It was never at school. It was at home! That's where it's going to happen. To my mother, or my father, or my sister. A fire will trap them. A sniper will shoot them. A car will lose control and ram into our living room, only it won't be an accident. Or maybe it will. I can't be sure, all I can be sure of is that it's going to happen.

I have to warn them before it's too late, but when I take out my cell phone, the battery is dead. They drained my battery! They don't want me warning my family!

I race this way and that, not sure what to do, until I find myself on the corner begging everyone who passes to borrow their cell phone. The looks they give me – dead-eyed gazes – chill me. They ignore me, or hurry past, because maybe they can see the steel spike of terror piercing my skull, driving all the way down into my soul.

My panic has subsided. The unbearable sense that something awful is about to happen has settled, although it hasn't entirely gone away. My parents don't know I left school early. The school did send out a robocall about "Kah-den Boosh" missing one or more classes, because the automated voice can't pronounce my name. I deleted it from voice mail.

I lie on my bed, trying to make sense out of chaos, examining the mystery ashtray that holds the remains of my life.

It's not like I can control these feelings. It's not like I mean to think these thoughts. They're just there, like ugly, unwanted birthday gifts that you can't give back.

There are thoughts in my head, but they don't really feel like mine. They're almost like voices. They tell me things. Today, as I gaze out of my bedroom window, the thought-voices tell me that the people in a passing car want to hurt me. That the neighbor testing his sprinkler line isn't really looking for a leak. The hissing sprinklers are actually snakes in disguise, and he's training them to eat all the neighborhood pets – which makes some twisted sense, because I've heard him complaining about barking dogs. The thought-voices are entertaining, too, because I never know what they are going to say. Sometimes they make me laugh and people wonder what I'm laughing at, but I don't want to tell them.

The thought-voices tell me I should do things. "Go rip out the neighbor's sprinkler heads. Kill the snakes." But I won't listen to them. I won't destroy someone else's property. I know they're not really snakes. "You see that plumber who lives down the street," the thought-voices tell me. "He's really a terrorist making pipe bombs. Go get in his truck and drive away. Drive it off a cliff." But I won't do that either. The thought-voices can say a lot of things but they can't make me do anything I don't really want to do. Still, that doesn't stop them from tormenting me by forcing me to think about doing those terrible things.

"Caden, you're still awake?"

I look up to see my mom at the door of my room. It's dark outside. When did that happen? "What time is it?"

"Almost midnight. What are you still doing up?"

"Just thinking about stuff."

"You've been doing that a lot lately."

I shrug. "A lot of things to think about."

She turns off the light. "Get some sleep. Whatever's on your mind, it'll look clearer in the morning."

"Yes. Clearer in the morning," I say, even though I know it will be just as cloudy.

Then she hesitates at the threshold. I wonder if she'll leave if I pretend I'm asleep, but she doesn't.

"Your father and I think that maybe it would be a good idea for you to *talk* to someone."

"I don't want to talk to anyone."

"I know. That's part of the problem. Maybe it will be easier to talk to someone different, though. Not me or your father. Someone new."

"A shrink?"

"A therapist."

I don't look at her. I don't want to have this conversation. "Yeah, sure, whatever."

61 Check Brain

Automobile engines aren't all that complicated. They look that way when you don't know much about them – all of those tubes and wires and valves – but mostly the combustion engine hasn't changed that much since it was invented.

My father's issues with cars don't end with plunging rearview mirrors. He basically knows next to nothing about cars. He's all about math and numbers; cars are just not his thing. Give him a calculator and he can change the world, but whenever the car breaks down, and the mechanic asks him what's wrong, his response is usually, "It broke."

The automotive industry loves people like my father, because it means they can make lots of money from repairs that the car may or may not need. It annoys my father no end, but he rationalizes it by saying, "We live in a service economy. We all have to feed it somehow."

It's not like the car manufacturers are much help. I mean, with modern technology, you'd think our cars could diagnose themselves, but no, all there is on the dashboard is this moronic "check engine" light that comes on whenever there's anything wrong – which proves that automobiles are more organic than we think. They're obviously modeled on the human brain.

There are many ways in which the "check brain" light illuminates, but here's the screwed-up part: the driver can't see it. It's like the light is positioned in the backseat cup holder, beneath an empty can of soda that's been there for a month. No one sees it but the passengers – and only if they're really looking for it, or when the light gets so bright and so hot that it melts the can, and sets the whole car on fire.

62 More Alive Than You Think

"There is much to teach you," the captain says, strolling the copperized deck, his hands clasped behind his back. The crisp woolen uniform he now wears is beginning to look almost as natural on him as his pirate outfit had. He even carries himself differently now. More regally. Clothes make the man.

As he does his rounds, he makes sure everyone is occupied with their particular trivial pursuits. Today my assignment is to be his shadow. Watch and learn.

"Journeys of discovery require more than just a working maritime knowledge," the captain lectures. "They require intuition. Impulsiveness. Leaps of folly as often as leaps of faith. Do you catch my drift?"

"Yes, sir," I tell him.

"Wrong answer," he snaps. "Best not to catch a drift. It could lead to influenza." Then he jumps on the weblike rope ladder on the mainmast. "Come join me on the ratlines." He climbs upward, with me right behind.

"Are we going to the crow's nest?" I ask.

"Absolutely not," he tells me, insulted by the suggestion. "Only to the sails." We climb high enough to reach the mainsail. "I'll show you a secret," he says. Then he pulls out a knife from his coat and slashes the sail – a gash a full foot wide. Wind pushes through the tear, making it spread like an opening eye.

"What was that for?"

"Observe," the captain says.

I watch the damaged sail … and witness it slowly repair itself. The sail heals like a membrane, until all that remains is a faint scar where the tear had been, a slightly deeper beige than the rest of the canvas sail.

"This ship is more alive than you think, boy. She feels pain. She can be hurt but can also heal."

As I cling to the rope ladder, a chill goes through me that has nothing to do with the blustering wind. "Is it Calliope's pain?" I ask.

The captain turns his eye to me. "I don't know. How is it that you know her name?"

I realize my mistake – but maybe it's the kind of folly of which the captain approves. "Crewmen talk," I say. Which is true, so it's not like I'm really lying. Still, the captain seems suspicious.

"Whether or not she feels the ship's pain is important to

know. 'Tis a question for which I would welcome an answer."

"I'll keep that in mind," I tell him. I wonder whether he's just given me permission to speak to her, or if he's trying to trap me for having done so.

63 People I Don't Know in Places I Can't See

"I feel everything," Calliope tells me as I rest in her metallic arms one night, suspended above an easy sea. "I feel not only the sails, but the hull. Not only the ship, but the sea. Not only the sea, but the sky. And not only the sky, but the stars. I feel everything."

"How can that be?"

"I don't expect you to understand."

And yet I do. "I have connections, too," I tell her. "Sometimes I feel *inside* the people around me. I believe I know what they're thinking – or if not *what*, then at least *how* they're thinking. There are times that I'm certain I'm tied to people on the other side of the world. People I've never met. The things I do affect them. I move left, they move right. I climb up, and they fall from a building. I know it's all true, but I can never prove what happens to people I don't know in places I can't see."

"And how does this make you feel?"

"Wonderful and terrible at the same time."

She tilts her neck to look into my eyes, instead of looking forward at the sea. It's a harder move than folding her arms to hold me. I hear the straining squeal of bending copper. "We are not all that different, then," she says.

And I know for the first time that I've truly pierced her loneliness. And she has pierced mine.

64 If Snails Could Talk

The doctor has a PhD in psychology from American University, which, to me, sounds a little too generic to be real. A framed diploma hangs proudly in the waiting room above a potted ficus with leaves a little too green to be real as well.

"I want you to feel you can talk to me about anything," the talk-doctor says, speaking with a calmness to his voice, and a deliberately slow cadence – like a snail might, if snails could talk. "Anything you say or do in here is kept in strict confidence, unless you want me to share it."

It sounds like he's reading me my anti-Miranda rights.

"Yeah. Confidence. I get it."

I get it, but I don't believe it for an instant. How do you trust a therapist when even the plant in his waiting room is a lie?

That's where my parents are now. They're in the waiting room leafing through copies of *Psychology Today* and *FamilyFun*, and talking about me. They were here in the room with the talk-doctor and me for the first few minutes. I thought they would launch at him a laundry list of all the things that have been going on, but they seemed uncomfortable when they tried to talk about me to a stranger.

"Caden's behavior has been" – my father had struggled for the words – "out of the ordinary."

Both he and Mom seemed relieved when the doctor asked them to leave the room.

"So," says the talk-doctor now that we're alone. "Out of the ordinary. Let's start there."

I know I have to hold it together in here. I feel as if my entire life depends on my holding it together. This man doesn't know me. He can't see into me. All he gets is what I give him.

"Listen," I say, "my parents mean well, and I know they think they're helping me, but this is their problem, not mine. They're totally stressed and overprotective. I mean, you saw them, right? They're so nervous, they make me nervous."

"Yes, I can see that you're anxious."

I try to stop talking with my hands, and to keep my heels consistently on the floor. I'm only partially successful.

"Tell me," he says, "have you been having trouble sleeping?"

"No," I respond. It's true. I haven't had *trouble* sleeping, I just haven't felt like sleeping. At all.

"And how are things at school?"

"School is school."

He's quiet for a painfully long stretch. I can't stand it. I start fidgeting with things within fidgeting distance. I reach for a small cactus on the table beside me to see if it's fake, too, but it's real, and I prick my finger. He hands me a tissue.

"Why don't we do some relaxation exercises?" the talk-doctor suggests, although I know it's only phrased like a suggestion. "Lean back, and close your eyes."

"Why?"

"I'll wait until you're ready."

Reluctantly I lean back and force my eyelids to close.

"Tell me, Caden, what do you see when you close your eyes?"

My eyelids snap open again. "What kind of dumb-ass question is that?"

"It's just a question."

"What am I supposed to see?"

"Nothing specific."

"Well, that's what I see. Nothing specific." I'm standing now. I don't remember standing. I can't recall when I began to pace the room.

The session drags on for a torturous eternity that is just another twenty minutes. We never do get through the relaxation exercises. I never answer his question. I never close my eyes for fear of having to tell him – to tell myself – what's there. Instead we play chess, although I don't have the patience to consider my moves, so I intentionally make bad ones to end the game quickly.

When it's time to leave, he tells my parents we should schedule weekly sessions, and that maybe, just maybe, they should consider having me also see someone with a license to write prescriptions. I knew he was a fake.

65 The Darkness Beyond

What do I see when I close my eyes? Sometimes there is a darkness there that goes beyond anything I can describe. Sometimes it is glorious, and sometimes it is terrifying, and I rarely know what it's going to be. When it's glorious, I want to live in that place, where the stars are just marking a vast unreachable shell, like they used to believe in days of old. The inside surface of a giant eyelid – and when I peel back the lid, there's a darkness that truly goes on forever – but it's not darkness at all. It's just that our eyes have no way to see that kind of light. If we could, it would blind us, so that eyelid, it protects us. Instead we see stars – the only hint of the light we can never reach.

And yet I go there.

I push past the stars into that dark light, and you can't imagine how it feels. Velvet and licorice caressing every sense; it melts into a liquid you plunge through; it evaporates into air that you breathe. And you soar! You don't need wings because it supports you of its own accord – of its own will resonating with yours – and you feel not only that you can do anything but that you *are* anything. Everything. You move through everything, and your heartbeat becomes a pulse of all things alive, all at once, and the silence between each beat is the stillness of things that exist, but do not live. The stone. The sand. The rain, and you realize that it is all necessary. The silence must exist for there to be a beat. And you are both those things: the presence and the absence. And that knowledge is so magnificent you can't hold it in, and it drives you to share it – but you don't have words to describe it, and without the words, without a way to share the feeling, it breaks you, because your mind just isn't large enough to hold what you've tried to fit into it …

… but it's not always like that.

Sometimes the darkness beyond is not glorious at all, it truly is an absolute absence of light. A clawing, needy tar that pulls you down. You drown but you don't. It turns you to lead so you sink faster in its viscous embrace. It robs you of hope and even the memory of hope. It makes you think you've always felt like this, and there's no place to go but down, where it slowly, ravenously digests your will, distilling it into the ebony crude of nightmares.

And you know the darkness beyond despair, just as intimately as you know the soaring heights. Because in this and all universes, there is balance. You can't have the one without facing the other. And sometimes you think you can take it because the joy is worth the despair, and sometimes you know you can't take it and how did you ever think you could? And there is the dance; strength and weakness, confidence and desolation.

What do I see when I close my eyes? I see beyond darkness, and it is immeasurably grand both above me and below.

66 Your Terrifying Awesomeness

But now my eyes are open.

And I stand at my front door, not in and not out, halfway between two places. I think back to the time I told Max that I was outside of myself. It's more than that now. I can't tell the difference between what's part of me and what's not. I don't know how to explain the feeling. I'm like the electricity in the walls. No – more than that! I'm in the high-tension wires traveling through the neighborhood. I'm moving through everything around me at lightning speed. I realize there is no longer an "I" anymore. Just the collective "we," and it takes my breath away.

Do you know how it feels, to be free from yourself and terrified by it? You feel both invincible and yet targeted, as if the world – as if the universe – doesn't want you to feel this dizzying enlightenment. And you know there are forces out there that want to crush your spirit even as it expands like a gas filling all available space. Now the voices are loud and blaring in your head, almost as loud as your mother as she calls you down to dinner for the third time. You know it's the third time even though you don't remember hearing the first two times. Even though you don't even remember going up to your room.

So you sit at the kitchen table, moving food around your plate, and you only shovel food into your mouth when someone reminds you that you're not eating. But it's not food you're hungry for. Maybe it's because you're not you anymore. You're everything around you. Now your body feels like an empty shell, so what's the point of feeding it? You have bigger things to do. And you tell yourself that your friends don't connect with you anymore because they're too frightened by your awesomeness. Almost as frightened as you are.

67 The Flesh Between

The captain gathers us around the table in the map room at dawn. The storm still looms in the distance no closer than the night before or the night before that. It retreats as we draw near.

These mission meetings are always populated by the same crew members: me, the navigator, Bone-boy, the girl with the pearl choker, the blue-haired girl, and our pudgy lore-master. Each of us has struggled to excel at our assigned positions. The navigator and I have it easy – my drawings and his charts are treated as beyond scrutiny. The others, well, they fake their way through. Choker-girl, our dark and miserable morale officer, has learned to fake positive comments when under the captain's glaring eye. The bone-boy reads whatever he thinks the captain wants to hear in the tossed bones, and the blue-haired girl claims she's found everything from gold doubloons to crates of diamonds in the shredded manifests of sunken ships.

The lore-master, however, has a dangerous streak of honesty.

"I can't do it," he tells the captain at our group gathering. "I can't make heads or tails of the runes in the book."

The captain seems to swell like a sponge in water. "We care not of heads and tails, only of the flesh between!" Then the captain calls for Carlyle, who has been lurking in the corner, as he always lurks during these meetings. "Keelhaul him."

The lore-master protests, beginning to hyperventilate at the suggestion, then the parrot flaps out of nowhere to the captain's shoulder.

"Clean the cannon!" the parrot says. "Have him clean the cannon!"

The captain swipes the bird off, dislodging several bright feathers, but the parrot is undeterred. "The cannon! The cannon!"

"Pard'n me, sir," Carlyle says, "but maybe the bird is right. A keelhauling will leave him useless, if not dead. And the cannon needs a good cleaning if we're to battle the beasts ahead."

The captain's eyeball fixes on Carlyle, burning at the insubordination – a lowly swabby second-guessing his order. But he holds his temper and waves his hand. "Do as you will," he says. "As long as the boy suffers for his indolence."

The parrot, now perched on a hanging lamp, looks at me and

shakes his head sadly at the captain's comment. I look away, not knowing what it means to be the focus of the parrot's attention, and how the captain might react to it.

It takes Carlyle and two other brawny crewmen to drag the lore-master out, kicking and screaming at the prospect of the cannon, and I wonder why that would be as terrifying to him as a keelhauling. Once he's gone, the captain returns to his agenda.

"Today is truly a momentous day," the captain tells us, "for we shall test the diving bell and see if Caden's knowledge of deep-sea exploration rings true."

I feel queasy, and it has nothing to do with the motion of the ship. "But … it's the wrong kind of bell," I say, feeling small and impotent.

"You should have thought of that before you suggested it," snarks the girl with blue hair.

"We're all screwed," says our morale officer.

68 Worm Inside

It's like this: You know the answers to everything. Your head is so full of answers, it's bursting. It's ready to explode and pour killing radiation on everyone. Your life will be declared a radio-active zone for hundreds of years if you can't release some pressure by showing the truth of what you know to anyone who'll listen. The lines, the *connections* you see between all things.

And you have to share it.

So you walk the streets, and spout out randomness at people, knowing there's nothing random about it at all. People look at you strangely, and even in their gazes you can see the connections between you, them, and the rest of the world.

"I can see inside you," you tell a woman carrying a bag out of the supermarket. "There's a worm in your heart, but you can cast it out."

She looks at you and then turns away, hurrying to her car, afraid of what you've told her. And you feel good. And not.

You feel pain down low, and you glance at your feet. You're barefoot. You've been walking around that way, and it's left your feet blistered, scraped, and bloody. You don't remember taking off your shoes but you must have. There's meaning to that,

too. Meaning to the way your flesh connects to the earth, telling gravity to hold you and everyone else down. And suddenly you know that if you put shoes on your feet, the world will let go and everyone will be hurled off into space, all because of a thin layer of rubber that would cut your connection to the ground. *You* are the antigravity lever of the world. As wonderful as knowing this is, the sheer awe of it is terrifying because of the power you have. And that worm you saw in the woman's heart has somehow migrated into you. That's not a heartbeat you're feeling, it's the worm eating its way through you and you can't get it out.

Beside the supermarket is a travel agency fighting to stay alive in an age where travel is all booked online. You push your way through the door.

"Help me," you say. "The worm. The worm. It knows what I know, and it wants to kill me."

But a woman in a pantsuit roughly pushes you out the door, yelling at you. "Get away from here, or I'll call the police."

For some reason that makes you laugh, and your feet are bleeding, and that makes you laugh, too, and in the parking lot, a BMW sits with a broken headlamp, and that makes you cry. Leaning against the wall, you slide down in a heap and your soul fills with tears. You think of Jonah, who, after enduring being partially digested by the whale, burst into tears on a mountaintop when the gourd vine protecting him from the sun was devoured by a worm and died. The same worm. You understand his tears. How, with the sun beating down on his head, he was so grieved that he wanted to die.

"Please," you say to anyone around you. "Please just make it stop. Please just make it stop." Until someone from the Hallmark store, a woman much nicer than the travel witch, kneels down to you.

"Is there someone I can call?" she says kindly. But the thought of her calling your parents to come get you is enough to make you rise to your feet.

"No, I'm okay," you tell her and you start moving away. You tell yourself you'll be fine if you can find your way home. There is no whale to digest you here. The thing that's eating you works from the inside out.

69 Your Meaning Is Irrelevant

Roll call. The sky is white, the distant horizon gray and sparking with faint lightning – not just ahead, but in all directions. The captain paces the upper deck, looking down on the crew, going on about the great importance of the mission, and the importance of this particular day.

"Today Seaman Caden's diving bell shall be put to the test, and the manner of our descent shall be once and for all determined." He looks very authoritative – even more so now in his uniform of brass buttons and blue wool – but authority and reason are two different things.

"That's not a bathyscaphe!" I call out. "It won't work! That's not what I meant by a diving bell!"

"Your meaning is irrelevant."

It takes more than a dozen crewmen to lift the woefully mis-cast Liberty Bell to the railing. Then, on the captain's order, the bell is hurled overboard. It sinks like a stone, and the rope – which has been gnawed upon by the feral brains – snaps, sending the bell to the irretrievable depths. A single bubble surfaces like a belch.

And the captain says, "Test successful!"

"What? How is that a successful test?" I shout.

The captain stalks toward me slowly, deliberately, his foot-steps clicking on the copper-plated deck. "This test," he says, "was to disprove your theory of how to achieve the bottom of the trench." Then he shouts, "You were WRONG, boy! And the sooner you accept your complete and overwhelming wrongness, the sooner you'll be of use to me, and this mission." Then he storms away, very satisfied with himself.

It is only after the captain is gone that the parrot lands on my shoulder – something he rarely does – and says, "We need to talk."

70 Silver Shark

Your father stands in your path as you're on the way out the door.

"Where are you going?"

"Out."

"Again?" He's much more forceful than the last time he asked, and he's not moving out of your way. "Caden, your feet are full of blisters from all this walking."

"So I'll get better shoes." You know he won't understand why you have to walk. It's this movement through the world that keeps you from blowing up. It keeps the world safe. It keeps the worm calm. Only it's not a worm now. Today, it's an octopus, with eyes instead of suction cups on its tentacles. It moves around inside you, inside your gut. Sliding around your organs, trying desperately to get comfortable. But you won't tell your parents that. They'll just tell you it's gas.

"I'll walk with you," he says.

"No! Don't do that. You can't do that!" You push past him and out the door. You're in the street. Today you have shoes and you realize now that wearing shoes won't stop gravity from holding things to the earth. That was silly. How did you ever think that? But you do know that if you don't walk, something terrible will happen somewhere and you'll see it in the news tomorrow. You know that beyond a doubt.

Three blocks from home you look over your shoulder to see your father's car slowly following you like a silver shark. Ha! And they think *you're* paranoid. There's something very wrong with your parents if they have to follow you when you walk.

You pretend you don't see the car. You just keep walking until long after dark. Not stopping, not talking to people. You let him follow you all the way around the neighborhood, then all the way home.

I awake to find the parrot watching me from the foot of my bed. I gasp. He hops closer. I can feel sharp claws on my chest. He doesn't dig his talons in, though. He just gingerly walks across my tattered blanket until his one good eye is looking back and forth between mine.

"I am concerned about the captain," he says. "Concerned, concerned."

"Why is that my problem?"

The navigator stirs in his sleep, and the parrot waits for him to be still, then leans closer to me. I can smell sunflower seeds on his breath.

"I am concerned that the captain doesn't have your best interests at heart," he whispers.

"Since when do *you* care about my best interests?"

"Behind the scenes, behind the scenes, I have been your greatest advocate behind the scenes. Why do you think you are in the captain's inner circle? Why do you think you weren't chained to the diving bell when it went down?"

"Because of you?"

"Let's just say I have influence."

I don't know whether to believe the bird, but I'm willing to entertain the idea that maybe he's not the enemy. Or at least not the *worst* enemy.

"Why are you telling me this?" I ask.

"There may be a need to…" Then he begins bobbing his

head nervously, so that his face makes figure eights in front of me.

"Need to what…?"

He begins to pace on my chest. It tickles. "Nasty business, nasty business." He calms down, is silent for a moment, then meets my left eye with his. "If the captain proves unworthy of the crew's trust, I need to know I can count on you."

"Count on me to do what?"

Then he puts his beak right up against my ear. "To kill him, of course."

72 Our Only Hope

You lie on your bed. Shirt off. A feverless fever burns through your brain. Rain falls outside like the end of the world.

"Bad," you mumble. "Something bad. Something bad will happen at school because I'm not there."

Your mom rubs your back like she did when you were little. "And when you were there, something bad was happening at home."

She doesn't get it. "I was wrong about something happening at home," you tell her, "but this time I'm right. I know. I just know."

You turn your head to look at her. Her eyes are red. You want to tell yourself it's not from crying. It's from lack of sleep. She hasn't slept. Neither has your dad. Neither have you. You haven't slept for two days. Maybe three. They're both missing work. They take turns tending to you. You want to be left alone, but you're afraid to be left alone, but you're afraid to not be left alone. They listen to you, but they don't hear you, and the voices tell you that your parents are a part of the problem. *"They're not really your parents, are they?"* the voices say. *"They're impostors. Your real parents were eaten by a rhinoceros."* You know that's from *James and the Giant Peach* – a favorite book when you were little – but it's all so muddled, and the voices are so persuasive, you don't know what's real and what's not. You know the voices aren't talking into your ears, but they're not exactly in your head either. They seem to call to you from another place that you've accidentally tapped into, like a cell phone pulling in a conversation in some foreign language – yet somehow you understand it. They linger there on the edge of your consciousness like the things you hear just as you're waking up, before the dream collapses under the crushing weight of the real world. But what if the dream doesn't go away when you wake up? And what if you lose the ability to tell the difference?

The voices can't be real, but they're very good at making you forget that.

"They're telling me it's the end of the world if I don't stop whatever is going to happen."

"Who's telling you?" your mother asks.

But you don't answer. You don't want your parents to know about the voices, so you just moan, and think about all the movies where one person is chosen to save the world. *"You're our only hope,"* those movies always say. So what if those heroes never faced their destinies? What if they just lay there in bed and let their mothers rub their backs? What if they did nothing? What kind of movie would that be?

73 The Honors

The captain calls me into his study. Just him and me. The parrot is nowhere to be seen. Last I saw, the parrot was down in the galley, hopping from shoulder to shoulder, peering in sailors' ears to make sure they still had brains. Now the parrot winks at me any time he sees me, to remind me of our secret conversation.

"Do you trust me, Caden?" the captain asks.

If I lie, he'll know it, so I tell him the truth. "No," I say.

My answer makes him smile. "Good boy. That means you're learning. I'm proud of you. More proud than you could know."

It throws me for a loop. "I thought you hated me."

"Far from it!" he says. "The trials I put you through are to burn away the chaff. To purify you. Make no mistake, boy, you are the brightest hope for this mission. All of my hopes are on you."

I'm not sure what to say to this. I wonder if he says this to all the crewmen, but somehow I sense that he's sincere.

"Truth be told, I am greatly concerned about things on my ship, boy. Not the ocean without, but the tides within." Then he leans close. "I know she speaks to you. Calliope. She tells you things that she tells no others. That's proof that you are special. That you are chosen."

I don't say a thing. Not until I know where this is going.

"If there are things she knows, you are the one she'll tell."

Then I realize that maybe I'm finally in a position to have a little bit of power. "If she tells me things, she tells me in confidence. Why should I break that confidence and tell you?"

"*I am your captain!*" And when I don't respond, he growls and storms back and forth behind his desk. "Or maybe you answer to the parrot." He pounds his fist against the bulkhead. "That mutinous fowl! He sows seeds of sedition among the crew even as he sits on my shoulder."

Then he grabs me and looks at me closely with his good eye, just as the parrot had. "Does Calliope say there'll be a mutiny? Does she say the bird will prevail?"

I stay calm. "I'll ask her," I tell him.

He is relieved. "Good boy. I knew you were loyal." Then he whispers, "When the time comes, I shall let you do the honors."

"What honors?"

He smiles. "The honors of killing the parrot."

74 In God We Trust

When I was younger, whenever I looked at dollar bills, I always had a strange sense that Washington was glaring at me. It was funny, and a little bit creepy. It wasn't just Washington. Hamilton was totally judgmental with that perpetual smirk. Jackson was the worst. That disturbingly high forehead, and superior gaze, accusing me of spending my money unwisely. Only Franklin was friendly, but it wasn't like I got to see him often.

Maybe this should have been a sign that something was seriously up with me. Or maybe everyone thinks nutty, quirky things like that. I mean, it's not like I thought they were really looking at me — it was just a funny thought I'd bounce around for no particular reason. It never stopped me from actually using money. At least not until recently.

We always look for the signs we missed when something goes wrong. We become like detectives trying to solve a murder, because maybe if we uncover the clues, it gives us some control. Sure, we can't change what happened, but if we can string together enough clues, we can prove that whatever nightmare has befallen us, we *could* have stopped it, if only we had been smart enough. I suppose it's better to believe in our own stupidity than it is to believe that all the clues in the world wouldn't have changed a thing.

75 Safety Locks

"We're going on a trip," your father tells you. You know he's been crying.

"What kind of trip? Is it a cruise?"

"If you like," he says. "But we've got to go; the ship sails soon."

You can't remember the last time you slept. Insomnia doesn't cover this. It's anti-somnia. A viral wakefulness that's so contagious, it would wake the dead if you got close enough. You truly believe this. You fear it. Every thought that comes into your head becomes a truth to fear.

The voices are still speaking, but they haven't slept either, so now they just grumble nonsense. You pick up the feelings behind their gibberish, though. Those feelings are not good. They brim with foreboding, bitter warnings, and hints at your importance in the universe.

You don't want to take this trip. You have to stay here to protect your sister. She's off with friends now. Away from home. But you need to be here when she gets back. And then you look into your parents' bloodshot eyes, and you realize they want to protect her, too. And that it's you she needs protection from.

You're in the car now. Your parents talk, but their words are as jumbled as the voices inside, and although you know the car is just the trusty family Honda, your parents in the front seat begin to feel further and further away. Suddenly you're in the back of a limo, and someone is sucking out the oxygen. You can't breathe. You try to open the doors and jump out on the freeway, but the doors won't open. Someone has put on the child safety locks. You curse and scream, and say the most horrible things. Anything to get them to stop and let you out, but they don't. They try to calm you. Your father can barely drive the car with the commotion you're causing, and you wonder if the horrible thing you're worried about is a car accident that will kill you all, and maybe you're the one causing it, so you put your head in your hands instead of trying to escape.

You go down a steep hill. Suddenly the car's not a limo anymore, it's a padded elevator, and you're going down the diagonal slope of the black pyramid, into its hidden depths – deep, deep underground.

The vehicle pulls into a parking lot at the bottom of a hill. A sign out front says SEAVIEW MEMORIAL HOSPITAL, but it's a lie. Everything is.

Five minutes later, your parents sit across from a chipmunk-cheeked woman with glasses too small for her face. They fill out paperwork, but you don't care, because you're not really here. You're watching from an untouchable distance.

To keep yourself from pacing, you focus on the fish tank. A liquid oasis in a desert of uncomfortable institutional chairs. Lionfish, clown fish, anemone. An ocean, condensed and captured.

There's a small child pounding the glass with his palm. The fish dart away, bumping their noses against the invisible barrier that contains their world. You know how this feels. Tormented by something incomprehensible and so much larger than yourself. You know how it feels to want to escape, only to be limited by the dimensions of your personal universe.

A mother calls to the boy in Spanish, then pulls him away when he doesn't come, and you begin to wonder, *Am I on the outside or the inside of that tank?* Because the rules of "here" and "there" don't have a clear place in your head anymore. You are as much the objects around you as you are yourself. Maybe you are in the tank with them. The fish may be monsters, and you may be afloat on a doomed vessel – a pirate ship, perhaps – unaware of the breadth and the depth of the peril it sails upon. And you hold on to that, because no matter how frightening that is, it's better than the alternative. You know you can make that pirate ship as real as anything else, because there's no difference anymore between thought and reality.

76 No Way to Stop It

I am trapped in a conspiracy of conspiracies. On one side, the parrot and I plot mutiny. Not so much with words, but with glances. Nods. Clandestine winks of his single seeing eye. My artwork seethes with secret messages for him. Or at least he thinks so.

On the other side, the captain and I plot the parrot's end. He, too, winks at me with his one working eye, and decorates the walls of his quarters with what he calls "the telltale visions of a captain triumphant."

"Share with no one the secret meaning of your creations," he whispers to me. "We shall feed the parrot to the beasts of the deep, as your drawings suggest, and none will be the wiser."

I know these two plots will come together like matter and antimatter, annihilating me in the explosion, but I see no way out. No way to stop it. It's coming as surely as are the beasts that protect the mysteries of Challenger Deep.

The hospital paperwork is signed. The deal with the devil is done. The lady with the cheeks and small glasses looks at you with a gaze of false but practiced kindness.

"It's gonna be okay, sweetie," she says, and you glance behind you, wondering if maybe she's talking to someone else. You and your parents are led to a different wing of the hospital. A specialized wing. Your parents grip each other. A single creature with four weeping eyes.

You think you're okay with this, because you still watch it all from a distance, until it's time for your parents to head for the door, and you realize there is no distance at all. You are here and about to be stranded terrifyingly alone. You are about to be keelhauled, and all the premonitions join together into one and you know for a fact beyond any doubt that something terrible will happen to you, to your parents, to your sister, to your friends, but mostly to you if they leave you here.

So you panic. You've never been violent, but now your life depends on fighting your way free from this. The fate of the very world depends on you being anywhere but here.

But they're shrewd. They're sly. Brawny men in pastel scrubs descend on you from nowhere. They grab you and hold you back.

"No!" you scream. "I'll be good! I won't do it anymore!" You don't even know what "it" is, but whatever it is you'll stop if you don't have to be left here.

Hearing your pleas, your parents hesitate by the door as if

they might change their minds — but a nurse in a pastel-pink outfit comes between you and them.

"The longer you stay," she tells your parents, "the harder it will be for him, and the harder it will be for us to do our jobs."

"They're killing me!" you scream. "They're killing me!" And just by hearing yourself say it, it becomes true, but your parents turn around and escape through a series of doors that open and close like canal locks, going out into a night that seems to have fallen from daylight only seconds ago. Now you think that maybe you were right. Maybe they're not your parents at all, but impostors.

Your adrenaline makes you almost stronger than the three pastel men holding you. Almost. In the end they wrestle you into a room, and onto a bed, and you feel a sharp sting in your ass. You turn just in time to see a nurse pulling away a hypodermic needle, its lethal load already delivered. In seconds your arms and legs are secured in padded restraints, and you feel the shot begin to take effect.

"You rest up, dear, everything will be fine," the nurse tells you. "You'll be better for this."

Then the poison they put in your ass reaches your brain, and your mind spreads thin like an oil slick on the surface of an ocean.

And you discover, for the first time, the White Plastic Kitchen. A place you will visit again and again. A gateway to all the places you don't want to be.

I have this dream. I'm lying on a beach someplace where they don't speak English – or if they do, it's only because so many American tourists are there, spending money they don't have on things they don't need, and burning lobster-red beneath an unforgiving sun.

The sun forgives me, though. It forgives all of us – my mom, my dad, and my sister. It sheds warmth and light upon us without any threat of consequence. No sunscreen required.

The sounds here are all sounds of joy. Laughter. Children playing. The voices of bargaining beach vendors who sell shiny wares with such charisma that people can't resist them. Happy tourists walk away festooned in silver and gold, their new jewelry jingling like Christmas bells with every step.

My sister plays in the gentle turquoise surf, looking for shells. The hiss of waves breaking at her ankles is a gentle sigh, as if the sea itself has found lasting contentment.

My parents hold hands and walk along the beach. My father wears his favorite white straw fedora, saved exclusively for tropical vacations, because it looks so ridiculous anywhere else. There's no talk of bills or taxes, and he has no numbers to crunch. Mom is happily barefoot, and no matter how warm the sun is, the sand stays cool. She has no one's teeth to clean today. They both stroll with an easy pace that speaks of no destination.

As for me, I sit in the sand, enjoying the gritty feeling as it sifts through my wriggling toes. In my hands is a tall glass with a cool drink beaded with condensation that catches the sunlight, refracting it like a kaleidoscope. I sit there on the beach, and I do absolutely nothing. I think absolutely nothing. I am satisfied just to be in the moment.

In this place, there is no kitchen except for an outdoor grill serving up shrimp further along the beach. The aroma is pleasing; a carnal incense like burnt offerings to the God of Infinite Vacation.

In this place there is no ship but the sleek racing yacht sailing out of the bay, blown by a custom-made zephyr, sending it off to points even more exotic than this.

Everything feels right with the world …

… and the sad thing is that I know it's a dream. I know it must soon end, and when it does I will be thrust awake into a place where either I'm broken, or the world is broken.

So I curse the perfect beach, and the cool, quenching drink that I can feel in my hand, but can never, ever raise to my lips.

79 Submitted for Your Approval

Consciousness is a relative concept when you're pumped full of psychoactive meds. It's not an either/or proposition. It's as if the interface between being asleep and being awake has gone supernova, exploding and swallowing everything around it with cosmic shrapnel. Nothing survives but an abiding sense of being *elsewhere*. A place where time isn't a straight, predictable line, but is more like a toddler's knotted shoelace. A place where space bubbles and twists like a funhouse mirror in four dimensions, and everyone's a scary clown. You are the little faceless figure falling through a world of shadow and substance at the beginning of *The Twilight Zone,* cottony thoughts leaking from your oblong head.

Rod Serling must have been severely psychotic when he came up with that show.

80 Salted Slug

Sometimes you realize you're on a bed in a hospital. Sometimes you're convinced it's the White Plastic Kitchen. And other times you're certain that you've been sewn to the billowing sails of a ship. The dizziness is real, and some of the faces are, too, but good luck figuring out which ones, and what they really look like. They tell you that you were only "restrained" on that first night when you appeared to be violent, but it still feels like you're tied to the billowing bed.

People come and go, talking to you, and you hear yourself respond, but don't feel your lips making the words. You don't feel your toes or fingertips either.

"How are you feeling?"

You're asked this a lot. Or maybe you're only asked it once, and the other times are just echoes.

"Salted snail," you hear yourself say in a medicated slur. "I think I peed myself."

"Don't you worry about that. We'll take care of it."

You think maybe they'll put you in one of those adult diapers, and then realize that maybe they already have, but you can't tell, and don't want to find out. You want to retreat into your shell, spiraling in and in and in, but you realize you don't have a shell. You're more of a slug than a snail. You have no protection at all.

Through all of it, the voices in your head are still talking at you, but they're too stoned to have much impact, and you realize this isn't all that different from chemotherapy for cancer. They bombard the whole body with bad crap, hoping it will knock out the disease, and leave the rest alive. The question is, will poisoning the voices kill them, or just make them really, really pissed off?

81 War of the Nemesi

"Today," says the captain in his most commanding voice, "I shall share a tale of these waters that I do not need a lore-master to verify, for this one I know by heart."

The parrot, growing wary, takes a healthy sidestep away, perhaps not wanting to associate himself with anything the captain says.

"It begins with a great captain, name of Ahab," he tells us, "and ends with another captain, name of Nemo."

And although I know I'm risking another brand on my

forehead or worse, I say, "Excuse me, but I don't believe those two fictional characters ever met."

"They did, boy!" says the captain, with far more patience than I expected. "In fact, they were fast friends – which was part of the problem. However, this story is less about them, and more about their great Nemesi."

I consider pointing out that *nemesi* might not actually be the plural of *nemesis*, but I figure I'll quit while I'm ahead.

"The *Nautilus*, that mysterious submarine that carried Nemo for twenty thousand leagues and more, was under endless siege by the giant squid that threatened to take her down to the depths. As the *Nautilus* raced away from the squid, it chanced to encounter the *Pequod*, and Ahab, in pursuit of the white whale. There was a collision, and the *Pequod* was sunk." Then he looks at me and says mockingly, "*You* would tell me that it was the whale that took the ship and its captain down, but Melville was wrong. His story was a fabrication told to him by Ishmael, who was sworn to keep the captain's secret."

The parrot whistles with either disgust or appreciation at the spandex flexibility of the yarn.

"Be that as it may," continues the captain, "Nemo rescued Ahab from the water, and in a single glance, the two captains realized they were men of like minds, and sailed off in the submarine until they found the Sea of Green, and thus lived happily ever after." He pauses, perhaps expecting applause, but receives none, so he continues. "Their beasts, however, found no such affinity for each other." Then the captain spreads out his arms and his eye goes wide. "Huge they were, the white whale and the giant squid. Grotesque freaks of nature, but of opposing sorts. Sentient and strange was the squid, confounding the sea around it with inky darkness. An eight-armed monstrosity – a beast of chaos that defied all logic. The whale, on the other hand, was all sense and seemliness. Its great echolocating brain could calculate dimension and distance. It knew everything worth knowing about the world it inhabited, while the squid saw nothing beyond the cloud of its own ink. Naturally they despised each other."

Then he pounds his fist on the table so hard it makes all of us jump, and the parrot flaps his wings powerfully enough to lose a few feathers. "Great men of the sea must never abandon their beasts!" the captain announces. "Now, thanks to those two neglectful men, their Nemesi are doomed to wage war against each other until the end of time, growing angrier and angrier with each passing year!" He takes a moment to stare each of us down before he says, "Any questions?"

We all look to one another. Clearly there are plenty of questions, but no one wants to put any forth. Finally Bone-boy apprehensively raises his hand, and when called on says,

"Huh?"

The captain takes a deep breath and empties his lungs in an exasperated sigh that I can feel like a gale. "The moral of the story is that we must not free ourselves from our beasts. Nay — we must abandon all else in this world *but* our beasts. We must feed them as much as we fight them, submitting to loneliness and misery with no hope of escape."

The girl with the pearl choker nods approvingly. "I get that."

But it sits so badly with me that I can't stop myself from voicing disagreement. "It's not right!"

All eyes turn to me. I can already see a *minus* being branded next to my F.

"Elucidate," the captain growls. I know it's a warning, but it's one that I refuse to heed.

"If those captains found a way to leave their monsters behind, they deserve whatever peace they find. They deserve resolution. And the beasts ... well, they deserve each other."

No one moves. No one but the parrot, who grooms himself. I can't help but sense he's proud of me for what I've said. It annoys me that I care.

Whatever patience the captain had is now gone. He looks like a volcano about to blow. "As usual, Seaman Bosch, your insolence can only be surmounted by your ignorance!"

And then the navigator comes to my rescue.

"Insolence, ignorance, ignoble, Chernobyl. Don't go nuclear, sir – the crew can't survive the radiation."

The captain considers this, then chooses to vent the pressure of his fury by safely releasing it in another gale-force sigh. "Opinions are like sandstorms, Seaman Bosch," he says. "They have no place at sea." Then he tweaks my nose like he might a naughty child, and dismisses us.

As soon as we've left the map room and are out on deck, the navigator scolds me. "When will you learn? You walk in step with the captain, or you walk the plank – which, being copper, will not give you the proper bounce for a graceful dive."

It occurs to me that, while I've seen crow's nest jumpers, I've never seen the ship's plank. But now as I look out across the open deck, there it is, poking rudely off the side of the ship like a middle finger. It doesn't surprise me that it appeared at its mention. I've learned not to be surprised by anything here.

Before we go below, the girl with blue hair turns to me.

Each time I talk back to the captain, I seem to earn a little more respect from her. "I'll bet our captain has a pretty bad beast, too," she says. "Do you think we'll ever run into it?"

I look up to see the parrot swooping from the map room to a high perch on the foremast.

"I think we already have," I tell her.

82 Deep in the Throat of Doom

In the middle of the night, I am abducted by crewmen I don't know and taken to clean the cannon. Punishment, no doubt, for talking back to the captain. I try to fight, but my limbs have turned to rubber just as completely as the ship has turned to copper. My arms and legs bend and stretch in strange directions, and give me no support when I try to stand, no assistance when I try to fight. My arms flap like noodles at my abductors.

Down a dark hatch we go where the massive cannon awaits. "Everyone must clean the cannon at least once each voyage," I am told. "You'll do it whether you like it or not."

The place is dark and dismal with a stench of grease and gunpowder. Cannonballs are stacked in pyramids, and there in the middle sits the cannon, impossibly heavy – the copper planks beneath it buckle from its weight. Its dark mouth is even more intimidating than the captain's eye.

"Isn't she a beauty?" says the master-at-arms – that grizzled, muscular career seaman, covered in leering skeletal tattoos.

Beside the cannon is a bucket of polish and a rag. I dip the rag in the polish with my rubbery arms, and begin to slather it on the barrel of the great gun, but the master-at-arms laughs. "Not like that, you fool." Then he grabs me with his powerful arms and lifts me off the ground. "It's not the outside that needs cleaning."

I hear more laughter, and for a moment think that there are others hiding in the room – but the laughter is from the skull faces of his tattoos. Dozens of voices cackle at me. *"Push him in!"* they yell. *"Shove him in!"* *"Cram him in!"*

"No! Stop!" But my pleas are useless. I am pushed headfirst into the mouth of the cannon, sliding down its cold, rough throat. Tight. Claustrophobic. I can barely breathe. I try to squirm, but the master-at-arms yells at me:

"Don't move! The slightest motion can set it off!"

"How can I clean it if I can't move?"

"That's *your* problem." He and his ink laugh long and loud – then there's silence … and then he begins pounding on the barrel of the cannon with an iron pole. In a constant rhythm so loud it resonates in my skull.

Bang! Bang! Bang! Bang!

"Hold still, please!" the skull tattoos yell. "Or you'll have to do this again."

After what feels like forever, the rhythm of the banging changes.

B-B-B-Boom! B-B-B-Boom B-B-B-Boom!

The endless percussive symphony makes my brain want to slide out through my ears and run away – and I realize that must be how it happens! That's what chases the brains out of sailors' heads! But I don't want to be another mindless sailor. I don't want Carlyle mopping my renegade brain into the sea.

Clang-Clang Bang! Clang-Clang Bang! Clang-Clang Bang!

The pattern of the pounding cycles through twice more, louder each time, until the world is all noise and my teeth are rattling in my head, and I know that no one is going to stop this. I am alone in the barrel of the gun and no one can save me.

83 Clockwork Robots

Your parents come once a day during visiting hour, like a pair of clockwork robots. You convene in the rec room, and each day you beg and bargain with them to take you away.

"There are *crazy* people here!" you tell them in a hushed voice so the ones you're speaking about can't hear. "I'm not one of them! I don't belong here!"

And although they don't speak the words, their answer is in their eyes. *Yes you are, and yes you do.* You hate them for it.

"It's only for a little while," your mother tells you. "Until you're feeling better."

"If you didn't come here," your father insists, "you would just have gotten worse. We know it's hard, but we know you're brave."

You don't feel brave, and you don't trust them enough to take their word for it.

"There's some good news," they tell you. "Your MRI came back clean. It means you don't have a brain tumor, or anything like that."

Until they mentioned it, it had never occurred to you that you might have had one. And now that it's been mentioned, you don't believe the results.

"It wasn't so bad, was it? The MRI?"

"It was loud," you tell them. Just thinking about it makes your teeth start to rattle again.

Your parents come and go, come and go. It's the only way you can measure the days. And they talk about you when they think you're not listening – as if somehow it's your sense of hearing that's been affected, not your mind. But you can still hear them across the room.

"There's something in his eyes now," they say. "I don't know how to describe it. I can't look at them." And that almost makes you laugh, because they don't see what you see when you look in *their* eyes. In everyone's eyes. You see truths no one else can see. Conspiracies and connections as twisted and sticky as a black widow's web. You see demons in the eyes of the world, and the world sees a bottomless pit in yours.

84 Lost Landscape

You can't get in your own head sometimes. You can pace around it, you can bang it against walls, but you can't get inside.

"That's not a bad thing," Dr. Poirot tells you. "Because right now the things inside aren't doing you much good, are they?"

"Not doing me much good," you repeat. Or is it him repeating you? You're never really sure, since cause and effect have become as shifty as time itself.

Dr. Poirot has a glass eye. You only know because your roommate told you, but now that you look, you can see that it is slightly smaller and doesn't track as well as the other. Dr. Poirot wears bright Hawaiian shirts. He says it's to make his patients feel more comfortable. Dr. Poirot prounounces his name Pwah ROW. "Like Agatha Christie's detective," he told you. "You're probably too young to know the character. Times change, times change."

Dr. Poirot has a cheat sheet that tells him everything about you. Even things you don't know yourself. How can you even begin to trust such a person?

"Forget the troubles of the outside world. Your job now is to rest," he says as he flips the pages of your life.

"My job is to rest," you echo, and are mad at yourself for being unable to offer anything but an echo. You don't know whether or not it's the meds making you do this, or your misfiring brain.

"Your mind is in a cast now," he says. "Think of it that way. It was broken and now it's in a cast."

You ask if you can have things from home, but don't know what to ask for. You have your own clothes to wear, but no belts or jewelry. Books are allowed, but no sharp pencils or ballpoint pens either. Nothing that can be used as a weapon against others, or against yourself. They do allow writing instruments in the rec room, but they are under constant guard by the pastels.

Later that morning, your breakfast, along with your morning meds, comes up in an epic projectile puke in the rec room. You had no internal warning, and it spews out all over the puzzle table like white-water foam.

The girl who seems to spend her life at that puzzle table throws a fit.

"You did that on purpose!" the perpetual puzzler yells. "I know you did!" She has blue hair with blond roots. The roots, you suspect, are accurate measures of how long she's been here. When you puke on her puzzle, she launches herself at you – pushes you hard against the wall, and you're too drugged up to fight back. You have a bad bruise on your arm now, but the pain of that is also numbed, like every other part of your nervous system.

A pastel persona is quick to restrain the perpetual puzzler before she can claw your eyes out, and another one escorts you away. There are always pastel personas around, quick to respond if someone gets out of line, and if it gets really bad, there's security dressed in black, but you don't think they carry weapons, because weapons are too easy for a desperate person to grab.

You hear the puzzler crying as you leave. You want to cry, too, for her lost landscape, but instead it comes out as a laugh, which makes you feel even worse, and so you laugh even louder.

You are in the White Plastic Kitchen again. There are shapes around you that sometimes make sense and sometimes don't. Monsters of malicious intent wear ever-changing masks. Voices join in a babbling chorus, and you can't tell what direction they come from, or what dimension – one of the standard three, or one that's only accessible through the part of your head that hurts all the time.

Tonight you sweat. The kitchen is too hot. And it only makes your head hurt worse.

"I have a brain tumor," you tell a disembodied mask with a clipboard hovering beside it.

"No you don't," it says.

"It's inoperable," you insist. You can't tell if the mask is male or female. You think that's intentional.

"Both your MRI and CAT scan showed nothing out of the ordinary," it says, looking at the clipboard – and you don't argue, because you don't want to be shoved back into the cannon.

The mask grows hands – or maybe it had hands all along that were just invisible until now. You feel pressure on your upper arm, and when you look, your whole arm is wedged into the crook of a guillotine.

"Hold still, I'm just checking your vitals," the he-she mask says.

The guillotine slices down. You watch your arm flop on the ground like a trout in a boat. You groan, and the mask says,

"Too small. Throw it back, yes?" And it tosses the arm out an open window that wasn't there a moment ago. Yet when you look, your arm is still attached to your body.

"Systolic's still high. We'll up your Clonidine," it says. "And if that doesn't work, we'll just pop your head like a balloon."

Some of these things are actually spoken. Some aren't. Yet you hear them all the same, and you can't tell which words are out loud, and which are sent to you telepathically.

"Let's have a look at that bruise. Is it tender?" He-she looks at the purple bit of flesh given to you by the blue-haired puzzle-girl.

"Hmm – nice and tender," he-she says or doesn't say. "Good! All our beef should cut like butter." Then you're left to slowly broil in your own juices.

86 Therapy Rodeo

You don't know what this stuff is they feed the kids within these painfully bare institutional walls. Chicken, maybe? Beef stew? The only thing you can clearly identify is Jell-O. There's lots of it. Little bits of peaches or pineapple are mired within it, suspended in red jiggling transparency. You can relate to their plight. Especially when the meds kick in. There are times when the world is gelatinous around you, and it takes such a gathering of willpower just to move the slightest bit, it hardly seems worth the effort.

You exist from meal to meal, in spite of the fact that food means nothing anymore, because you have neither a feeling of hunger nor a sense of taste. It's a side effect of your magical medical cocktail.

"Only temporary," Dr. Poirot says. "Only temporary."

Which doesn't really mean much to you, because time no longer moves forward. It doesn't move sideways anymore either. Now it just spins in place like a little kid making himself dizzy.

You learn to measure time by therapy sessions.

Three times a day, for an hour at a time, they corral you into a circle and force you to listen to things that are so awful you can't purge them from your mind. A girl describes, in graphic detail, how she was repeatedly raped by her stepbrother, before trying to slit her own throat. A boy explains step-by-step what it's like to shoot up with heroin, and sell yourself on the streets to earn money for more. The demons these kids ride are awful, and you want to turn away, run away, cover your ears, but you're forced to listen because it's "therapeutic." You wonder what freaking moron decided it was a good idea to torture screwed-up kids by making them listen to one another's living nightmares.

You tell your parents about it, and to your surprise, they are as furious as you.

"My son's fifteen!" your father says to the head pastel. "You're exposing him to horrors no kid should be exposed to – much less one who's sick – and you call that therapy?"

Way to go, Dad. It's the first sign that maybe he's not an impostor after all.

Your parents' complaints bring about results. A new "facilitator" takes over the therapy group to help rein things in, and keep the therapy rodeo from being overly traumatic to impressionable young minds. "I'm not here to brainwash you," he tells us. "I'm just here to help you speak your mind."

His name is Carlyle.

87 All That We've Worked For

"The dreams you're having trouble me," the captain says. "They reek of malevolence and subversive intent."

We sit in his study, just the two of us. He smokes a smoldering pipe stuffed with seaweed skimmed from the ocean. The parrot's perch is empty.

"But dreams give you insight," I point out.

The captain leans closer, the acrid smoke of his pipe stinging my eyes. "Not these dreams."

I keep expecting the parrot to voice an opinion, forgetting that he's not in the room. I've become so used to the captain and the parrot as a team, it makes me uneasy.

"The masked demons you speak of in your dreams of the white kitchen threaten to undo all that we've worked for," the captain says, "and our journey will be for naught."

I wonder if the parrot has suffered the same fate as his father, and has had an unwanted visit to the galley, which is nowhere near as sterile and bright as my dream-kitchen. Has he had an appointment with the chopping block? I've often thought I'd like the parrot gone, yet the thought of his absence brings me foreboding.

The captain could not have done away with him, because the captain and I are in cahoots. As long as I am a key part of both the captain's and the parrot's schemes, then both are safe if I make no move one way or the other. There are times I want them both to survive. There are times I want them both dead. But I live in fear of only one of them remaining.

"Listen to me well," the captain instructs. "You must not go to the white kitchen. Keep your eyes closed to the brightness of its light. Resist that place with every fiber of your being. Everything depends on you staying here with us. With me."

88 Toxic Tide

You don't so much sleep as borrow eight hours from death. When the meds peak, and you can't get in your head, you can't dream either. Maybe in the earliest hours of the morning, just before waking up, you'll slide into your own unconscious mind, but you'll wake all too soon.

You come to know the pattern of your particular chemical bombardment. The numbness, the lack of focus, the artificial sense of peace when the meds first hit your system. The growing paranoia and anxiety as they wane. The worse you feel, the more you can get into the treacherous waters of your own thoughts. The greater the threat from inside, the more you long for those waters, as if you've grown accustomed to the terrible tentacles that seek to draw you into their crushing embrace.

Sometimes you can see why you need the cocktail. Other times you can't believe you even thought that. And so it goes, waxing and waning like a tide, both toxic and healing at the same time.

When the tide is high, you believe in the walls of this place. When the tide is low, you start to believe other things.

"Once your brain chemistry begins to settle," Dr. Poirot says, "what's real and what's not real will become increasingly clear."

You're not entirely convinced that's a good thing.

89 Streets Green with Blood

"He looks at maps all day long," Carlyle, the therapy guy, tells you. "We call him the navigator."

The kid sitting at the table in the corner of the rec room pores wide-eyed over a map of Europe. You can't help but be curious.

"Why do you have it upside down?" you ask him.

He doesn't look up from his map. "Gotta break up the known patterns to see what's really there." It sort of makes sense. You've been there, so you know what he means.

With a green marker he draws purposeful lines between cities as if he knows exactly what he's doing. The map is a wild web of green. "Solve the pattern, and it solves everything," he says, and it gives you a chill, because it reminds you so much of yourself. You sit down across from him. He's older than you. Seventeen, maybe. He has a faint goatee trying hard to express itself, but it's six months short of becoming a reality.

Finally he looks up at you with the same intensity with which he scoured the map. "Name's Hal," he says, putting up his hand to shake, but taking it down before you can shake it.

"Short for Haldol?"

"Cute. Short for Harold, but that's a parental designation. I am no more Harold than I am Seth, the Egyptian god of chaos. Although Seth is my middle name."

He jiggles his marker in his fingers and mumbles words that rhyme with "middle," and somehow that leads him to bring his pen down on Vienna.

"Mozart!" he says. "The violin was his instrument of choice. Here is where he died in poverty." He holds the pen on the point of the city. Green ink bleeds into the suburbs. "This is where it will start," he says. "I thought I had it yesterday, but I was wrong. This time I'm right."

"What will start?" you ask.

"Does it matter?" Then he mumbles, "Matter, flatter, fatter, hatter. Mad Hatter!"

He leaps up from the chair and asks the nearest pastel persona if they can put on *Alice in Wonderland* – the creepy one with Johnny Depp – because there's something important about it, and he must view it immediately.

"We don't have that one," the pastel tells him. "How about the Disney cartoon version?"

Hal waves his hand in disgust. "Why is everyone here so useless?" he says, then looks at you. "Present company excepted."

It makes you feel good to be, for once, excluded from the ranks of the useless.

90 Atlas Drugged

They make Hal your roommate. Your old roommate, whose name and face you've already forgotten, was discharged that morning. Hal is moved in before the bed is cold.

"You seem to get along," a pastel persona tells you. "Hal hasn't been able to share a room with anyone, but you he likes. Go figure."

You're not sure whether that's a compliment or an insult.

Hal arrives with an overstuffed portfolio of maps torn from atlases and pilfered from AAA.

"My mother brings new ones sometimes," he tells me. "Every addition is a step in the right direction."

He has written mysterious things on the lines that he draws between cities. And he orates random thoughts of profundity with such authority that you want to write them down and hang them on the wall, but they only allow writing instruments in the rec room.

"Man is often lost in a technological, physiological, astrological lack of logical existence that can best be described as a whole lot of nothing lightly dashed with an obvious hint of Scotch," Hal says. You wish you could remember it so you could recite it to your parents, and show them that you, too, are profound – but these days things just don't go in one ear and out the other, they actually teleport, avoiding the space between.

Hal speaks of mathematics, Euclidean perfection, and the golden mean. You tell him about the invisible lines of meaning you feel stretching and winding through and around the people in your life. He gets all excited, which excites you, too.

"You get it!" he says. "You see the big picture." And although your big picture isn't the same as his, they seem to layer neatly over each other, like parts of a musical score, incomprehensible to someone who can't read music until all the instruments begin to play.

"Your artwork is a map," he tells you. "Lines and curves that contain continents of meaning, points of commerce and culture. Trade and travel routes in every curve." He traces his finger along the lines of your latest piece, which is taped up on the wall.

"What we perceive as art, the universe perceives as directions," he proclaims. Directions to where, however, neither of you is sure.

91 Not in the Olympics at All

You empty your lunch plate mindlessly. When you stare at the empty plate, for just a few moments you're in the Olympics. You're the discus thrower. You spin round and round, fighting the chemical-induced thickness of the air, and hurl the plate, certain you're about to win a gold medal. It hits the wall but doesn't shatter because it's plastic. Then you realize you're not in the Olympics at all. How disappointing. The pastels are there on either side of you in an instant, certain that you've just had a violent outburst, and want to prevent another one.

"You can't break down the walls that way," Hal calmly tells you from another table in the dining room. "You can't break the windows either. I've tried. Tried, fried, lied, and untied. They won't even let us have shoelaces. *Shoelaces!* It's because they know how much I hate freaking slippers."

92 The Greater Unknown

Ever since I came out of the cannon mostly intact, the other sailors look at me in awe.

"He's a special one," the captain says.

"That he is, that he is," says the parrot.

The two of them playact with each other, pretending to be cordial, but only so it will make the final betrayal even sweeter. Even though I trust neither of them, I know that eventually I'll have to choose a side.

"Be my second eye," the captain says, "and you shall have riches and grand adventures beyond imagining."

"Be *my* second eye," says the parrot, "and I will offer you something the captain never will. A way off this ship."

I can't decide which offer is the better one, because I don't know which is the more frightening unknown: the captain's adventures, or life ashore.

I try to pose the quandary to Carlyle but, not knowing where his true loyalty lies, I must couch my question so it doesn't give him reason for suspicion.

"If two equally dangerous creatures attack our ship simultaneously from opposite sides," I ask him, "how do we decide which one to take down, since we only have one cannon?"

"I wouldn't know," Carlyle says. "Lucky for me I don't make the decisions around here."

"But if you did…"

He stops mopping for a moment and considers it. "If I did, things would be a whole lot better," he says. Then he adds, "Or a whole lot worse."

It maddens me that Carlyle refuses to commit to any sort of opinion. Even about himself.

"If it's vision and wisdom you want, then you know who you should ask," he says. Then he looks toward the bow, letting his gaze complete the thought.

Calliope has no answer for my quandary about the two beasts.

"I deal in futures, not hypotheticals," she tells me, almost insulted that I asked. "You're on your own with this one."

I almost tell her the truth of the matter, but then realize that she's right. Even if I tell her the real beasts are the captain and the bird, her answer will be the same. Only I can decide. It can be no other way.

The storm still postures on the horizon, but we get no closer, and the captain becomes increasingly frustrated.

"The ocean current is like a treadmill beneath our keel," the captain tells me. "It pushes us back at the same rate the wind pushes us forward. We sail at a fine clip, yet go nowhere."

"We need a stronger wind," I tell him.

"Or a lighter ship," he suggests, burning me an evil eye. He still holds me responsible for the transmutation of our ship into copper. Then he softens, and grabs my shoulder. "But sturdier than wood we now are – and the pale green of things is a better camouflage against the sky and sea. It protects us from the loathsome, scanning eyes of the beasts."

94 Critical Mass

Today you are in a hospital. Or at least this morning. This hour. This minute. Where you'll be three minutes from now is anyone's guess. You've begun to notice, though, that, bit by bit the sense of being outside of yourself has diminished with each passing day. A critical mass is reached, and now your soul collapses in upon itself. You're back inside the vessel of your body.

Just one. Just you. Just an individual.

Me.

I don't quite know when it happens. It's like the movement of an hour hand, too slow for the naked eye to see, but look away for a moment, and the hand has magically leaped from one number to the next.

I am here in the White Plastic Kitchen, but it's not as white as I remembered, and the table I lie upon has mellowed into a bed. My body feels like rubber and my brain like chewing gum. The light above me hurts my eyes. What is it that everyone needs to see so desperately that they need so much light? And why do I still feel as if I'm about to be eaten?

No one comes, and nothing happens forever and forever. Then I realize there's a light switch across the room. I can turn it off. I can, but I can't because I'm the pineapple chunk in the Jell-O. Nothing can motivate me out of this bed but an urgent need to go to the bathroom. Since I'm not feeling that right now, I can't move. Apparently neither can Hal. I can't tell if he's asleep or just trapped in the same Jell-O mold across the room. I doze and I wake, unable to really tell the difference. Then the ground begins to roll beneath me, and I relax, knowing it won't be long until I'm back on the sea, where I make sense, even if nothing else does.

95 Windmills of My Mind

How do you explain being *there* and being *here* at the same time?

It's sort of like those moments when you're thinking about something big that burned itself a powerful memory. Maybe it's the time you scored the winning goal in the play-offs. Or maybe it's the time you got hit by a car on your bike. Good or bad, you're bound to relive it in your head now and then – and sometimes after you've gone there, it's a shock to come back. You have to remind yourself that you're not there anymore.

Now imagine being like that all the time – never knowing for sure when you're going to be here, or there, or somewhere in between. The only thing you have for measuring what's real is your mind ... so what happens when your mind becomes a pathological liar?

There are the voices, and visual hallucinations when it's really bad – but "being there" isn't about voices or seeing things. It's about *believing* things. Seeing one reality, and believing it's something else entirely.

Don Quixote – the famous literary madman – fought windmills. People think he saw giants when he looked at them, but those of us who've been there know the truth. He saw windmills, just like everyone else – but he *believed* they were giants. The scariest thing of all is never knowing what you're suddenly going to believe.

96 Divine Dealer

My friend Shelby comes to visit with my parents. She slowly moves toward me through the Jell-O. It's amazing she can move through it at all.

"I visited you before – do you remember? Do you know who I am?"

I want to be angry at the question, but I can't feel anger. I can't feel anything. "No, and yes," I tell her. "No I don't remember, but yes I know who you are."

"You were pretty out of it the last time."

"I'm not now?"

"Everything's relative."

I sit there saying nothing. I think it's awkward for her. I don't feel that. I feel patient. I can wait forever.

"I'm sorry," she says.

"Okay."

"I'm sorry for thinking that you … you know."

"Thinking that I…?"

"That you were *using*."

"Oh. That." I pull back pieces of the last conversation we had in school. It feels like several lifetimes ago. "I *was* using," I tell her. "And God was my drug dealer."

She doesn't get it.

"Tripping on my own brain chemicals. The dope I was doing was already inside."

She nods in a sort-of understanding way, and changes the subject. I'm cool with that. "So Max and I are still working on the game."

"That's good."

"When you get out we'll show you what we've got."

"That's good."

She has tears in her eyes now. "Stay strong, Caden."

"Okay, Shelby. I'll stay strong."

I think my parents join us for a game of Apples to Apples, but I don't think the game goes well.

97 Can I Trust You?

The girl stands silhouetted against a huge picture window that stretches floor to ceiling, corner to corner, in a room the hospital has labeled the "Vista Lounge." It's designed to give the patients a sense of freedom and open air in the midst of claustrophobic sterility. It doesn't work.

The girl is almost always there. She stands like a monolith looking out of the giant window. A dark silhouette against the bright outside world, staring forever forward.

I'm almost afraid to go up to her. The first few times I saw her, I kept my distance – but right now, that feeling of being a chunk of pineapple congealed in Jell-O isn't as strong as other times. I'm here – not Elsewhere – and I resolve to take advantage of that fact. It requires a tremendous effort of will for me to stride forward and move toward her. In a few moments, I'm close enough for her to see me out of the corner of her eye.

She makes no move, gives no acknowledgment that I'm there. I can't quite tell her ethnicity. The girl has silky brown hair and rich skin the color of polished oak. I've never seen anyone stand so rigidly for so long. I wonder if it's her medication, or if this is the way she is. I find it fascinating.

"What's out there?" I dare to ask.

"Everything that's not in here," she says coldly, with the hint of an accent. The accent is enough to tell me that she's from India, or maybe Pakistan.

The view from the window is of a series of rolling hills, and a row of hillside homes that light up at night like a string of Christmas lights. Beyond the hills is the sea.

"I saw a hawk dive down and fly off with a baby bunny," she tells me.

"Well," I say, "that's something you don't see every day."

"I could feel it die," she says, and she touches her body in a place that her liver might be. "I felt it here" – and then she reaches up and touches the side of her neck – "and here."

Silence for a moment, and then she says, "Dr. Poirot tells me these things aren't real. And that when I'm better, I'll know that. Do you believe him? Because I don't."

I don't answer her because I'm not sure if I can trust anything the parrot says.

"The hawk was my hope, and the rabbit was my soul."

"That's very poetic."

Finally she turns to look at me. Her dark eyes burn with fury. "It wasn't meant to be poetic, it was meant to be true. You work for Poirot, don't you? He sent you. You're one of his eyes."

"Poirot can take a flying leap," I say. "I'm here because…" I can't bring myself to finish the thought, so she finishes it for me.

"Because you have to be. Like me."

"Yeah. Exactly." We've finally reached an understanding.

It's not exactly comfortable but at least it's a step down from awkward.

"The others talk about me, don't they?" she asks, turning her gaze back out toward the horizon. "I know they do. They say terrible things behind my back. All of them."

I shrug. Mostly the kids here don't seem to notice anything unless it intrudes on their idea of personal space. Of course, for some of them, personal space can stretch the distance between the earth and the moon.

"I've never heard them say anything," I tell her.

"But if you do, will you tell me? Can I trust you?"

"*I* can't trust me," I tell her.

That makes her smile. "Admitting you can't trust yourself makes you all the more trustworthy." She turns to me again. Her eyes study my face, moving up and down, then side to side like she's checking the distance between my ears. "I'm Callie," she says.

"Caden."

And I stay with her, looking out of the window, waiting for hawks to kill rabbits.

98 Decomposed Potential

I used to be afraid of dying. Now I'm afraid of not living. There's a difference. We go through life planning for a future, but sometimes that future never comes. I'm talking about personal futures. Mine, to be specific.

There are times I can imagine people who know me looking back ten years from now, and saying things like "He had such potential," and "What a waste."

I think of all the things I want to do and want to be. Groundbreaking artist. Business entrepreneur. Celebrated game designer. "Ah, he had such potential," the ghosts of the future lament in mournful voices, shaking their heads.

The fear of not living is a deep, abiding dread of watching your own potential decompose into irredeemable disappointment when "should be" gets crushed by what is. Sometimes I think it would be easier to die than to face that, because "what could have been" is much more highly regarded than "what should have been." Dead kids are put on pedestals, but mentally ill kids get hidden under the rug.

99 Running on Saturn's Rings

There's a motivational poster in Poirot's office. It's an Olympic runner bursting through the tape at the end of a race. The caption reads, "You may not be the first, you may not be the last, but you will cross the finish line." It makes me think of the track team I didn't actually become a part of. His poster is a lie. You can't cross the finish line if you drop out before the first track meet.

"Does it speak to you?" asks Poirot when he catches me staring at it.

"If it did, you'd probably change my medication," I tell him.

He chuckles at that, and asks how I'm getting along. I tell him that everything sucks, and he apologizes for it, but does nothing to make things less suckful.

He has me fill out a questionnaire that seems more than pointless. "It's for the insurance," he says. "They love paperwork." But looking at my file in front of him, he's nurturing a paperwork fetish as well.

"Your parents tell me you're an artist."

"I guess."

"I've asked them to bring you some art supplies. We don't allow what could be a hazard, of course – the staff will determine what you can have. I'm sure you'll be able to express yourself creatively."

"Goody for me."

He takes in my attitude like a scent in the air, and writes something down. I suspect it will result in a tweak in my cocktail. In addition to the occasional shot of Haldol, I now take four pills, twice a day. One to shut down my thoughts, another to shut down my actions. A third to address the side effects of the first two. And a fourth so the third doesn't feel lonely. The result leaves my brain somewhere in orbit beyond Saturn, where it can't bother anyone, especially me.

Somehow I can't imagine a runner that far out crossing the finish line any time soon.

"I have been concentrating on my legs," Calliope tells me as she holds me in her familiar cold embrace above the sea. I am bruised from the hardness of her copper hands, which have turned even greener than the rest of the ship. What began as traces of oxidation in the corners of her eyes and in the folds of her flowing copper hair have spread across her, so that her sheen has dulled into pale acceptance.

"You don't have any legs," I remind her.

"I think now that I do. Legs and feet. Toes and toenails. My concentration has made it so." Then she whispers, "You cannot tell anyone, especially not the captain. He would not approve."

"He fears you," I remind her.

"He fears anything he can't control – and he's not above hacking my legs off if he thinks it will keep me from walking away from him." She shifts, but her grip on me never loosens. "If I have feet, they are embedded behind me, in the forecastle of the ship. Find that place just below the main deck, where the starboard and port sides meet to form the bow. Find that place, tell me if I have legs, and tell me if you can free them."

"Callie doesn't sit in front of the window because she likes to, she sits there because she *needs* to."

I learn this from the girl with blue hair – the perpetual puzzler who guards her new puke-free jigsaw landscape with her life. She likes to talk to me only when she has something nasty to say about someone else. "She's my roommate, and believe me, she's a total freak. She thinks the outside world goes away when she's not looking."

I watch as the blue-haired girl tries to fit a puzzle piece into a place it clearly doesn't go. Then she touches her nose twice, and tries to fit the same piece in the same spot, then touches her nose twice again. Only after repeating this pattern three times does she move on to another piece.

"She doesn't think the world goes away," I explain. "She *fears* that it goes away. See, there's a difference. It's the fear she's trying to avoid."

"Either way it's idiotic."

I want to lash out at her. Tell her that she's the idiot. Maybe flip the whole table and send puzzle pieces flying in all directions. But I don't – because it's not about idiocy. I suspect Callie is brilliant. And maybe the blue-haired girl is, too. No, it's not about intelligence, it's about the rearview mirror on the floor. It's about the freaking useless "check engine" light, and the only people qualified to look under the hood can't get the damn thing open.

No, I don't lash out. Instead I ask, "What are you afraid will happen if you don't touch your nose twice?"

She snaps her eyes to me like I've slapped her in the face, but she sees I'm not making fun of her, I'm asking the question for real. I really want to know.

She looks back down to her puzzle, but doesn't try to fit any pieces into place. "If I don't," she says quietly, "then I feel like I'm falling. If I don't, then my heart starts beating so fast, I'm afraid it will explode. If I don't, then I can't breathe, like the air has been sucked away." Then, ashamed, she touches her nose twice, and tries to fit in a new piece.

"You're not a freak," I whisper to her.

"I never said I was."

I get up to leave, but she grabs my wrist and squeezes, forcing my hand to open. Then she shoves a puzzle piece into my palm. It's blue. A piece of sky. No distinguishing marks to identify where in the sky it could belong. The hardest kind of piece to place.

"You can borrow this," she says. "Just bring it back before I'm done with the puzzle, okay?" Then she adds, "It's my name. Skye. Stupid name, right?"

And although I have no use for the puzzle piece, I take it, and I thank her – because I know it's not about how useless it is to me; it's about her choice to part with it.

"I'll keep it safe," I tell her.

She nods, and returns to her puzzle ritual. "Callie likes you," she says. "Don't blow it by being a creep."

Hal rarely has visitors. When he does, it's just his mother. Hal's mother is a very beautiful woman. She barely looks old enough to be the mother of a seventeen-year-old. When she comes, it seems like she's just been to the hair salon, but I think she always looks like that.

Not only does she stand out from the other parents, but she stands apart. She seems to coat herself in a protective aura, like a hazmat suit that no one else can see. This place can't touch her. Hal's wild, profound non sequiturs can't move her.

During her latest visit, I overhear her complaining about a fly that seems attracted to her perfume, and won't leave her alone.

"The flies are awful secret police that tear us as if we were carrion," Hal tells her. "Our thoughts are only skin."

Unfazed, she sips a Diet Coke, and talks about the weather. It's "unseasonably cool." I can't even recall what season it is, except that it must not be winter, since it's the only season that can't be unseasonably cool.

Hal's mother's nails are too long to do anything effectively, and they are always painted with such precision it almost draws attention away from her chest, which, like a Renaissance sculpture, was clearly worked on extensively by masters of their art.

I once asked Hal what she does for a living.

"She's a collector," he told me, but would not elaborate.

She didn't raise Hal. He was raised by grandparents until they died, then put into foster care.

"She was deemed an unfit mother, in spite of the fact that she goes to the gym every day," Hal once told me. He also told me that the first map he defaced was a map of the state. He drew lines between all the places he'd lived. He found the patterns very arresting.

When Hal's mother sits with him, she speaks in brief, practiced sound bites. She poses questions like a talk show host, and supplies news to him like an anchorwoman. She taps her nails on the table with such severity that after a while it's the only noise I can hear in the rec room and I have to leave, because I can feel her nails digging into my brain, and then I start to believe they actually are, and the rest of my day is ruined.

Beautiful people are often forgiven for many things – and maybe she's gotten through life that way, but I don't forgive her for anything – and I don't even know what awful things she's done other than showing a lack of parental fitness. The thing that infuriates me most about her, though, is that she has the gall to make me appreciate my own parents more.

103 Magic Mantras and Latex Poodles

My father has the irritating habit of saying the same thing whenever something bad happens. "This, too, shall pass," he says. What annoys me is that he's always right about it. What annoys me even more is that he always reminds me later when it does pass, as a smug "I told you so."

He doesn't say it to me anymore because Mom told him it was trite. Maybe it is, but I find that I say it to myself now. No matter how bad I'm feeling, I make myself say it, even if I'm not ready to believe it. *This, too, shall pass.* It's amazing how little things like that can make a big difference.

It's like that old Nike ad. "Just do it." My mom likes to tell the story about how she had gained so much weight when Mackenzie was born, and exercise was so daunting, she didn't know where to begin, so she just ate and got fatter. Finally she started telling herself "Just do it," and it was the magic mantra to get her exercising regularly again. She dropped the weight before Mackenzie turned two. On the other hand, there was this bizarre cult that committed mass suicide wearing brand-new Nikes as their own warped homage to "Just do it."

I suppose even a simple slogan can be twisted into whatever shape we want, like a balloon animal – we can even make it loop back around on itself, becoming a noose. In the end, the measure of who we are can be seen in the shapes of our balloon animals.

104 Mutinous Mutton

A figurehead can only see things in front of the ship, and nothing within it, so Calliope can just guess at the way into the forecastle, where her legs – if they exist – would be embedded. She guesses that I can get there from the lower decks, but she's wrong. The only way into the forecastle is through a grate on the main deck. The grate is locked by a steel padlock, its shine a mocking contrast to the muted green coat that covers the rest of the ship. I peer down into the grate, but see only darkness.

"Looking for something special, something special?"

The parrot's shrill voice makes me jump. Following his voice, I look over the front of the bow to see him perched on Calliope's head. She doesn't try to shake him off. She doesn't reach up to grab him. I wonder if he even knows she has come to life. Perhaps she remains so still because she doesn't want him to know.

"Nothing special," I tell him, knowing I can't get away without an answer he'll believe. I look down into the square grate above the forecastle. "I'm just wondering what's down there."

"Stowage," he tells me. "Stowage and steerage and sewage and queerage," he says, mimicking the voice of the navigator, then he laughs, pleased with his impersonation. It isn't even close, though. He has the voice, perhaps, but not the cadence. Cadence, Caden, maiden, mutton. That's more like it.

"Wits about you!" the parrot reminds me. "Do not be distracted by shiny things, and do not forget what I said about the captain. What may need to be done."

"Mutton, mutiny, destiny, desperately," I tell him, putting his own impersonation to shame.

"Very good, very good," he says, "I have faith in you, Seaman Bosch. Faith that you'll do the right thing when a thing is right to do." Then he flies off to the crow's nest.

That night the parrot makes sure mutton is on the menu, just to remind me of our conversation — although I don't know where one finds sheep at sea, and I fear it may not be mutton at all.

105 Out of Alignment

"There are many ways to view the world," Dr. Poirot tells me on one of my clearer days, when he knows I'll digest it, and not just repeat back what he says. "We all have our constructs. Some see the world as evil, some see it as a basically good place. Some see God in the simplest of things, some see a void. Are they lies? Are they true?"

"Why are you asking me?"

"I'm just pointing out that your construct has gotten out of alignment with reality."

"What if I like my 'construct'?"

"It can be very seductive, very seductive. But the price to live it is severe."

He holds his silence for a moment, letting his words sink in, but lately thoughts tend to float rather than sink.

"Your parents and I — the entire staff here — we want what's best for you. We're here to help you get better. I need to know that you believe that."

"Why does it matter what I believe? You'll do it anyway."

Poirot nods, and offers what I think is an ironic smile, but a squirrelly voice in my head tells me it's sinister. The voices can be muffled by the meds, but they can't be silenced entirely.

"I believe you want to help me," I tell him. "But in five minutes I might not believe it."

He accepts that. "Your honesty will help in your recovery, Caden."

And that pisses me off, because I didn't realize I was being honest.

Back in my room, I ask Hal to weigh in on the subject. Does he believe everything they do here is for our own benefit?

Hal is slow to answer. He's been more antisocial than usual since his mother's visit. Apparently that's a pattern. They've upped his antidepressant, which doesn't seem to make him any less depressed, but helps him to forget that he is.

"What they do here has no bearing on the price of tea in China," he finally says. "Or for that matter, the price of china in Turkey."

"Or," I add, "the price of turkey in Denmark."

He looks up at me sharply, and wags a finger. "Don't bring Denmark into the equation, unless you're ready to deal with the consequences."

And since I'm not, I suggest no further nations.

106 The Skin of Who We Were

Callie and I are not in the same therapy group. I ask to be switched into hers, but I don't think such requests are honored.

"I'm sure it's the same as your group," Callie tells me at breakfast one day, "except that no one in my group is a first-timer. We're probably all a little less naive. We were arrogant enough to think we were done with this place. Now we're more humble. Or more pissed off. Or both."

"Hal's in my group, and he's not a first-timer," I point out.

"Well, he may have been in and out," Callie says, "but I think his first time never really ended."

I join her in front of the picture window of the Vista Lounge whenever I can. Whenever my feet allow me to stay in one place.

Today, while she stands valiantly observing the world, I draw the random things that come to mind. They've bent the rules, allowing me to have markers outside of the rec room. I think that's a sign that I'm making progress. No pencils, though. Felt-tip markers are less likely to cause injury, either intentional or accidental.

Sometimes Callie and I talk, sometimes not. Sometimes I hold her hand – which, strictly speaking, we're not supposed to do. No physical contact allowed. Human interaction here must come verbally or not at all.

"It's good when you do that," she tells me as I take her hand one day. "It keeps me from falling off."

Falling off what, I don't know. I don't ask. I figure she'll tell me if she wants to.

Her hands are cold. She says she has poor circulation in her extremities. "It's genetic," she tells me. "My mother is the same.

185

She can chill a beverage just by bringing it to you."

I don't mind the chill of her hand. Usually I'm too warm. Besides, her hand warms quickly when I hold it. It's good to know I can have that effect on her.

"This is my third time here," she confides in me. "My third episode."

"Episode."

"That's what they call it."

"More like a miniseries."

She smiles at that, but doesn't laugh. Callie never laughs, but the sincerity of her smile makes up for it.

"They tell me that when I'm ready to stop looking out of this window, I might be ready to go home."

"Are you getting close?" I ask, selfishly wanting her to say no.

She doesn't answer. Instead she says, "More than anything I want to be out of here ... but sometimes home is harder than here. It's like jumping into a cold ocean on a hot summer day. You want to do it more than anything, but you don't want to feel the shock of the cold water."

"I actually like that feeling," I tell her.

She turns to me, grins, and squeezes my hand. "You're just weird." Then she returns her gaze to the view, which doesn't change today. Not as much as a single hawk in the sky in search of a rabbit.

"At home they expect you to be fixed," she says. "They say they understand, but the only people who really understand are the ones who've been to That Place, too. It's like a man telling a woman he knows what it feels like to give birth." She turns to me, forsaking her view for a moment. "You will never know that, so don't pretend you do."

"I don't. I mean I won't. But I do kind of know how it feels to be you."

"I believe that. But you won't be with me at home. Just my parents and my sisters. They all think medicine should be magic, and they become mad at me when it's not."

"I'm sorry."

"But if I endure it," she says, "eventually I will settle in. I will find myself as I was before. We do, you know. Find ourselves. Although it's a little harder each time. Days pass. Weeks. Then we squeeze ourselves back into the skin of who we were before all this. We put the pieces back together and get on with things."

That makes me think about Skye, the puzzler, and the jigsaw piece she gave me. I keep it in my pocket as a reminder, although I can't recall what it's supposed to remind me of.

107 The Foc'sle Key

The navigator might be brilliant, but I don't dare ask him about the forecastle, and how to get in, because he's also curious. He'll want to know why I'm asking. I haven't told him about the time I spend with Calliope, because I know he can't keep a secret. He will blurt it out in so many rhymes and alliterations, everyone will know. Besides, the navigator has been moodier than usual. He's begun to close me out the way he closes out others.

Something about me being suspicious and pernicious.

Instead, I seek out Carlyle at midnight, and ask him. I find him mopping aft, back toward the mizzenmast, clearing the deck of grime and the occasional brain.

"The fo'c'sle?" he asks, pronouncing *forecastle* in the proper seaman's way. "What do you want with the fo'c'sle?"

"I just want to know what's down there."

He shrugs. "We store the forward mooring ropes there," he tells me. "Although it's been so long since we've seen port, I wouldn't be surprised if the ropes have evolved into higher forms of life."

"If I wanted to get in there, where would I find the key?"

"Why would you want to?"

"I have my reasons."

He sighs and looks around to make sure we're unobserved. He respects my privacy on the matter, and doesn't ask my reasons again. "There's only one key to the padlock, and the captain has it."

"Where does he keep it?"

"You're not going to like it," Carlyle warns me.

"Tell me anyway."

For a moment Carlyle ponders the gray suds in his bucket, then finally says, "It's behind the peach pit, in the socket of his dead eye."

No matter how rational the world seems to be, you never really know what crazy crap is around the bend. I saw this in the news once: some socialite in a Manhattan high-rise takes an elevator from the penthouse to the basement garage, dropping down sixty-seven floors – sixty-eight if you count the mezzanine – to get her Mercedes and go to a gallery on Madison Avenue, or whatever it is that Manhattan socialites do with their time.

What she doesn't know is that a water main burst just a few minutes ago next to her building. So the elevator reaches the basement, and as the doors begin to open, the elevator is flooded by freezing water. What is she going to do? There isn't even a worst-case scenario for this, because it's beyond anyone's imagination.

In five seconds the water's at her waist, then at her neck, and then she drowns, never knowing what the hell happened, or how such a horrific thing is even possible. I mean, think about it: drowning in an elevator in a skyscraper. That's wrong on sixty-seven different levels, not counting the mezzanine.

The weird thing is, hearing stories like this makes me feel a kind of kinship with the Almighty, because it proves that even God has psychotic episodes.

I go to the crow's nest to ponder the obstacles and consequences to getting this particular boss key. The way I see it, it's an impossible task. I sit at the bar, sipping my cocktail and sharing my dilemma with the bartender, because bartenders are known to give good advice, and I know that the crow's nest personnel have neither love for, nor loyalty to, the captain. I've met several bartenders here. They work varied shifts, because the crow's nest operates twenty-four hours a day. Today's bartender is a slender woman with eyes a little too small for her face. She compensates with mascara and turquoise eye shadow, so that her eyes look a bit like two peacock feathers.

"Best to forget it," the bartender advises. "I mean literally. The less you remember it, the less important it will seem, and the less important it seems, the less anxious you'll be."

"I don't want to be less anxious," I tell her. "At least not until I get that key."

She sighs. "Sorry, I wish I could help you."

She appears a bit miffed that I'm not taking her advice. Or maybe she's miffed that I'm hanging out at the bar. The crow's nest folk don't seem to like when I hang around too much. Like any other service establishment, they want to move the customers in and out as quickly as they can. I prefer to take my time.

On the barstool next to me is the master-at-arms. He has no cocktail, he's just chatting up the bartender. She doesn't seem to mind *him* being there. The leering tattoos on his arms regard me with emotions that range from curiosity to disdain, then the skull with a penchant for show tunes launches into a rousing "Hello, Dolly!," which happens to be the name of the bartender. It makes all the other skulls complain.

"How can you stand it when your ink acts up?" I ask him.

For a moment he looks at me like I'm from Mars, then he says rather slowly, "I just … don't … pay attention." I suppose "not paying attention" takes a great deal of discipline. I know when my voices get out of hand, it's like being in the middle of the New York Stock Exchange. At least he can muffle his with long sleeves and layers.

"Have you ever seen the captain up here?" I say, but the master-at-arms seems to be ignoring me now, so I direct the question to the skull with a rose in its mouth, figuring it might be the mellowest one. "Does the captain ever come to the crow's nest?"

"Never," says the tattoo through clenched teeth. "He'd prefer that no one did. The captain doesn't like anyone messing with sailors' minds but him."

"Then how come he doesn't just shut the place down? I mean, he's the captain, he can do anything he wants on his ship, right?"

"Ha!" says the dice-eyed skull. "Shows how much *you* know."

"There are some things that not even the captain can control," says the skull with the rose.

"What kinds of things?"

And the theatrical skull sings, "*Storm fronts that linger upon the horizon; white plastic places where every thought dies in; swabbies and cocktails and parrots' bright wings; these are a few of his least-favorite things."*

The other skulls all groan, and I smile. If the captain isn't all-powerful, perhaps getting that key isn't as impossible as I thought.

110 Garden of Unearthly Delights

Hal and I sit in the rec room. He's absorbed in his maps and I'm absorbed in my drawings, trying to be here and not somewhere else.

"I wrote myself a chaos language," Hal tells me. "Full of symbols and signals and sigils and cymbals. But due to its chaotic nature, I can't remember it."

"Were the cymbals to wake you up when you got too boring?" I ask him.

He points a finger at me. "Watch yourself, or I will mark you in your sleep with a sigil of hair loss, and you will turn into your father."

Sigils, as I recall from some dark comic book series, are symbols of medieval magic from back in the day when so few people were literate that literacy itself was seen as borderline magical. A man who could read was considered a genius. A man who could read without moving his lips was proclaimed either divine or demonic, depending on the agenda of whoever was doing the proclaiming.

Today Hal is doing all the proclaiming, which is how it usually goes.

"Symbols have power!" he announces. "You see a cross, it makes you feel something. You see a swastika, it makes you feel something else. Yet the swastika is also an Indian symbol meaning 'It is good,' showing that symbols can be mortally corrupted. That's why I make up my own. They are meaningful to me, and that's all that matters."

He draws a spiral punctured by a sine wave. He draws two question marks at odd angles bisecting each other. He's right — they are powerful. He's *made* them powerful.

"What do they mean?" I ask.

"I told you, I forgot the language." Then he looks over at my sketch pad, noticing that I have copied his symbols and am adding on to them, turning them into figures that battle one another. I have corrupted his symbols. I wonder what he will do.

"Your last name is Bosch," he says. "Are you related?"

I assume he's asking if I'm related to Hieronymus Bosch — an artist who painted some pretty bizarre things that scared the crap out of me when I was little, and still dance around my head on bad days.

"Maybe. I don't know."

He nods, at home with uncertainty, and says, "Don't put me in your Garden of Earthly Delights, and I won't write death-symbols on your forehead."

Thus, Hal and I reach a mutual understanding.

I open my eyes in the middle of the night, and feel the familiar numbness of semiconsciousness combined with medication. My head is a fogged-in airport. All thoughts are grounded. Still, I can sense that I'm being watched. I force myself through my pharmacological haze and roll over to find someone standing beside my bed. In the dim light coming from the hallway, I can see green pajamas covered in cartoon sea horses. I hear a clicking sound, and it's a few moments before I realize that the sound is the chattering of teeth.

"I'm cold," Callie says. "And you're always so warm."

She makes no move, she just chatters. I look across the room to see Hal snoring away. Callie's waiting for an invitation. I throw back my covers. It's invitation enough, and she climbs in.

She *is* cold. Not just her hands and feet, but her whole body. I pull the covers over both of us and she turns her back to me, making it easier to hold her and share my body warmth. We lie close like a pair of spoons. I can feel the ridges of her spine against my chest. I can feel her heart beating so much more rapidly than mine. Our bodies form a symbol, I think, as powerful as one of Hal's – and it occurs to me that the most meaningful symbols of all must be based on all the different ways two people can embrace.

"Don't get any ideas," she says.

"No ideas," I repeat groggily. I couldn't have any such "ideas" even if I wanted to. When the meds are dialed this high, it takes away all stirrings. I'm actually glad for that – at least at this particular moment – because there are no expectations, and not the slightest hint of awkwardness. This is about one thing: keeping her warm.

I'm worried, though. I know there are several pastels on duty and they have regular rounds, checking each room. Surveillance cameras are everywhere, too. The hospital makes every effort to monitor all aspects of our behavior, but there's still room for human error. The fact that Callie is here proves it.

"What if they see us?" I ask.

"What are they going to do, throw us out?" she answers.

And I realize I don't care what they see, what they say, or what they do. Not Poirot, or the pastels, or even my parents. They have no part of this moment. They don't have the right.

I hold her tighter, pressing against her until I feel just the slightest bit cold, which means she's taking some of my body heat. After a while her teeth stop chattering, and we lie there, breathing in unison.

"Thank you," she finally says.

"You can come whenever you're cold," I tell her. I think to give her a gentle kiss on the ear, but instead I just snuggle a little closer and whisper into it. "I like being hot for you."

Only after I say it do I realize the joke. I let her think that I intended it.

She says nothing. Her breathing slows, I doze off, and when I open my eyes again, I'm alone in my bed, left to wonder if it happened at all. Was it just another mind trick?

It isn't until morning that I find her slipper on the floor near my bed – left there not accidentally, not carelessly, but with mischievous purpose.

At breakfast I will bring it to her, kneel before her, and slip it on her foot. And, just like in the fairy tale, it will be a perfect fit.

112 Abstract Angular Angst

In group, Carlyle hands out pieces of sketch paper and markers. "We're going to give our mouths a rest today," he tells us. "There are other ways to express ourselves. Today we'll take advantage of nonverbal expression."

The creepy kid everyone calls Bones looks at Skye and offers her a nonverbal and sexually explicit gesture, which elicits another nonverbal gesture from Skye that involves a particular finger. Bones snickers, and Carlyle pretends he didn't see the exchange.

"The object today is to draw the way you're feeling. It doesn't have to be literal, and there is no right or wrong way to do it. No good or bad."

"This is kindergarten crap," announces Alexa – the girl with bandages on her throat.

"Only if you make it so," Carlyle tells her.

People look at their pages like the screaming blankness is already invading their fragile minds. Others stare at the pale green walls around them as if the answers might be there. Bones grins evilly and gets to work. I know exactly what he's going to draw. We all do. And none of us is claiming to read minds today.

This assignment is no problem for me. It's what I do most of the time anyway. Sometimes with more passion and urgency than other times. Carlyle knows this, and perhaps this is why he chose an art project for today.

In a few minutes my paper reflects a jagged inner landscape of sharp edges and deep crevasses. No sense of gravity or perspective. Abstract angular angst. I like it. And will until I hate it.

Others are not so quick to draw.

"I can't do this," complains Skye. "My head doesn't see feelings as pictures."

"Try," Carlyle says gently. "Whatever you put down is fine. You're not being judged."

She looks at her blank page once more, then pushes it at me. "You do it."

"Skye, you're missing the point..." Carlyle says.

Still, I take the piece of paper, ponder Skye for a moment, and get to work. I draw a sweeping abstract something that's a cross between an amoeba and a manta ray with eyes and mouths in unexpected places. It takes me about a minute. When it's done, Skye gapes at me, wide-eyed. I expect her to offer me a single-digit gesture, but instead she says, "How did you do that?"

"What?"

"I have no idea what the hell that is, but it's exactly how I feel right now."

"Skye," says Carlyle, "I really don't think—"

"I don't care what you do or don't think," Skye says. "He got me right."

"Me next," says Bones. He flips over the phallus he's drawing, so I can work on the other side of the page.

I glance at Carlyle. He raises his eyebrows and shrugs. "Go for it," he says. I like the fact that Carlyle rolls with the waves rather than fighting them. Good sea legs.

For Bones, I draw a squiggle that turns into a vaguely suggestive porcupine. When I'm done he laughs. "Man, you are a true arteest of the soul."

Others are anxious for their turns. Even the crew members

who are totally out of it look to me like somehow what I draw is going to save their lives.

"All right," says Carlyle, leaning back against the green copper bulkhead of the map room. "Caden can draw it, but when he's done, you each need to explain what it means."

They thrust their parchments before me, and I feverishly translate their feelings into line and color. For the lore-master, I offer a prickly something-or-other covered with eyes. For Alexa and her pearl choker, I offer a tentacled kite caught in an updraft. The only one who won't offer me his parchment is the navigator. Instead he draws his own map in silence.

Everyone claims that I've gotten them right, and while they compare their inner selves, I go to Carlyle, a bit concerned. "Do you think the captain will approve of this?"

Carlyle sighs. "Let's just be here in the moment, okay?"

And although it makes me edgy, I agree to try.

113 Who They Were

Vincent van Gogh cut off his ear, sent it to the woman he loved, and in the end took his own life. In spite of an artistic vision so startlingly new it took years for the world to appreciate it, his artwork couldn't save him from the depths of his tortured mind. That's who he was.

Michelangelo – arguably the greatest artist mankind has ever seen – became so pathologically obsessed with sculpting *David* that he didn't bathe, or take care of himself for months. He had gone so long without removing his work boots, that when he took them off, the skin of his feet came off with them. That's who Michelangelo was.

Recently, I saw a story about a schizophrenic artist living on the streets of Los Angeles. His paintings were gorgeous abstract masterpieces, and people were comparing him to the masters. Now his works sell for tens of thousands of dollars because some rich person turned the media spotlight in his direction. He wore a suit and tie at the gallery opening, and when it was done, even with doors wide open to him, he went back to living on the streets. Because that's who he was.

And so who am I?

114 Happy Paper Cup

"I'm sorry, I didn't get that."

"I asked if you've noticed any difference in the way you've been feeling, Caden."

"Difference in the way I've been feeling."

"Yes. Have you noticed any?"

Dr. Poirot has the annoying tendency to nod, even when I don't speak, which makes it difficult for me to know if I've answered the question or not.

"Have I noticed any what?"

He taps his pen on the desk thoughtfully for a moment. It

distracts me and I forget not just the gist of the conversation, but its entire direction as well. It's one of those days. What were we talking about? Dinner, perhaps?

"Mutton," I say.

"Mutton," he says. "What about mutton?"

"I can't be sure, but I think we're eating the crewmen with no brains."

He considers this very seriously, then he grabs his little pad and scribbles out a new prescription for me. "I'd like to add Risperdal to your medication regimen," he says. "I believe it may keep you here with us more of the time."

"Why don't you combine the Ativan, the Risperdal, the Seroquel, and the Depakote into a single pill?" I suggest. "AtiRisperQuellakote."

He chuckles, then tears out the prescription, but knows better than to hand it to me. It goes into my chart, which will go to the pastels, who will bring it to the pharmacy, and a new pill will find its way into my happy paper cup before dinner.

115 Double, Double, Toil and Trouble, Fire Burn and Cauldron Bubble

About 99 percent of a pill is made up of other stuff that has nothing to do with the medication. They add extra ingredients for color, coating, and to make the pill stick together. Stuff like xanthan gum, which is made from bacteria; Carbopol, which is an acrylic polymer like house paint; and gelatin, which is made from cow cartilage.

Somewhere deep in the secret recesses of Pfizer, or Glaxo-SmithKline, or one of the other big pharmaceutical companies, I imagine there's a high-security dungeon where three hunch-backed witches stir a massive industrial cauldron of crap I don't want to know about, but I must ingest on a daily basis.

And the generic versions aren't even brewed by real witches.

116 Dirty Martini

It finally happens.

My brain escapes through my left nostril and goes feral.

I'm out of my body, scurrying on the deck in the middle of the night. The ship is fogged in. There's no hint of stars, or what lies before us – or maybe it's just that my mind's eye can't see all that far. The other brains hiss when I get close. We are solitary creatures, I realize. Solitary and suspicious. This close to the deck, I can see the sticky black caulking spread between the copper planks. That black sludge seethes with intentions I'd rather not know about.

My gnarled purple legs are rootlike, sparking with intelli-gence, or maybe it's just a series of short circuits. Those twisted dendritic legs get stuck in the pitch, and the stuff begins to pull me down like I'm a dinosaur in tar. I know if I can't get free I will be dragged into the narrow space between the copper planks, and crushed – digested by the pitch. It takes a huge amount of will, but finally I tear myself free.

Where will I go?

I cannot let Calliope see me like this. I'm horrible. So instead I head aft and make my way like a gecko up the bulkhead toward the captain's ready room, squeezing myself as flat as I can to slip in under the door. If it's true that I play a crucial part in this mission, then he will help me. He will find a way to fix this.

The captain sits at his desk with a half-melted candle, studying one of my drawings for symbols and signs. When he looks up to see me, the glare of his eye is like a flamethrower.

"Get that thing out of here!" he bellows.

He doesn't recognize me. Of course he doesn't – to him I am just another piece of useless vermin infesting his ship. I try to explain, but I can't. I have no mouth.

I hear footsteps. A door creaks open, and hands, dozens of hands, hundreds of hands grab at me. I wriggle and squirm. I can't let them get me! The hands grasp and claw, but I twist free from them and bolt out the door, tumbling down the stairs, into … wetness. The deck is wet with soapy water, and Carlyle pushes his mop toward me. The mop is huge! A wall of filthy brown snakes. His mop hits me and I slide through the slick flood, trying to grab on to something, but it's no use. I see the drainage hole in front of me, and there's nothing I can do. In a moment I'm in free fall. Then I'm in the cold sea, submerged beneath the waves.

I hurt. I hurt everywhere – and I know I'm going to die this

way. My body, on the ship, will go through the motions of living, but I will be gone.

Then, in the midst of my panic, I feel something. Something huge. It moves beneath me. Hard scales brush past my raw nerve endings. It's one of the creatures the captain speaks of. It's here, and it's real. I recoil in terror. In a moment it's gone, diving deep … but only so it can gain momentum as it rises again – this time with its mouth open. I kick, I struggle, and finally I break the surface.

I can see nothing. No ship. No sea. The fog is cotton-dense. I feel the rush of water as the creature rises toward me.

Then, out of nowhere, the parrot swoops down, his wings

wide, and he grabs me, his talons digging into the ridges and convolutions of my gray matter. He pulls me from the water, and we soar upward.

"Unexpected, unexpected," the parrot says, "but not irreversible."

We rise high above the ship, out of danger, and out of the dense fog bank. All I can see of the ship is the mainmast and the crow's nest poking through the fog, but the sky above it is clear. The stars are as plentiful as the Milky Way seen from space. In an instant, I've gone from absolute terror to absolute wonder.

"I can give you a gift of unlimited horizons," the parrot squawks loudly, "but only if you do what must be done. The time has come. Do away with the captain, and all that you see from horizon to horizon will be yours."

I want to tell him about the creature beneath the waves, but I can't communicate at all. I want to believe the parrot can read my mind, but he can't.

"All is well," he says. Then he drops me.

I plummet toward the fogged-in ship. The crow's nest swells before me, envelops me, and I find myself splashing in bitter liquid. I am at the bottom of a huge cocktail glass, sitting there helplessly like an olive in a dirty martini.

There are eyes all around. They study me with faces too distorted in the curved glass to recognize.

"You know," I hear the bartender say, "they put Einstein's brain in a jar of formaldehyde. If it's good enough for him, it's good enough for you."

"It happens like that sometimes," Carlyle says. He doesn't have a mop, so that helps me to know where I am. The clock says it's long after therapy group, but sometimes Carlyle hangs in the dining area, talking. Helping.

"It happens like that," I echo. I didn't participate in group today. I had other concerns.

"Everyone reacts differently to medication. That's why Poirot keeps changing it up on you. He's got to find the right cocktail."

"The right cocktail," I say. I know I'm repeating him. I know it, but I can't stop. My thoughts are rubber and anything that comes in bounces out again by way of my mouth.

I had an "adverse reaction" to the Risperdal. Neither Poirot nor the pastels would tell me exactly what that meant. Carlyle was more forthcoming. "I'm not supposed to bother you with the details, but you deserve to know," he told me. "You had a rapid heartbeat and tremors. You were pretty incoherent. I know it sounds awful, but it really wasn't so bad."

I have no memory of these things. I was Elsewhere.

Carlyle pushes a plate of food toward me, reminding me that I need to eat.

I do, trying to focus on chewing and swallowing, but even when I attempt to concentrate, my mind drifts. I think about Calliope, whom I haven't seen for days. I must get up to the bow. I think about the bartenders, and wonder what diabolical things they'll be putting into my cocktail. Spleen of chameleon.

Testicle of tarantula. Eventually I realize that I'm sitting there with a fork in the air, and food drooling out of the side of my mouth. I feel like I could have been like that for hours, but probably not, because Carlyle would let it go on only for a few seconds. He reminds me to chew and swallow. Then he reminds me to chew and swallow again. This has been a setback. We both know it.

Carlyle takes the spoon out of my hand and sets it down. "Maybe you'll eat more later," he says, realizing this meal isn't happening.

"Maybe I'll eat more later." It is not lost on me that the fork has magically transformed into a spoon.

118 Zimple Physics

The ship heaves and drops, heaves and drops. A lantern hanging from the low ceiling of my cabin swings with the motion, and shadows reach and retreat, each time seeming to get a little bit closer.

The captain personally supervises the return of my brain to my head. Getting toothpaste back into the tube doesn't even begin to describe it.

"Zis is accomplished by creating a vacuum within ze cranium," the ship's doctor explains. "Zen ze errant brain is introduced to ze left nostril, at vich time it is zucked in to fill ze void. All zimple physics." The ship's doctor, who I've never seen before, and never see again, looks and sounds suspiciously like Albert Einstein, whose brain, I've heard, is in a jar. When the operation is over, I still feel somewhat out-of-body. The captain looks at me and shakes his head in disappointment.

"Lie down with dogs, get up with rabies," he tells me unsympathetically. I don't think that's the actual expression, but I get the point. "If you choose to trust the bird and those blasted bartenders, then this is what you can expect. Put your faith in me, boy, not in their brain-sucking concoctions. I thought you'd know better by now!"

The captain looms over me, seeming so much larger than life when I'm this incapacitated. He turns to go, and I don't want him to. The navigator is nowhere in sight, and I don't want to be left alone right now.

"It swam past me…" I tell him.

He slowly turns back to me, studying me. "What swam past you?"

"Something huge. It had scales. They felt like steel. Then it dove deep, and launched itself toward the surface. I could feel its hunger. It wanted to devour me." I don't dare tell him that the parrot rescued me before it could.

The captain sits on the edge of my cot. "That," he says, "was the Abyssal Serpent – a very formidable adversary. Once it sets its eye on you, it will track you until you, or it, are no more. It will never let you be."

And although this is not the best of news, the captain smiles.

"If the Abyssal Serpent sees you as worthy of its attention, that speaks very well of you. It means there's much more to you than meets the eye."

I look away from him, rolling to face the wall, trying to escape the prospect of the serpent. "If it's all the same to you," I tell him, "there are certain eyes I'd rather not meet."

119 Little Chatterbox

My anxiety level is spiking again, and I pace around the nurses' station, making Dolly, the morning charge nurse, nervous.

"Honey, don't you have group now?"

"I don't think so."

"Then isn't there something you'd rather be doing?"

"I don't think so."

She complains to the other nurse that we patients don't have enough structured time, and in the end, she gets the orderly with the scary tattoos to escort me away.

"Why don't you watch some TV in the rec room?" he suggests. "A bunch of your friends are watching *Charlie and the Chocolate Factory*," he tells me. "The original one – not the creepy one with Johnny Depp."

I find myself instantly irked. "First of all, just because we've got Oompa-Loompas bouncing around our brains, that doesn't make us all friends. And secondly, the original was called *Willy Wonka and the Chocolate Factory* – although technically not, because the book was first, and it was Charlie in the book – but that still doesn't make you right."

He chuckles and that ticks me off even more. "Well, aren't we the little chatterbox today?"

What is he, a kindergarten teacher for the Hells Angels? "I hope all your skulls eat you in your sleep," I tell him. He doesn't laugh at that and I feel I can claim a minor victory.

120 The Maps Say Otherwise

Hal's mother pays one of her surprise visits. I'm not in the rec room to see it. I can't even sit long enough to draw – I'm pacing back and forth on deck to counteract the motion of the sea again. They'd give me an extra Ativan if I asked, but I don't. The bartender is much too free with the cocktails, and the thought of climbing to the crow's nest just makes me more anxious.

When we're both back in our room, Hal tells me of his current maternal adventure. She stayed longer than usual this time. She even played a game of checkers with him. This is what's commonly referred to as "a red flag."

"So what's wrong?" I ask him.

"She's moving to Seattle," Hal tells me. "She's very excited, and wanted me to know."

"Why Seattle?" I ask.

"She's in the process of collecting a new husband, and that's where he lives."

I can't quite tell how Hal feels about this. "So, that's good, right? You'll go there when you're done here."

Hal stares at the ceiling, lying flat on his bed. "The maps say otherwise."

"She's not taking you?"

"I see no path to the Pacific Northwest." A moment of silence, then he says, "Her fiancé finds me 'off-putting.'"

I'm about to point out that, as his mother, she can't just leave him, but then I remember that he's already been removed from her custody.

He rolls to face the bulkhead. I feel the ship rise and fall, riding a slow, powerful swell.

"It's okay," Hal tells me, "I've got better places to be."

121 Mentally We Roll Along

The following morning's group features a couple of new faces, and an absence of some old faces. Everyone has a different graduation day, and the population is constantly rolling. Sometimes there are warm good-byes, other times exits are stealthy. It all depends on what the individual wants.

"They can beam people in and out of this place," a kid named Raoul tells me. "I've seen it." Rather than argue with Raoul's construct of reality, I just tell him that I'm not allowed to talk to people with too many consecutive vowels in their name.

Today in group, Skye, who is nearing the end of her puzzle,

seems slightly less angry. "There's a reason for all of this," Skye tells the group, looking to Carlyle for validation. "My mother says God never gives us something we can't handle."

To which Hal says, "Your mother's an asshat."

"Hey!" barks Carlyle, and Hal is banished from the rest of the session. Rule one: disparaging remarks are punishable by early dismissal. Unless of course early dismissal is what you were aiming for. Then it's not a punishment at all, but a pleasant perk of rudeness.

"Caden," Carlyle says, looking for a moderate among extremes, "what do you think about what Skye said?"

"Who, me?"

I think he might say something snarky like "No, the Caden hiding in the air vent," but instead he says "Yes, you," as if I wasn't just trying to buy time, but actually thought he might be addressing air-vent-Caden. Carlyle can be disappointingly unbanterful.

"I don't think God gave us this any more than he gives little kids cancer, or makes poor people lottery winners," I say. "If anything, he gives us courage to deal."

"What about the ones who can't deal?" asks Raoul.

"That's easy," I answer, with wide, soulful eyes and a totally straight face. "Those are the people who God really, really hates."

I'm hoping Carlyle expels me from the group, too, but no such luck.

If you think about it, the public perception of funky brain chemistry has been as varied and weird as the symptoms, historically speaking.

If I had been born a Native American in another time, I might have been lauded as a medicine man. My voices would have been seen as the voices of ancestors imparting wisdom. I would have been treated with great mystical regard.

In the Dark Ages my parents would have sent for an exorcist, because I was clearly possessed by evil spirits, or maybe even the Devil himself.

And if I lived in Dickensian England, I would have been thrown into Bedlam, which is more than just a description of madness. It was an actual place — a "madhouse" where the insane were imprisoned in unthinkable conditions.

Living in the twenty-first century gives a person a much better prognosis for treatment, but sometimes I wish I'd lived in an age before technology. I would much rather everyone think I was a prophet than some poor sick kid.

123 Bard and Dog

Raoul, the new kid, has visitations from famous dead people. Most notably Shakespeare. Whether it's his ghost, or the product of time travel, no one is quite sure.

"So what does he say?" I ask him as we loiter around the nurses' station. Raoul suddenly gets very guarded.

"Leave me alone!" he says. "You're gonna tell me it's not real – but I got theories, okay? I got theories."

He storms away from me, probably thinking I'm going to make fun of him, but I'm not. I have developed a great respect for delusions and/or hallucinations – although I'm not sure which Raoul suffers from. Does he see the bard? Does he just hear him? Or does he think *I'm* Shakespeare when I talk to him?

There was a time, before I wound up here, when I would have thought all this was funny. When I was a member of the world, and not a member of "the club." The world just loves to laugh at the absurdity of insanity. I guess what makes it funny to people is that it's a gross distortion of something very familiar. For instance, Raoul's much ado about nothing comes by way of his father, a failed Shakespearean actor who gave up the dream and started a theater camp for underprivileged children.

I feel bad that I was mean to him in group, so now I feel helpful in the worst way. And what could be worse than me trying to help? So I follow Raoul to the rec room where Skye works away on her puzzle, and a bunch of other kids watch a talking dog movie – as if any of us really needs to add talking dogs to our mental stew.

Raoul plops himself down at a table and I sit across from him. "Is it a tragedy or a comedy?" I ask.

He turns his chair away from me but doesn't get up to leave, which means he's just posturing now. He wants to see where this is going.

"Shakespeare wrote tragedies and comedies, so which do you feel like you're in when he talks to you?" Actually the bard also wrote love sonnets, but if Shakespeare's reciting sonnets to him, that's a whole other issue.

"I … don't know," says Raoul.

"If it's a tragedy," I tell him, "remind Shakespeare that he's got a comic side, too. Challenge him to make you laugh."

"Go away!" he says, and when I don't leave, he joins the dog watchers – but I can tell he's really not watching, he's thinking about what I said – which is all I wanted.

I'm no Poirot, and I'm not even a Carlyle; I don't know if I've given him good advice or not, but it seems to me that these worlds we touch upon can get so dark, anything we can do to lighten them must be a good thing, right?

124 Hating the Messenger

I've been desensitized to the horrors of group therapy. The graphic details, the tearful confessions, the furious rants. They're all so much background noise. Carlyle is a good facilitator. He tries to be a fly on the wall, and lets us talk among ourselves, giving advice and guiding us only when he needs to.

Alexa does the same thing almost every day. The second she gets the floor, it's like a filibuster – especially when there's someone new in the group. She keeps reliving the horrors inflicted on her by her stepbrother, and how it felt to cut her own throat – she just uses different words, and different lead-ins, to trick us into thinking she's taking us somewhere new.

Is it insensitive for me to want her to stop? Is it cruel for me to want to scream at her to shut the hell up after the millionth time I've heard the story? I realize I'm feeling a little clearer than usual today. A little more verbal. I can put thoughts together. It may not last, but I'm determined to use it while I've got it.

In today's retelling, she's standing in front of the mirror, looking deep into her own eyes, and deciding there's nothing in them worth saving, but before she raises the Swiss Army Knife to her throat, I shout out—

"Excuse me, but I've already seen this movie."

All eyes turn to me.

"Spoiler alert," I continue. "The girl tries to kill herself, but she lives, and her scumbag stepbrother takes off and disappears from everyone's lives. It was a real tearjerker the first few times, but now it's old – even for cable."

"Caden," says Carlyle carefully, like he's trying to figure out whether to cut the yellow or the blue wire on a bomb. "You're being a little harsh, man."

"No, I'm being honest," I tell him. "Aren't we supposed to be honest here?" Then I look back toward Alexa, who stares at me, maybe terrified of what's coming next. "Every time you relive it, it's like he's doing it to you again and again," I tell her. "But it's not even him anymore – it's you. Now *you're* the one making yourself his victim."

"Oh, so I should just forget it?" Tears well in her eyes, but I have no sympathy today.

"No, don't ever forget it," I tell her. "But you have to process it and move on. Live your life, otherwise he took your future away from you, too."

"You're just mean!" she shouts at me. "I hate you!" Then she buries her face in her hands and sobs.

"Uh … I think Caden's right," says Raoul apprehensively. Hal nods his approval, Skye looks off to her left like she couldn't care less, and the others just watch Carlyle, either too afraid or too medicated to have an opinion.

Carlyle, still fretting over which wire to cut, cautiously says, "Well, Alexa has a right to feel what she feels …"

"Thank you," Alexa says.

"… but maybe Caden does have a larger point that we all should consider." Then he asks what "moving on" means to each of us, and calm conversation continues. Even though I meant what I said, I'm also relieved he found the right wire to cut.

After the session is over, Carlyle calls me aside. I know what this is about. He's going to lecture me about how I behaved in group today. Maybe he'll even threaten to tell Poirot about it.

So I'm shocked when he says, "That was actually very insightful of you back there." Then, seeing my surprise, he says, "Hey, credit where credit is due. It might not have been the best way to say it, but Alexa needed to hear it, whether she knew it or not."

"Yeah, and now she hates me."

"Don't sweat it," Carlyle says. "When the truth hurts, we always hate the messenger."

Then he asks me if I'm aware of my diagnosis – because the doctors always leave it to parents to tell us. My parents have floated a few mental-illness buzzwords, but only in the vaguest way.

"Nobody tells me anything," I finally admit. "At least not officially to my face."

"Yeah, it's like that at first. Mainly because diagnoses change, but also because the words themselves carry so much baggage. Know what I mean?"

I know exactly what he means. I had overheard Poirot talking to my parents. He was using words like *psychosis* and *schizophrenic.* Words that people feel they have to whisper, or not repeat at all. The Mental-Illness-That-Must-Not-Be-Named.

"I've heard my parents say 'bipolar,' but I think that's just because it sounds like a nicer word."

He nods in understanding. "Sucks, doesn't it?"

I laugh at that. It's actually nice to have it stated so clearly. "No, it's a walk in the park," I tell him. "When the park is Yellowstone, and Old Faithful is blowing boiling steam up your ass."

Now it's his turn to laugh. "Your meds are working if you've got a sense of humor again."

"It's a fluke," I tell him.

He grins. "As time goes on, you'll find more and more flukes."

"That's a whole lot of whales," I say.

"Not necessarily," he answers. "Dolphins have flukes, too."

And that sends me right to the wall in Mackenzie's room. I begin to wonder if that wall has been painted over to erase any hint of my illness from her room. After all, those samurai dolphins could be seen as psychotic.

125 Promenade

I sit in the Vista Lounge drawing while Callie looks out the window. This is how our free time goes, what little of it there is. My stomach is acting up today. Gas, or indigestion, or something. Being here with Callie makes my discomfort seem unimportant. The big picture window loses heat to the overcast day, making the lounge chilly, but I can't keep Callie warm during the day, when eyes are everywhere. I imagine she comes to my room every night to borrow my warmth – but I think that happened only once. Still, this is one time I'm happy to believe my imagination.

Bland Muzak plays in the Vista Lounge through speakers that are built into the ceiling, so we couldn't grab them and rip them out if we tried. Muted brass instruments drone on like Charlie Brown's parents. *Bwah-wa-wah, Bwah-mwah-wa-wah.* Even the tunes here are medicated.

Callie glances at my sketch pad. "You draw differently than you did before you got sick, don't you?"

I'm surprised that she would know that, but maybe I

shouldn't be. I feel like we've known each other much longer than we actually have.

"I don't 'draw' anymore," I tell her. "Lately I just push stuff out of my head."

She grins. "I hope you have something left inside when you're done."

"Yeah, me, too."

Then she grabs my arm gently. "I want to walk," she says. "Will you walk with me?"

This is a new request from her. Once she's fixed in front of the Vista Lounge window, she rarely leaves until someone makes her leave.

"Are you sure?" I ask.

"Yes," she says. Then again, "Yes, I am," as if she needs to say it twice to convince herself.

We go out into the hallway and walk – an old-fashioned promenade, arm in arm, in defiance of the no-physical-contact rule. No one stops us.

The ward is designed as an oval. "Like a big fat zero," Hal once pointed out, finding great significance to that. Here, you can walk the hall without pacing, because once you start walking, you never reach the end. Today I measure laps by how many times I pass the nurses' station, but quickly lose count.

"Don't you want to go back to the window?" I ask Callie. Not because I want to, but because *she* should want to.

"No," she says. "There's nothing more to see today."

"But…"

She turns to me, waiting for me to continue. I wish I could, but I have no idea what my "but" was about. So I walk her to her room.

"You should finish your drawing," she says. "I want to see it when it's done."

Since I was just sketching Muzak impressions, I'm less interested in the finished product than she is.

"Sure," I tell her. "I'll show it to you." Our conversations never feel this awkward. Even when we say nothing, it's less awkward than this. My stomach rumbles and begins to ache. It seems to echo the discomfort in the air between us. Finally she tells me what's on her mind.

"I'm worried," she says. "I'm worried that we won't set each other free."

I'm not sure I catch her meaning, but I'm unsettled, even so. "That's not up to us. It's Poirot who decides that."

She shakes her head. "Poirot just signs the papers."

We stand at the door to her room. Angry Arms of Death passes by, giving us an *I've-got-my-eyes-on-you* sort of look before moving on.

"We'll leave here," she tells me, "but we won't leave together. One of us will be left behind."

And although I don't want to think about that, I know it's true. A harsh reality amidst the harsh unreality.

"We have to promise to free each other when the time comes," she says. "I promise... Can you?"

"Yes," I tell her, "I promise, too." But I know it's easier said than done. And I think, if thoughts are worth a penny, how much less promises must be worth. Especially the ones you're likely to break.

126 A Fine Kind of Pain

My gut is the sea, roiling and stirring with deep dark acidity and malevolent intent. The discomfort within has evolved into sheer misery. Just as my stomach rumbles with gaseous unpleasantness, so does the ocean beneath the hull of our ship.

"The Abyssal Serpent is stalking us," the navigator tells me.

"Just as some people feel rain as the tightness of their joints, you feel that nasty-ass creature coursing through your bowels." Then he goes to one of his maps of a nonexistent world, and picks up a pencil he's not supposed to have in our cabin. "Tell me where you feel it and I'll plot a course for us that will confound its pursuit."

I point to the places within where I feel my gut gurgling and aching, growling and straining. He translates my angry intestines, and with steely concentration draws a tangled knot of lines on his map – a path crossing itself over and over in every direction but straight. Then he runs the modified map up to the captain.

"It's a fine kind of pain," the captain reassures me, when he comes to check on my condition. "Go with your gut and it'll never steer you wrong."

127 Have You Considered That Maybe It Was Intentional?

The nurse says it's not food poisoning, since no one else got sick but me. I suspect that I got it from the eggplant parmesan my mom brought for me. She sneaked it in because we're not supposed to get food from the outside. I hid it in my closet, and forgot about it, but then found it and ate it the following day. Best argument ever for refrigeration. I'm too embarrassed about it to tell anyone that my writhing tortured gut is my own stupid fault – although Hal knows, because he saw me hide the plate. I know he won't tell, though. He doesn't tell the pastels or the doctors or Carlyle anything anymore. I can barely move from the pain, except to thrash back and forth on my bed. The pastels give me medicine that does absolutely nothing. It's like trying to put out a forest fire with a water gun.

I moan loudly, and Hal looks up from his crazy-ass atlas long enough to say, "Have you considered that maybe it was intentional? Maybe your parents poisoned you."

"Wow, thanks, Hal, that's just what I need to hear."

The fact is, I already thought of that, but hearing him say it out loud makes the concern that much more real, and it ticks me off. Like I'm not already paranoid enough.

He shrugs. "Just trying to give you perspective, perplexive, perspiration, expiration. If you expire, I'll give you a twenty-one gun salute, but your next of kin will have to provide the twenty-one guns."

128 Intestinal Time-share

I'm shackled to the table in the White Plastic Kitchen again. I'm lucid enough to know it's a dream. Lucid enough to know that my stomach is giving me no relief, even in my sleep.

The monsters with masks that look like my parents are there, and now a creature with Mackenzie's face is there, too. The mask looks like a cross between my sister and Edvard Munch's

The Scream; blond hair and a terrified yowling mouth – although from behind the mask I can hear laughter.

The three of them press their pointed Vulcanoid ears to my bloated belly, and my belly speaks to them in guttural evil growls like Satan himself has purchased a time-share in my intestinal tract. They listen, nod, answer questions in the same guttural language.

"We understand," they say. "We will do what must be done."

Then, the foul thing inhabiting my stomach begins to dig its way out.

129 Against Us

The sea rolls with regular relentless surges. My bedroll is wet beneath me. The pale green tarnished copper ceiling drips with condensation.

The captain stands above me, looking down. Assessing with his good eye. "Welcome back, lad," he says. "We thought we had lost you."

"What happened," I croak.

"You were keelhauled," he tells me. "Taken in the middle of the night from your quarters, brought on deck, turned inside out, then tied to a rope, and hurled overboard."

I don't remember any of this until the moment he speaks of it – as if his words themselves are my memory.

"Someone got tired of hearing you moan about your gut,

so they cleaned it out by exposing your innards to the sea, and dragging you over the barnacle-covered keel of the ship, then back up the other side. Whatever was causing your distress has surely been scraped off."

As he says it, I can feel every barnacle. I can feel my lungs on fire as they fight for oxygen that's no longer there. Screaming soundlessly into the deep, then filling my lungs with killing seawater, then blacking out.

"Many a sailor dies of it, or is left broken beyond repair," the captain tells me. "But you seem to have endured it well."

"Am I still inside out?" I ask weakly.

"Not as I can tell. Unless your insides bear a close resemblance to your outsides."

"Was it done on your orders?" I ask.

He looks insulted. "If it had been on my orders, mine would have been the last face you saw when you went down, and the first you saw upon coming back up. I always take credit for my acts of cruelty. To do otherwise is cowardice."

He orders the navigator, who watches us from his bunk, to go fetch me some water. Once he is gone, the captain kneels beside me and whispers.

"Hear me well. Those who appear to be your friends are not. Those who seem one thing are another. A blue sky can be orange, up can masquerade as down, and someone is always trying to poison the meal. Do you catch my drift?"

"No," I tell him.

"Good. You're learning." He looks around to make sure we

are still unobserved. "You've had your suspicions about these things for quite some time, haven't you?"

I find myself nodding, even though I don't want to acknowledge it.

"I tell you now that your fears are founded. It's all true; forces are watching at every minute of every day, scheming against you. Against us." He grabs me by the arm. "Trust no one on this ship. Trust no one off this ship."

"How about you?" I ask. "Can I trust you?"

"What about 'trust no one' did you not understand?"

Then the navigator returns with the cup of water, and the captain spills it out on the floor, because not even the navigator is beyond suspicion.

130 Stay Broken

My intestinal distress passes, proving it was nothing more than spoiled eggplant. Poirot would call it a victory that I realized my parents didn't intend to poison me. That I understood such a feeling was just paranoia.

"The more you can disbelieve the things your illness tries to make you believe, the sooner you'll be well enough to go home."

What he doesn't get is that even though part of me has come to sense the things that might be delusional, there's the other part of me that has no choice but to believe them. At this moment I see poisoned eggplant as very unlikely. But tomorrow, I might be raving that my parents are trying to kill me, and I'll believe it as completely as I believe the earth is round. And if I suddenly have a notion that the earth is flat, I'm likely to believe that, too.

My one point of stability is Callie, but she's beginning to concern me. Not that she's getting worse, but that she's getting better. She doesn't spend as much time by the window of the Vista Lounge anymore. Such a lack of obsessive behavior might tempt Poirot to send her home.

I say an awful prayer that night. The kind that could get me damned if I believed in that stuff, which I might, or might not. It's still up in the air.

"Please stay broken, Callie," I pray. "Please stay broken as long as I am."

I know it's selfish, but I don't care. I can't imagine not seeing her smile. I can't imagine not keeping her warm. No matter what I promised her, I can't imagine being here without her.

131 Cardboard Forts

My parents bring Mackenzie to visit for the first time. I know why they haven't done it until now. Because I'm scary sometimes. Maybe scary in a different way than I was at home, but still scary. And then there's everyone else. Mackenzie's tough, but a psychiatric ward for young people is no place for a young person.

My parents had warned me they were going to bring her, in spite of their reservations.

"She's convinced things are much worse than they are," my mom had told me. "You know her imagination. And it will be good for you to see each other. Dr. Poirot agrees."

So during visiting hour one day, when those of us with visitors are escorted into the rec room by the pastels, I find her sitting at a table with my parents.

I hesitate when I spot her, having totally forgotten she was coming. It's like I'm afraid that if I get too close I might break her. I don't want to break her, and I don't want her to see me like this. But it's visiting hour. You can't run away from visiting hour. I cautiously approach my family.

"Hi, Caden."

"Hi, Mackenzie."

"You look good. Except for your bed-hair."

"You look good, too."

My father stands and pulls out the one chair at the table that isn't occupied. "Why don't you sit, Caden."

I do as I'm told. I sit down, and do my best to keep my knees from bouncing, but only succeed when I give it all of my attention. When I give it all of my attention, though, I lose the conversation. I don't want to lose that. I want to shine for Mackenzie. I want to give off an everything's fine kind of vibe. I don't think I'm succeeding.

Mackenzie's lips move, and her eyes emote. I catch the tail end of what she's saying. "... and the Dance Moms practically gouged one another's eyes out, so Mom, who's like totally not one of them, found me a calmer dance studio where the people aren't psycho." Then she looks down, and goes a little bit red. "Sorry. I didn't mean that."

I'm not feeling much of anything right now, but if I could feel bad because she's feeling bad, I would – so I say, "Well, there's psycho, and there's *psycho*. There's no medication for Dance Mom Syndrome. Except maybe cyanide."

Mackenzie giggles. My parents are not amused.

"We don't use that word here, Mackenzie," Mom says. "Just like we don't use the *C* word."

"Cyclops," I say. "Because the doctor has only one eye."

Mackenzie giggles again. "You're making that up."

"Actually," says Dad with a weird sort of pride, "he's not. The other eye is glass."

"Both his wings work, though," I tell her. "But there's nowhere to fly."

"Why don't we play a game?" Mom quickly says. The last game I remember playing was Apples to Apples when Shelby came. Or was it Max? No, I think it was Shelby. Although I know how to play the game, the concept was out of my reach at the time. The rules are pretty straightforward: an adjective is put down, like maybe "awkward," and everyone has to throw down a noun that best fits. Throwing down an absurd card only works when you're ironic, not medicated. Last time, I think the cards I played made everyone else profoundly sad.

With all the visitors engaged in playtime pursuits, however, Apples to Apples is the only game left on the shelf, and Mackenzie grabs it, not knowing the sordid history.

"I have an idea," says Mom when Mackenzie sits down with the box. "Why don't we use the game to build a house of cards?" Mackenzie begins to protest, but Dad gives her a bulgy-eyed *don't-argue-we'll-explain-later* sort of look.

I grin at the house of cards idea, getting the irony that they don't. The parrot would call that a good sign. He'd suggest I try to play the game after all. For that reason, I don't.

Dad starts with the concentration of an engineer laying the foundation of a bridge. Each of us adds cards in turn. We don't seem to get more than ten cards up before the house falls. Four attempts. The fourth time we actually get further, building a second level before the whole thing flattens.

"Oh well," says Mom.

"It's a tough thing to do, even when the sea is calm," I point out.

Mom and Dad simultaneously try to change the subject again, but Mackenzie won't let them. "What sea?" she asks.

"What sea, what?" I say.

"You said the sea was calm."

"Did I?"

"Mackenzie…" Dad begins, but Mom gently touches Dad's shoulder to stop him.

"Let him answer," Mom says gently.

I suddenly feel very, very uncomfortable. Shamefully embarrassed. Like I've been caught on a date with my finger up my nose. I turn away, looking out of the window, where I see rolling hills of freshly mowed grass. It grounds me. If only for the moment.

Still, the captain must be somewhere, listening to every word I say.

"It's … like that sometimes," I tell Mackenzie. It's the only thing I can say that will keep me from imploding in on myself.

And Mackenzie says, "I get it."

Then she reaches her hand out and puts it on mine. I still can't look directly at her, so I look at her hand.

"Remember when we used to make forts out of cardboard boxes on Christmas?" she says.

I smile. "Yeah. That was fun."

"Those forts were so real, even though they weren't, you know?"

No one says anything for a moment.

"Is it Christmas?" I ask.

Dad sighs. "It's almost summer, Caden."

"Oh."

Mom has gotten teary eyed, and I wonder what I did to make her cry.

132 Without Whispering

It's late afternoon. Almost sunset. The sun, low on the horizon, casts a hypnotic reflection on the sea. Our sails are full of a steady wind as we head relentlessly west. If indeed the sun still sets in the west.

I'm on deck with Carlyle. He hands me his mop, and lets me do some of his dirty work.

"Somehow I don't think the captain would approve," I tell him. "Or the parrot."

He seems to have no opinion about the captain, but of the parrot he says, "That bird sees everything. I gave up keeping secrets from him long ago."

"So then ... whose side are you on?"

Carlyle smiles, and dumps some water from his bucket for me to mop up. "Yours."

He watches me for a few moments, then says, "You remind me of me when I used to be in your shoes."

"You?"

"Yep." He closes his laptop, to give me his full attention. There are others in the rec room with us, but they're mostly just watching TV. We're the only ones talking. "You're lucky. I was also fifteen when I had my first episode, but I didn't end up in a place as nice as this."

"You?" I say again.

"At first they thought bipolar one, but when the delusions got increasingly psychotic, and I started to have auditory hallucinations, they changed my diagnosis to schizoaffective."

He says the words without whispering. He says them without the fearful gravity people on the outside give the words. The idea that Carlyle is one of us troubles me, because what if he's lying? What if he's making it up to mess with my head? No. That's just paranoia. That's what Poirot would say, and Poirot would be right.

Carlyle explains that schizoaffective is a cross between bipolar and schizophrenia. "Oughta be called 'tri-polar,'" he says. "'Cause first you get manic, thinking you're king of the universe, then you go off the deep end, seeing things, hearing things – *believing* things that aren't true. Then when you come down, you fall into a depression once you realize where you've been."

"And they let you work here?"

"I'm cool as long as I'm on my meds. Learned it the hard way, but I learned. Haven't had an episode for years. And anyway, I don't technically work here – I volunteer in my free time. I figured I got this thing, and a master's in psychology, I might as well use them."

It's all too much for me to take in. "So what do you do when you're not mopping up our mental crap?"

He points to his laptop. "Software company. I design games."

"No way."

"Hey, the meds can muddle your imagination, but they can't kill it."

I'm amazed, thrilled even. When I turn to look out over the deck, other crewmen are busy with tasks assigned by the captain, or just milling around. It's a gorgeous sunset, filled with just about every color.

Carlyle wrings out his mop and looks around, satisfied with the cleanliness of the deck. "Anyway," he says. "Just because it's a long voyage, it doesn't mean you're on it forever."

He leaves me with that thought as he goes belowdecks. It's only after he's gone that I see the captain. He's standing at the helm, his favorite place for looking down on the rest of the ship – and right now he's looking straight at me with an acid gaze from his singular eye that could dissolve me into nothing.

133 Crestmare Alley

Nature, whether natural or not, unleashes its fury with a vengeance as we finally sail into the churning winds of the stalled storm front. The sky instantly turns from unrelenting day to an end-of-time kind of twilight as the ship pitches and rolls like a cork. Lightning flashes around us with thunder less than a second behind.

As I stand on deck, not knowing what to do, I watch the sails shred then heal, shred then heal above me, the scars on the fabric becoming as thick as the ratline ropes. I wonder how much they can stand before they fail. The captain barks orders to scrambling crewmen, who disgorge from the main hatch like ants from a flooding anthill. I'm thinking they should be going the other way. Better down than on deck, where they can be washed away, but perhaps they fear the wrath of the captain more than the wrath of heaven.

"Take down the sails!" the captain orders. "Secure the riggings!" He kicks a crewman in the behind. "Faster! Do you want us to lose a mast?"

The storm has been looming for more than a week – plenty of time to prepare the ship for this onslaught, but the captain chose to do nothing, sticking to a unique philosophy.

"Preventative measures are the bane of spontaneous action," he said. "I prefer the glory of heroism amidst panic."

Well, now he has panic. Whether or not heroism will save the day is yet to be seen.

The captain sees me standing there with no particular orders. "Take the helm," he tells me, pointing to the upper deck. "Man the tiller. Turn us into the waves!"

I am shocked that he has actually asked me to take control of the ship. "*Into* the waves?" I ask, not sure I heard right.

"Do as I say!" the captain yells. "These waves are thirty-footers if they're an inch. If they hit us broadside, we may capsize – and I prefer to sail this ocean right-side up."

I leap three steps at a time to the helm, grab the tiller, and struggle to turn it. The parrot swoops past me, squawking something, but I can't hear him over the thunder and crashing waves.

I finally get the tiller to move, pulling the stubborn rudder, but not soon enough. A wave hits us at an angle, crashing over the starboard bow. The crew is washed across the deck, grabbing on to anything they can for purchase.

Finally the ship comes about, challenging the waves. The bow pitches downward into a trough, and a wave hits us head-on. I can't help but think of Calliope and how she's faring through this. Do the waves batter her as they batter the rest of us? If she feels everything, does she feel the pain of the ship as it struggles to stay in one piece?

White water floods the deck, then drains away, leaving behind crewmen coughing for air. I have no idea if anyone has been lost to the sea.

I feel a sudden pain in my shoulder. The parrot has rounded back and landed on me, digging his talons in to keep from being torn away by the wind. "It's time, it's time," he says. "You must dispatch the captain."

"What? In the middle of this?"

"Kill him," insists the bird. "Throw him overboard. We'll say he was lost at sea, and you'll be free of him."

But my allegiance is still uncertain, and right now, saving my own life is more important than ending someone else's. "No! I can't!"

"He is the cause of this storm!" shouts the bird. "He's the one who tore you from your life! This all begins and ends with him! You must do it! You must!" Then a gust of wind tears him from my shoulder.

Whether he's lying or speaking truth, I don't have time to consider. Another wave hits us. This time I'm pitched off the helm and down to the main deck, becoming one of the many struggling to remain aboard against the pull of the sea.

When I look up, I see something the sea brought aboard. A creature that stares at me from the mainsail boom. The thing has a pointed equine face with flaring nostrils and angry red eyes. It's a horse – but it has no hind quarters. It has no legs at all, just a prehensile tail coiled around the boom. It's a sea horse the size of a man, with bone-hard spikes up and down its body.

"Crestmare!" someone yells.

Then the captain leaps to the boom and in one smooth move slits its throat. The thing falls dead, dropping at my feet, its eyes going dark. "I should have known," the captain says. "We are in Crestmare Alley." Then he orders me back up to the helm. "A new course of action," he says. "Our backside to the waves."

"Retreat?" shouts the navigator through the window of the map room. "My maps say we must pass this way."

"I said nothing of retreat! This is a duel – and a duel begins back-to-back."

Once more at the tiller, I force the rudder to one side, and the waves do the rest. We are easily spun 180 degrees.

I know I should be looking forward, but I can't help but turn my eyes aft. In a long flash of lightning, I see another wave coming at us from behind, higher than all the others – and at the wave's crest, I see too many fiery red eyes to count. Apparently the crestmares don't know the rules of a duel.

I hook my arm around the tiller as the wave hits. The stern disappears beneath the wave, the main deck is flooded, and the surge hits the helm, submerging me. As I hold my breath for what seems like forever, twisting with the force of the water, I hold tight to the tiller. I think we've been taken down and are on our way to the bottom, but then the water clears, and I'm gasping salty air.

When my eyes clear enough to see, I witness something hell itself could not have conceived. Dozens of crestmares maneuver around the deck, their tails giving them the agility of monkeys. They wrap their sharp bodies around crewmen like snakes. One creature opens its mouth and reveals sharklike teeth

that plunge into the neck of its screaming victim. Then it takes the dying sailor over the edge and into the sea.

A crestmare leaps toward me and I swing my fist, knocking it aside, but it curls its tail around my arm and twists its body, and in an instant, it's there breathing into my face again. I think it will take off my head in a single bite, but instead it speaks.

"It's not you we want … but we'll go through you if we have to."

Then it head-butts me, leaving me back down on the deck, and swings away.

That's when I see the captain. He's set upon by three crestmares – one constricted on each leg, and a third around his chest. He holds the third one by the neck as it snaps at his face. He tries slicing at it with his dagger, but it knocks the dagger away, and it clatters to the deck.

You must dispatch the captain, the parrot had said – but maybe I don't have to. Maybe the crestmares will do it for me. If they kill him, though, and drag him into the sea, what of Calliope? Without his key, she can never be free.

Before another wave has a chance to flood the deck, I scramble for the captain's dagger, then plunge it into the back of the head of the crestmare trying to bite him. It falls dead, then I go after the two on his legs. Another one leaps at us, but I knock it down, and crush its head beneath my heel.

Freed from the crestmares, the captain is disoriented. He gasps to regain his wind. If ever there were a time he'd be too weak to fight me, this is it. I grab a board from a broken crate, and swing it at the back of his head so hard that the force of it sends the peach pit flying out from behind his eye patch, along with a small silver key that clatters on the deck. The captain goes down. He doesn't know what hit him.

Another wave looms behind us – the crest full of red eyes like the leading edge of a lava flow. Let the crestmares get the captain now, I don't care. I have what I want.

Before the wave hits, I hurl myself forward toward the locked trapdoor of the forecastle, and fumble with the key in the padlock.

I feel more than hear the wave hit the stern of the ship. The rush of water moves closer along the deck, but I don't turn to look. Finally the padlock clicks open. I pull it free, lift the hatch, and throw myself in just as the wave reaches the bow, washing me down into the forecastle.

I stand up. There's water to my waist – the forecastle is half flooded. Mooring ropes are curled on either side of me. Then, right in front of me, dim, but clearly visible, I see a pair of legs protruding from the point that marks the tip of the bow. Calliope was right! She is more than a part of the ship; she has her own legs, but they're badly corroded from being so long in this dank place. Then I see why she can't free herself – there's a bolt through her lower back, keeping her attached to the bow. I can set her free!

"Calliope! Can you hear me?" I shout. In response she moves her copper foot. I struggle with the bolt, but my bare hands aren't strong enough – and I curse the shipbuilder who left her like this.

Then from behind me I hear:

"You might want this."

I turn to see Carlyle holding out a wrench, like somehow he's been here all along, just waiting for me.

I take it from him. It's the right size – and I know I'll have enough leverage to loosen the bolt ... but I hesitate.

If I do this, what will happen? Tearing her from the ship could condemn her to a watery grave. She's made of copper, which means she might sink like a penny in a fountain. But what if she doesn't sink? What if she swims? If I free her from the ship now, will she take me with her? Can I continue this voyage without her?

"Hurry, Caden," says Carlyle. "Before you're too late."

With the sound of crestmares above and the raging sea below, I hold the wrench on the bolt, struggling to set Calliope free. I put my full weight behind the wrench, and the bolt begins to turn. I jerk harder until it's loose, then work the wrench until the bolt falls free.

As soon as it plunks into the dark water of the flooded forecastle, Calliope begins to wriggle in the tightly cinched hole, pulling herself forward. I can imagine her straining her arms, pushing against the ship as if birthing herself from the bow. She frees her hips, her legs follow, and in an instant she's gone, leaving only a porthole-sized gap where she had been.

I look out through the hole to see that she has not sunk – but neither does she swim. Instead, she runs, her spirit lighter than air, lighter than the copper of her flesh, more willful than gravity. She runs on the surface of the waves! A single ray of sunlight pierces the clouds like a spotlight to follow her, and her corroded, oxidized shell peels away, revealing shining copper from head to toe. I want to cry for joy, but a dark shape falls from the ship up above into the waves, then another then another. The crestmares! In a moment the sea is infested with them, racing like a cavalry charge toward a single shining figure in the distance.

It's not you we want, but we'll go through you if we have to.

It wasn't the captain they were after – it was Calliope! The captain must have known! That's why he turned to face her away from them.

"Run!" I scream, even though I know she can't hear me. "Run and don't ever stop running!"

In a moment she is like a tiny flame on the horizon chased by the surge of crestmares, then I can't see her anymore, and I pray that she has the strength to run for as long as she has to.

When I climb out of the forecastle, the storm has ended, as if a switch has been thrown. The waves subside; the clouds begin to break apart. The captain stands midship with arms crossed, his good eye fixed on me. His dead socket is bare and dark, but somehow staring as well.

"Am I to be keelhauled?" I ask. "Or worse?"

"You had the gall to steal something from me," he says.

Around him the crew tenses in anticipation of what he might do.

"You had the gall to steal from me – and by doing so, you saved us all." He claps me on the shoulder. "Heroism amidst panic."

The navigator comes to him with his peach pit. "I found this.

Does that make me a hero, too?" The captain takes it from him without answering. He pops it back in place, but somewhere in the storm, the eye patch was lost. There is nothing to hide the awfulness of his peach-pit eye.

"Bring us around," the captain says. "A westerly heading once more, Master Caden."

"Master?"

"I've just promoted you to Master of the Helm. The wind no longer guides us," he says. "You do."

134 On the Other Side of the Glass

I hear from Skye that Callie is leaving.

"She's in our room, packing right now," Skye tells me as she works on the same puzzle she's been working on forever. I wonder if she remembers giving me a piece, and if she'll ever ask for it back. "You'll never see Callie again. Poor you." Skye seems to take both delight and misery from the fact. "Life is about suffering. Deal with it."

I don't dignify her with a response. Instead I go to Callie's room. On the way I run into Carlyle, and I can tell by the sympathetic look on his face that it's true. Callie is leaving.

"You may want this," he says, and reaching over the nurses' station, he pulls a rose from a flower arrangement. He hands me the rose.

"Hurry, Caden," he says. "Before you're too late."

Callie is in her room with her parents, packing up what few belongings she has. I have never met her parents. On the days they've come during visiting hour, the three of them retreated to a corner of the Vista Lounge and talked in hushed tones, letting no one in their little circle of three.

When Callie sees me, she doesn't smile. In fact, she seems almost in pain. "Mom, Dad, this is Caden," she tells them. Was she going to leave without saying good-bye? Or was it so painful she just didn't want to think about it?

The rose in my hand seems such an awkward gesture now, I lay it down on her bed rather than handing it to her.

"Hello, Caden," says her father in an accent much stronger than hers.

"Hi," I say, and turn back to Callie. "So, it's true – you're leaving."

Her father speaks instead. "Discharge papers are already signed. Our daughter comes home today."

In spite of his attempt to speak for her, I direct my words at Callie. "You could have told me."

"I wasn't sure until this morning. Then it happened so fast…"

Skye's words are still in my head. *You'll never see Callie again.* I am determined to prove her wrong. I pull a crumpled piece of paper out of the trash, then ask her parents for a pen, because I know I won't exactly find one lying around.

Her mother hands me a pen from her purse, and I write on the scrap of paper as legibly as I can.

"Here's my email address, so you can write to me," I say.

We're not allowed email here, but my in-box will still be there if and when I get out of this place.

She takes the paper and holds it tightly in her fist, treasuring it. I can see tears in her eyes. "Thank you, Caden."

"Maybe you can give me yours, too?"

Callie hesitates, and looks to her parents. She's so different around them – so subdued that I don't know what to think.

Her parents look to each other, as if I've asked something unthinkable.

And that's when I realize that I can't take her email address. Not because of her parents, but because of her. Because I promised I'd set her free.

"Forget it," I say like it's nothing, even though it's everything. "You can write to me first. And if you do, I'll write back."

Callie nods, and gives me a pained but sincere smile. "Thank you, Caden."

Her father tries to take the slip of paper from her, but she clutches it to her chest, as if she's still holding me.

I think about how Callie was when I first met her. She is now clearer. It's in the way she holds herself, the way she speaks. It's in her eyes. She is on the other side of the glass now. Part of the outside world she so needed to observe.

I want to hug her, but I know I can't in the presence of her parents. Their boundary of appropriateness is a no-fly zone miles wide. I shake her hand instead, and she meets my gaze, surprised by the gesture, and maybe a little disappointed, but she understands the necessity. Strange, but shaking her hand feels much more awkward than keeping her warm in my bed.

We must be holding each other's hands for too long, because her father finally says, "Say good-bye to him, Callie."

But in subtle defiance of him, she doesn't actually say good-bye. Instead she says, "I will miss you very, very much, Caden."

"I will always be there on the horizon," I tell her.

And with infinite sorrow, she says, "I believe that. But sadly I am no longer looking out of that window."

135 Which Is More Horrifying?

"I want to leave," I tell Poirot at my next assessment.

"You will, you will. I assure you that you will."

But his assurances mean nothing to me. "What do I have to do to get out of here?"

Instead of answering me, he pulls out one of my recent works of art from his drawer. He uses them against me like bullets to the brain.

"Why all the eyes?" he asks. "It's fascinating, but why all the eyes?"

"I draw what I feel."

"And you feel this?"

"I don't have to tell you anything."

"I'm concerned about you, Caden. Deeply concerned." He bobs his head a bit in thought. "Maybe we need to adjust your medications."

"Adjust my medications, adjust my medications, that's all you ever want to do is adjust my medications!"

He maintains his composure as he looks at me. I see his eyes — both the live one and the dead one — in the numbers of the ticking clock, in the motivational posters on the walls. Everywhere. I can't escape.

"This is the way it's done, Caden. This is what works. It's not as fast as you would like, I know. But give it time, and it will get you where you need to be. Where you *want* to be." He begins to write a new prescription. "I'd like to try you on Geodon."

I slam my fists against the arm of my chair. "I'm angry! Why can't you let me be angry? Why do you have to medicate away everything I feel?"

He doesn't even look up at me. "Anger isn't a productive emotion right now."

"But it's real, isn't it? It's *normal*, isn't it? Look at where I am and what's happened to me! I have a right to be angry!"

He stops writing and finally looks at me with his one good eye, and I think, how can this man possibly have perspective on me when he has no depth perception? I expect him to call for Angry Arms of Death to restrain me. Maybe order me up a shot of Haldol to send me to the White Plastic Kitchen. But he does neither of those things. He taps his pen. Considers. Then says, "That's a reasonable argument. It's a sign that you're getting better." He puts away his prescription pad. "We'll stay the course for one more week, and then reassess."

I am escorted back to my room, feeling much worse than

I did before my evaluation. I don't know which is more hor-
rifying – the thought of being here for another week, or the
thought that maybe the medication that I so despise might
actually be working.

136 Becoming a Constellation

Something's up with the navigator. He's more into himself,
more lost in his charts than ever before. He refuses to look at
my drawings, and now that my gut has gone silent, he refuses to
take guidance from it. He's in a mood, but it's more than that.
His skin is paler, and there's a rash on his arms that's beginning
to peel.

"Accompany me to the crow's nest," he says in one of his
rare social moments. "I'm in need of a view."

We climb to the little barrel atop the central mast. As always,
what appears to be only a yard in diameter is dozens of yards
across once we climb inside. It's an off hour. Just a few other
sailors sit alone watching the jumpers, or just watching the olives
in their drinks wink at them. The navigator gets his cocktail
from the bartender. It's not time for mine yet. I'll have to come
back later.

His drink swirls with blue sparkles in a cloudy orange brine.
"I am far too numb," he tells me. Then he slowly pours his cocktail on the ground. Radioactive liquid pools in a depression in
the copperized wood, but as I watch, it's sucked in by the black

pitch between the metallic planks. The pitch appears to writhe and squirm, but I know it must just be a trick of the light. The bartender is at the far end of the bar, serving someone else, and doesn't see what the navigator has done.

"It's our secret," he says. "If I am to navigate us to the dive point, I need my brilliance to be untainted. I must calculate our journey without any outside interference. Interference, perseverance, persecution, evolution. I'm evolving, is the thing; I'm a god becoming a constellation."

"The constellations are mostly demigods," I point out. "And they didn't get to be constellations until after they died."

He laughs at that, and says, "Death is a small sacrifice to become immortal."

137 Lost Horizon

Without Calliope on our bow, I feel a profound loneliness that nothing can penetrate.

"Take it day by day," Carlyle tells me, "and each morning you'll feel a little bit better."

But I don't. The captain acts as if Calliope never existed. For the captain there is no history, no yesterday, no memory. "Live for the moment and the moment after," he once told me. "Never for the moment before." It's a creed that defines him.

Calliope was our eyes on the horizon, and without her, it seems the horizon is gone. The sea fades into a haze that blends into the sky. There is no telling where one ends, and the other begins. Now the heavens are unpredictable and the sea fickle. Up above, clouds will billow out of nowhere into dark monstrosities, pregnant with malevolent intent, and a clear blue sky is like a magnifying glass for a punishing sun. As for the sea, there is no rhythm to the waves anymore; no reason to the ocean's temperament. One moment the sea is as smooth and tranquil as a mountain lake, the next, it's roiling with rogue waves.

"We have crossed the point of no return," the captain tells me as I struggle at the tiller to keep the ship zigzagging like a cargo ship in wartime. Traveling a straight line would be suicide now. The best chance of avoiding and confounding the beasts that lie below is to be as unpredictable as the sea and sky.

My hands are rough and calloused from manning the tiller. My palms are faintly green, for like everything else on the ship, the tiller wheel has turned to copper and has oxidized green in the salt sea air.

"Was there ever a point of return?" I wonder out loud.

"Pardon?" says the captain.

"You said we crossed the point of no return, so does that mean there was a time we could have gone back?"

There is little warmth to the captain's grin. "Well, now we'll never know, will we?"

I suspect there was never a returning point. This journey was destined for me before I set foot on deck. Destined from the moment I was born.

The navigator races up from below, waving a brand-new

navigational chart in his hands. His scribbled knots of lines are measured in leagues and compass degrees with painstaking detail. The captain looks it over, nods, and hands the chart to me. My zigzags are not random at all. Or at least it's not my randomness that we follow, it's the navigator's.

The captain slaps him on the back with pride. "This will most certainly get us to where we are going."

The navigator beams with the captain's attention. "I'm plugged into the power now – deeply connected to the deep," the navigator says. "Connected, infected, ingested, digested – I can feel our destination in my gut. It's the only nourishment I need!"

The captain knows that the navigator hasn't been drinking his cocktail. Perhaps that's part of the reason why the captain is so proud of him. The captain turns to me. "You should follow his lead, Master Caden. Our navigator's vision is clear. Is yours?"

But there are other things that come with this "clarity of vision," as the captain calls it. The navigator's charts are more convoluted than ever, and yet he is adamant that they are the key to getting us where we're going. And the scary thing is that I believe him.

"Shun the crow's nest and your enlightenment will be sweeter than its poison intoxication," the captain tells me. "Look at the navigator!"

I worry, though, that the navigator's enlightenment is as dangerous as fireworks in the hands of a child. If he's tuned into the deep, what is the deep telling him? The depths certainly do not mean us well. Now, when the navigator walks, I notice that the pitchy ooze that fills the crevices of the ship sticks to his heels. When he touches a wall the ooze grows thicker, drawn to his hand as if he's become a gravity well for the darkness – and it occurs to me that the dark must be in love with the light. Yet one must always kill the other.

138 Marksman on the Fields of Color

In a moment when the sea is calm and the sky clear, the captain pulls out a pistol. An old-fashioned one. A flintlock, I think it's called. The kind of weapon that Aaron Burr used to kill Alexander Hamilton in their infamous duel.

"I hear you are an expert shot," the captain says. This strikes me as odd, because I've never fired a gun in my life.

"Who told you that?" I ask, not wanting to deny it.

"Word gets around," he says. "It's well known that you've dispatched many an adversary on the fields of color."

"Oh. You mean paintball."

"A marksman is a marksman in any medium, and the time of action is upon us." Then he puts the gun in my hand, also giving me a small pouch of gunpowder, and a single lead shot. "One shot is all you'll need to do away with the bird."

I look at the gun, trying to appear less frightened of it than I am. It's a heavy thing. Much heavier than it looks. I turn my eyes up to the sails, but can't find the parrot. He has made himself scarce since baring his intent to kill the captain. Now he perches high in the ratlines and the high beams of the masts. The time of action is upon us, but I remain ambivalent as to what action I should take. It does feel good, though, to be at the wheel, and in the captain's good graces.

"Wouldn't it be more satisfying to do it yourself?" I suggest.

The captain shakes his head. "Even with one eye, that plumed serpent of a bird is too shrewd to be caught unawares. The deed must be done by someone he trusts, and who I trust to do it." He grasps me by the shoulder with something resembling pride. "Lure him into a liaison. Keep the weapon concealed until the last moment."

I slip the pistol into my belt and cover it with my shirt. The captain nods his approval. "When we are free of the parrot, then we shall truly be free."

I realize that my choices are impossible, and I have no idea what I'm going to do.

139 The Rest Is Silence

If you want to talk to anyone about mental misfirings, Raoul's got the right idea. Talk to Shakespeare.

My brain fries when I try to read Shakespeare, but my English teacher would not accept "my hound hath eaten my volume" as an acceptable excuse for avoiding *Hamlet*. Funny thing, after reading for a while, I actually started to understand it.

The doomed prince of Denmark is a dude faced with an impossible choice. The ghost of Hamlet's dead father tells him to avenge his murder by killing his uncle. For the rest of the play, Hamlet agonizes. Should I kill my uncle? Should I ignore the ghost? Is the ghost real? Am I insane? If I'm not insane, should I pretend to be insane? Should I end the agony of impossible choices by ending my life? Will I dream if I kill myself? And will those dreams be any better than the nightmare of my dead father telling me to kill my uncle, who, by the way, is now married to my mother? He agonizes, and ponders, and talks to himself until he's stabbed by a poisoned blade, and all his tormented self-analysis gives way to eternal silence.

Shakespeare had a thing about death. And poison. And insanity. Hamlet's beloved Ophelia really does go insane and drowns. King Lear loses his mind with what we, in modern times, would call Alzheimer's. Macbeth is totally delusional and has hallucinations of ghosts and a pesky floating dagger. It's all so on target, it makes me wonder if Shakespeare was writing from experience.

Regardless, I'm sure people accused him of being "on something," too.

I have yet to follow the captain's order to kill the parrot. I have yet to take the parrot's dire warning that I must kill the captain. I am paralyzed by my inability to act, one way or the other.

But everything changes the day we face our next threat from the deep.

It begins with a disturbance off the port bow; a patch of bubbling white water marking something beneath the surface.

The captain orders quiet on deck, but it's hard to order quiet when you have to whisper, so he sends Carlyle to tell the seamen on deck individually to hold their tongues, and whatever other parts of their anatomy are making noise.

"Turn us twenty degrees starboard," the captain whispers to me.

I turn the tiller. We are riding a swift tailwind today, and the ship veers starboard quickly, moving us away from the disturbance.

"What *was* that out there?" I ask.

"Shhh," the captain says. "It'll be fine as long as they don't hear our passage."

Then, to our starboard side, I see another patch of churning water even closer to the ship than the first. The captain takes a deep breath and whispers, "Hard to port."

I do as I'm told, but I crank the tiller too quickly, and the rudder creaks. I can feel the vibration amplified in the belly of the ship, like the menacing tone of a cello. The captain grimaces.

The ship veers away from the strange patch of sea, and for a moment I think we're out of danger, but then, directly in front of us, the water begins to froth, and in that churning foam, I catch a glimpse of something I wish I hadn't. A barnacle-covered creature as pale as a corpse, and the dark, oily tentacle of a second creature gripping on to the first. The monstrosities dive, and the water settles.

"Were those … what I think they were?" I ask the captain.

"Aye," the captain says. "We trespass now in the realm of the Nemesi."

We sail in silence waiting … waiting – then suddenly the whale, wrapped by the clinging body of the squid, does a full breach, barely fifty yards to starboard. The creatures are massive. Together they are more than double the size of our ship. The whale writhes, its fluke beating powerfully against the air as it leaves the water, revealing how completely the squid's tentacles envelop it, squeezing the whale with life-crushing force. They plunge back into the sea, creating an enormous wave that hits the ship broadside, and tips us within inches of capsizing.

While the rest of us slide along the tilting deck, the captain never loses his footing. He grabs me as the ship rights itself, and puts me back at the tiller. "Steer us clear of these beasts," he tells me. "Feel their presence and steer us clear."

And although I can sense great malevolence beneath us, the feeling has no direction. It's as if they're everywhere, and there's no way for me to know which way to turn.

"They are too consumed with each other to notice our

presence," the captain says. "Only if they hear us will their attention be turned. Guide us true, and we'll pass through unscathed."

I think back to the captain's tale of the Nemesi. "But if their quarrel is with each other, why would they attack *us*?" I ask.

The captain whispers into my ear. "The whale abhors chaos; the squid detests order. Is this ship not the bastard child of both?"

His words give me a glimmer of understanding. Although the Nemesi might sense a bit of themselves reflected in the ship, they see only that which they loathe. It makes us the mortal enemy of two mortal enemies.

"We might be able to sustain the wake of a close breach," the captain says. "But if they hear us, we're done for."

The next breach is off our port bow. The whale comes only partially out of the water this time, so its wake is less severe than before. Just as the captain said, the whale doesn't see us. Its eyes are rolled back into its head, seeing nothing. It thrashes back and forth, biting a tentacle the girth of a redwood. The squid lets loose an earsplitting screech. I crank the tiller to turn us away from them – but slowly this time so that the rudder won't moan.

And then from up above I hear a screeching almost as loud as the squid's.

"Over here!" the parrot yells. "Over here! We're over here."

And just before the whale sinks beneath the surface its eyes roll from sightless white to shiny black, and I swear it locks its gaze on me.

Our stealth destroyed, the captain now rages in venomous fury at the parrot. "The feathered demon would sink the ship rather than see me victorious! Do away with him now, Caden!" the captain orders. "Before he does away with us!"

I reach down to feel the flintlock pistol still in my belt, but silencing the parrot will do no good. It's too late – the creatures know we're here. When the captain sees me make no move to apprehend the parrot, he grabs me and hurls me from the helm to the main deck. "Do your duty, boy! Unless you want to be in the belly of one of those beasts!"

The parrot perches high on the foremast, squawking at a volume far too loud for such a small bird. I climb the ratlines toward him. When he sees me, he smiles. At least I think it's a smile. It's so hard to tell.

"Come see! Come see!" he calls to me. "The view is better from up here!"

He doesn't know I'm here to kill him. I still don't know if I can.

"Perspective! Perspective!" the parrot hoots. "Now do you understand?"

When I look down, I can see the situation with much greater clarity. From up here, I can see that the two beasts have separated. They circle the ship on opposite sides – for the moment the two enemies are united in purpose.

"The Nemesi will end this voyage. The captain will go down with the ship," the parrot says. "As it should be. As it should be."

Just then, the squid shoots a tentacle out of the water,

grabbing on to the bow. The ship lurches. I hold on to the ropes for my life. The dark creature curls a second tentacle around the bowsprit in a powerful grasp, and tears the bowsprit right off the bow. Had Calliope still been there, she would have been torn in half.

A violent shudder nearly knocks me from the ropes. I look down to see that the whale has battered our starboard side, nearly buckling it. The captain orders the master-at-arms to fire the cannon, but the whale submerges too quickly to be fired upon. The squid has now pulled itself completely out of the water and onto the bow, its tentacles wrapping around the lower half of the foremast like black vines. The bow dips low from its weight, and crewmen scream and scramble. I climb higher to get away from the seeking tip of the highest tentacle.

On deck, Carlyle jabs at the squid with a mop handle sharpened into a harpoon, but the creature's flesh is too thick for him to do much damage.

"Grab my talons," the parrot says. "I'll carry us away from here."

"But what about the others?"

"Their fate is not yours!"

"We're too far from land."

"My wings are strong!"

His voice is almost convincing, but I still can't believe. He's small. He seems powerless compared to the captain.

"Trust me," the parrot says. "You have to trust me!"

But I can't. I just can't.

And then I see the navigator. He's come up from below, racing toward the captain, oblivious to the battle that rages around him. Even from this far away I can see he's in worse shape than before. His pale skin peels with the wind. It comes off in page-like layers that flutter behind him to the deck, and are pulled in by the hungry pitch. He grabs one of the peeling pages, and shows it to the captain – a new navigational chart – but the captain pushes him aside, navigation being the furthest thing from his mind.

The whale rams us again, and finally the navigator looks around him to see the big picture. There's an expression on his face that chills me. A look of steely determination – and I think *parchment, judgment, sacrament, sacrifice.* I know what he's going to do even before he begins climbing the mainmast. He's going to the crow's nest. And he's going to jump.

"Not good," says the parrot, seeing what I see. "Not good, not good, not good."

"If you want to save someone, save him!"

"Too late," says the parrot. "Ours is not an exact science, but we do what we can do."

I will not accept that. The navigator is halfway up the mainmast now. A tentacle whips toward him but misses, grasping one of his trailing pages instead, crumbling it. The navigator never takes his eyes off the crow's nest, just above him. I have to save him!

The distance between the foremast and the mainmast is too far for me to jump, and if I climb down, I'll be climbing right into the gaping maw of the squid. But there might be a way to safely cross the distance. I turn to the parrot.

"Take me to the navigator!"

The parrot shakes his head. "Better if I don't."

And although I have no idea where I rank in the scheme of things, I muster my most authoritative voice and say, "That's an order!"

The parrot sighs, digs his talons painfully into my shoulders, beats his wings, and lifts me away from the ratlines of the foremast. He spoke the truth; even with wings so small, he has the strength to bear my weight. We sail above the battle, and he drops me into the crow's nest, just moments after the navigator gets there.

It takes a second for my eyes to adjust to the deceptive dimensions of the crow's nest; tiny from the outside, huge on the inside. I look around. The place is devoid of crewmen. There's nothing but shattered glass around the empty bar. Finally I spot the navigator at the far side, climbing to the leapers' ledge. I barely recognize him, so much of him has peeled away.

"No!" I shout. "Stop! You don't have to do this!" I try to get to him, but the broken glass beneath my feet slows me down.

The look of determination on his face has dissolved into a faint grin of acceptance. "You have your destination, and I have mine," he says. Even his voice now has the semblance of rustling paper. "Destination, violation, violence ... silence." And before I can reach him, he hurls himself into the wind.

"No!" I grab for him, but it's too late. He falls toward the sea, layers of parchment peeling away as he falls, page after page until there's nothing left of him. He's completely gone before he ever reaches the water. All that remains are a thousand pages wafting in the wind like confetti, settling piece by piece into the sea.

I stare at the flurry of parchment, unable to believe that he's gone. The parrot tries to bring a wing over my eyes. "Don't look, don't look." I push the parrot away in disgust.

Down below, the squid's passion for destruction is suddenly quelled. It releases its hold on the ship, and slithers back into the water. The whale, on a ramming run, dives under the ship instead of ramming it. In a few moments the creatures breach far off our port bow, once more intertwined in their familiar hateful embrace, forgetting us completely. The Nemesi have their sacrifice. The ship is saved.

"Unexpected," says the parrot. "Very unexpected."

I turn to him in fury. "You could have stopped him!" I shout. "You could have saved him!"

The parrot bows his head in mock reverence and gives off a low whistle. "We do what we can."

The things I feel cannot be put into words. Once more my emotions are talking in tongues. But that's all right – because the time of words is over. Now is the time of action. I give voice to my tumultuous fury by pulling the pistol from my belt. It's already loaded. I don't remember loading it, yet I know that it is. I press the pistol to the parrot's breast. I pull the trigger. The shot rings out as loud as a cannon blast, tearing through the parrot's chest. His single seeing eye locks on mine with the shocked gaze of the betrayed, and he offers me his final testimony.

"You've seen the captain before," the parrot says, his voice weaker with each word. *"You've seen him before. He's not … what you think … he is."* The parrot wheezes one final breath and goes limp. The time of words is over for both of us now. I grab the parrot's limp body and hurl it from the crow's nest, watching it arc across the sky like a feathery fireball, until it is taken by the sea.

141 Like He Never Existed

My parents are beside themselves when they hear about Hal. I wish no one had told them. Talking to them about it is just reliving it, and unlike Alexa, I don't have a need to relive nightmares if I can help it.

I sit in the Vista Lounge staring out of the window like Callie used to, not wanting to be on this side of the glass, but not wanting to be on the other side either. I'm numb. I can't think clearly. Part of it is the meds, and part of it isn't.

"It's a terrible thing," my mother says.

"What I want to know is how it could even happen," says my father. They sit on either side of me, trying to comfort me, but I'm already cocooned in invisible bubble wrap. Comfort isn't the issue.

"He took my plastic pencil sharpener," I tell them. "He pried the little blade off the plastic part, and slit his wrists with it."

"I know what happened," my father says, getting up to pace the way I often do. "But it shouldn't have. There are cameras, aren't there? And there are nurses up the wazoo. What the hell were they doing? Twiddling their thumbs?"

The commotion is over now, but the waves haven't settled. It will be a while before the sea is calm.

"You have to know, Caden, that it wasn't your fault," my father says. But somehow the only words that stand out to me are *your* and *fault*. "If he didn't use that sharpener, he would have found something else."

"Yeah, maybe," I say. I know my father speaks logic, but I think the logical part of my brain is still scurrying around belowdecks.

My mom shakes her head sadly, and purses her lips. "When I think of that poor boy…"

So don't I want to say to her, but I stay quiet.

"I understand his mother plans to sue the hospital."

"His mother? She's part of why he did it!" I tell them. "The hospital should be suing *her*!"

My parents, who have no context for that discussion, have no comment.

"Well," says my dad. "One way or another, heads will roll, that's for sure. Someone's got to be held accountable."

Then my mother tries to lighten the conversation with talk of my sister's dance recital, successfully filling the time with non-morbid talk until visiting hour is over.

I wasn't the one who found Hal. Angry Arms of Death did.

I caught a glimpse of the bathroom when they hurried Hal away, though. It looked like someone slaughtered an elephant in there.

And now it's back to business as usual. The staff puts on cheery faces and won't talk about it. Best not to upset the patients. Pretend like it never happened. Like he never existed.

Only Carlyle is human enough to talk about it in group.

"The good news," Carlyle tells us, "is that it happened in a hospital. They rushed him straight to emergency."

"Is Hal dead?" asks Skye.

"He lost a lot of blood," Carlyle tells us. "He's in intensive care."

"Would you even tell us if he died?" I challenge.

Carlyle doesn't answer right away. "It wouldn't be my place," he finally says.

And then Alexa touches her neck and compares and contrasts this to her own suicide attempt, as usual, making it all about her.

142 Are You Now, or Have You Ever Been?

My parents have wondered if I am, or have ever been, suicidal. My doctors wonder. The insurance questionnaires wonder. It's not like I haven't idly thought about it – especially when depression digs in its nasty claws – but have I ever actually crossed the line and been suicidal? I don't think so. Whenever those thoughts spring up, my sister is the fail-safe. Mackenzie would be screwed up for the rest of her life if she had a brother who killed himself. True, my continued existence could make her life miserable, but misery is the lesser of two evils. A brother who *is* a problem is easier to deal with than a brother who *was* a problem.

I still can't figure out if it's bravery or cowardice to take your own life. I can't figure out whether it's being selfish, or selfless. Is it the ultimate act of letting go of oneself, or a cheap act of self-possession? People say a failed attempt is a cry for help. I guess that's true if the person meant it to be unsuccessful. But then, I guess most failed attempts aren't entirely sincere, because, let's face it, if you want to off yourself, there are plenty of ways to make sure it works.

Still, if you've got to bring yourself within inches of your life just to cry for help, something's wrong somewhere. Either you weren't yelling loud enough to begin with, or the people around you are deaf, dumb, and blind. Which makes me think it isn't just a cry for help – it's more a cry to be taken seriously. A cry that says "I'm hurting so badly, the world must, for once, come to a grinding halt for me."

The question is, what do you do next? The world stops, and looks at you lying there with your wounds bandaged, or your stomach pumped, and says, "Okay, you have my attention." Most people don't know what to do with that moment if they get it. Which makes it definitely not worth the cost of getting there. Especially if that failed attempt accidentally succeeds.

Hal's pencil-sharpening happened on Saturday. Dr. Poirot comes to see me first thing Monday morning. He would have come sooner but he was away at a conference taking care of business while Hal was taking care of his own business.

I am alone in my room when Poirot arrives. Hal's bed is stripped, his belongings removed by the pastels. The emptiness on Hal's side of the room is like a living void. During the night I could hear it breathing.

"I'm very sorry about what happened. Very sorry," Poirot says. His bright Hawaiian shirt mocks the somberness of the day. I'm lying flat on my back, and I do my best not to look at him, or acknowledge him in any way.

"I know you developed a friendship with Harold. It must be particularly painful."

I still don't say a word.

"A thing like this … it should never have happened."

In spite of myself, I have to respond to such an accusation. "So you're blaming me?"

"I didn't say that."

"Didn't you just?"

Poirot sighs, pulls up a chair, and sits down. "You'll be getting a new roommate today."

"I don't want one."

"Can't be helped. Bed space here is limited. Another boy is coming in, and it's the only bed available."

I still won't look at him. "It was YOUR job to take care of Hal. To keep him safe from everything – including himself!"

"I know. We failed. I'm sorry." Poirot looks over to the void on the other side of the room. "Had I been here at the time—"

"What? Would you have flown in and stopped him?"

"I would like to think that I might have sensed the level of Harold's despair. But maybe not. Maybe it would have happened anyway."

Now I finally look at Poirot. "Did he die?"

Poirot keeps a practiced poker face. "His wounds are extensive. He's receiving the best possible care."

"Would you tell me if he died?"

"Yes. If I felt you could handle it."

"And if you felt I couldn't handle it?"

Poirot hesitates, and for the life of me, I can't tell whether or not he's covering up a lie. "You'll just have to trust me," he says.

But I don't. And I don't tell him that Hal stopped taking his meds. Hal swore me to secrecy. Whether he's dead or alive, I won't betray that trust. Of course, if I had squealed on him, I know he might have been too medicated to do what he did. I guess that moves the finger of blame even more in my direction. It makes me more determined to push it away.

"You should have saved him," I tell Poirot. "You're right; you failed."

Poirot takes it like a slap, but turns the other cheek. "Busy day, busy day. There are other patients I need to see." He gets up to go. "I promise to check in on you later, all right?"

But I don't answer him and resolve never to speak to him again. From this moment on, Poirot is dead to me.

144 Other Places

"Caden, we've been thinking," says my mom the following day. She glances at my dad to make sure he's on the same page. "With what's happened here, maybe you'd rather be elsewhere."

"I can go home?"

My dad reaches out to grab my upper arm with firm reassurance. "Not yet," he says. "Soon, though. But in the meantime, there are other places."

It takes a moment for me to understand what he's suggesting. "Another hospital?"

"Where this sort of thing doesn't happen," my mom adds.

That makes me cough out a single guffaw. Because "this sort of thing" can happen anywhere. Even if Hal was given his own personal bodyguard, it wouldn't have protected him from himself. I know there are other "facilities" like this one. The other kids tell stories about hospitals they've been in. They all sound worse than this. As much as I hate to admit it, my parents chose this place because it was the best one around. So maybe it is.

"No, I'll stay," I tell them.

"Are you sure, Caden?" My father tries to read me with eyes that make me look away.

"Yeah, I like it here."

That surprises both of them. It surprises me. "You do?"

"Yes," I say. "No," I say. "But yes."

"Well, why don't you think about it?" my mom says, maybe disappointed by my decision – but I don't want to think about it any more than I want to think about Hal. This place is a hell that I'm familiar with. What is it they say? The devil you know is better than the devil you don't.

"No, I'm sure," I tell them.

They accept my decision, but there's a kind of longing in them that remains unsatisfied.

"Well, we just wanted to give you the option," my dad says. They go on to talk about Mackenzie, and how she misses me, and how they might bring her to visit again, but they seem to be getting further away. And suddenly I realize something terrible about my parents. They are not poisoners. They are not the enemy …

but they are helpless.

They want to *do* something – anything – to help me. Anything to change my situation. But they are as powerless as I am. The two of them are in a lifeboat, together, but so alone. Miles from shore, yet miles from me. The boat leaks, and they must bail in tandem to keep themselves afloat. It must be exhausting.

The terrible truth of their helplessness is almost too much to bear. I wish I could take them on board, but even if they could reach us, the captain would never allow it.

Right now it sucks to be me – but until now, it never occurred to me that it also sucks to be them.

I have a new cabinmate who I don't know, and who I don't wish to know. He's just another member of the faceless crew. Now *I'm* the old-timer – the one who knows the ropes – the way the navigator was when I arrived. As much as I don't like being the newbie, I don't like being the salty sea dog either.

The captain comes to visit a few nights after the navigator unraveled into the sea. He sits on the end of my bed and regards me with his seeing eye. I think his weight should buckle the flimsy cot, but it doesn't. It's as if he's weightless. Insubstantial, like a ghost.

"I'll tell you this, boy," the captain says gently, "but I'll deny it in the light of day." He pauses to make sure he has my full attention. "You are the most important crewman on this vessel. You are the soul of our mission, and if you succeed – and I know you will – there will be much glory to be had. I foresee many voyages together, you and I. Until one day you'll find yourself a captain."

I cannot deny that it is an enticing vision the captain has put forth. To have a purpose is very desirable. And as for future voyages, I've grown accustomed to the nature of this ship and these waters. More time before the mast may not be out of the question.

"Only one member of this crew will make the dive," the captain says, "and I've chosen you. You alone will achieve Challenger Deep and discover the riches it holds."

My feelings on this are as deep and dark as the trench itself. "Without a proper vehicle, I'll be crushed by the pressure, sir, and—"

He puts up his hand to silence me. "I know what you believe, but things are different here. You already know that; you've already seen. The dive is dangerous, I won't deny that, but not in the way you think."

Then he clasps me on the shoulder. "Have faith in yourself, Caden, for I have faith in you."

That's not the first time I've heard it. "The parrot had faith in me, too," I tell him.

The mention of the bird makes him bristle. "Do you regret ridding us of that traitor?"

"No…"

"The parrot would have seen you never complete this journey." He stands and begins to pace the small space. "The parrot would have put an end to our adventures forever and ever!" Then he points a crooked finger at me.

"Would you rather be a cripple in his world, or a star in mine?"

Then he storms out, not waiting for an answer – and a moment after he's gone, there's a twinge of memory. *You've seen the captain before,* the parrot had said. For the first time I realize he was right … but that twinge of memory escapes from me, and is sucked into the foul-smelling pitch that holds the ship together.

I can feel the presence of the Abyssal Serpent more and more with each passing day. It trails behind the ship – behind *me*. It matches our pace. It doesn't attack like the crestmares, or the Nemesi. It just stalks. Which is even worse.

"It'll never let you be, boy," the captain tells me as we look aft into our wake. I cannot see the serpent, but I know it's there, swimming just deep enough to hide from my eyes, but not from my soul.

"No doubt the serpent has plans for you," the captain says. "Plans that involve digestive juices – but I think it likes to be hungry. It enjoys the pursuit as much as the devouring. That's its weakness."

When the captain retires for afternoon tea, or whatever a man like him does with his free time, I climb to the crow's nest, to get as far away from the Abyssal Serpent as possible.

I have come to despise the crow's nest almost as much as the captain does. I am never surprised by the odd sights I see up here. Today there are heads rolling about like tumbleweeds with the motion of the sea. One bumps into me as it rolls past. "Sorry," the head says. "Couldn't be helped." I think I recognize the face, but its trajectory takes it underneath a chair, where it gets temporarily stuck, so I can't be sure.

There is a new bartender today. No one sits at the bar, because there is a chill to her demeanor. She gives off waves of unapproachability like a force field. Still I approach, if only out of spite.

"Where's Dolly?" I ask.

The new bartender points to one of the rolling heads. I recognize Dolly immediately. "Hello, Caden," her head says as it tumbles in the aftermath of a sudden swell. "I'd wave if I could."

"It's unfortunate," says the new bartender, "but the unraveling of the navigator made it clear that changes had to be made."

And then another cranial casualty bounces past. One with short red hair. I hurry to catch it. Picking it up, I look into a pair of familiar eyes.

"Carlyle?"

"Sorry to tell you this, Caden, but I won't be leading your group anymore."

I'm speechless. Unable to swallow the news. "But ... but..."

"Don't worry," he says. "There'll be someone new this afternoon."

"We don't want someone new!"

There's no one else in the hall. I stand between him and the exit. I knew people would get smacked down, and maybe fired for what happened to Hal, but why Carlyle?

"You had nothing to do with it!" I tell him. "You weren't even there that day!" The chilly new charge nurse eyes me from the central nurses' station, wondering if my raised voice is a problem.

"They felt my group was ... psychonoxious. At least for Hal."

"Do you believe that?"

"It doesn't matter what I believe. The hospital's gotta spank somebody, and I was an easy target. It's just the way things work."

He looks around a bit nervously, as if getting caught even talking to me would make it worse for him. "Don't worry about me," he says. "It's not like I don't have other things to do. I was volunteering here, remember?" He gets past me and heads for the door.

"But … but … who will mop the feral brains?"

He chuckles. "Plenty of that going on without me," he says. "You take care, Caden." Then he touches his security card to the reader. The inner door opens, admitting him into the little air lock designed to keep patients from escaping. Then, once the inner door closes, the outer door opens to the world beyond, and Carlyle's gone.

I don't know what to do. I don't know who to yell at. The bartender won't have it, and although Angry Arms of Death is around, he and his skulls are just happy that they're not rolling around with Dolly and the rest.

I leave the crow's nest, and burst in on the captain to voice my complaint, telling him that Carlyle's headless body just walked the plank – but the captain is unfazed.

"Swabbies come and go," he says, with a head under each arm. "I'm going below to do some bowling. Care to join me?"

"Well, good morning! I'm Gladys, your new facilitator for morning group."

The room tone is as belligerent as a classroom in an alternative high school. And today there's a substitute teacher.

"The first order of business is getting to know one another."

Gladys doesn't look like a Gladys. Although I really don't know what a Gladys should look like, except for the ones in old black-and-white TV sitcoms. She's in her midthirties, with permed blond hair and a slight deviation in her facial symmetry that's worse when she smiles.

"Why don't we start by giving our names."

"We know our names," someone says.

"Well, I'd like to know them, too."

"You do," says someone else. "I saw you reading our files before you came in."

She gives us a mildly asymmetrical smile. "Yes, but it would be nice to attach names to faces."

"That would probably hurt," I offer. I get a courtesy chuckle from Skye and a couple of others – but a courtesy chuckle isn't enough to keep the snark going. Just to get this over with, I say, "I'm Caden Bosch."

It goes around clockwise from me. To my surprise, nobody gives names like "Dick Hertz," or "Jen Italia." I guess I threw a wet rag on the possibility by giving my actual name.

My new roommate has joined the group, along with a random new girl. A couple of people who I already can't remember were discharged a few days ago. The faces change, but the production remains the same, like a Broadway show.

Very few people share today. I know I don't want to share anything with Gladys. Ever. Then someone subtly begins calling her GLaDOS, which is the name of the evil computer in the classic *Portal* games — and if this session wasn't a travesty before, now it definitely is. A bunch of us take turns making game references that fly under her radar — like the kid who asks if there'll be cake when we're done.

"No," Gladys says, asymmetrically perplexed, "not that I know of."

"So…" says the kid, "you're telling me that *the cake is a lie?*"

Even the kids who have no idea what he's talking about snicker, because it doesn't matter if they don't get it — the only thing that matters is that GLaDOS doesn't get it.

I might feel sorry for her under normal circumstances, but I have no clear idea what normal circumstances are anymore, and anyway, I don't want her to have my sympathy. I know Carlyle's firing wasn't her fault, but she's the piñata in the room, and I don't mind swinging a bat along with all the others.

I lie on my bed and wait for the world to end.

It must end eventually, because I can't imagine it going on like this. This procession of gray days in a mental fog must eventually cease.

I have not heard from Callie. I don't expect any communication from her here; we are not allowed phones or computer access, and I don't expect she'll write a letter. I went so far as to ask my parents to check my emails. I gave them all my passwords because privacy has little meaning anymore. I don't care if they read my spam, which, at this point, is all I'll be getting, in addition to something from Callie. But she hasn't written. Or my parents tell me that she hasn't. Would they tell me if she had? I trust their answer just as much as I trust anyone who tells me that Hal is still alive. If everyone has convinced themselves it's okay to lie to me for my own good, how can I believe anything anyone says?

Are they lying when they tell me I've been here for six weeks? Probably not. It feels more like six months. The fog and the monotony make it next to impossible to measure the passing time. They don't call it monotony, though. They call it routine. The routine is supposed to be comforting. We have a genetic predisposition for same old-same old that dates back to the earliest vertebrates. Safety in sameness.

Except when they choose to create change.

Like sticking me with a new roommate who I refuse to talk

to. Or like firing the one person who made me see the slightest glimmer of hope.

I silently curse everyone for these things, knowing deep down I should be cursing myself, because none of it would have happened if I had broken my promise to Hal, and told on him.

"If you continue making progress," one of the nurses told me earlier today, "I see no reason why you shouldn't be going home in a couple of weeks." Then she added, "But don't quote me on that." Noncommittal is rampant among the committed.

I don't feel the progress the others see. I'm so encapsulated in the moment that I don't remember what I was like when I arrived. And I think if *this* is better than *that*, is this what I can look forward to when I go home? Same old-same old?

A nurse arrives in my room with our evening meds. First she tends to my roommate, and then to me. I look into my happy little paper cup. My current but ever-changing cocktail now provides me three meds in the evening. A green oblong pill, a blue-and-white capsule, and a yellow tablet that dissolves in your mouth like flavorless candy. I take them one at a time with a cup of water she gives me that's slightly larger than the cup the pills are in. Then, knowing the drill, I open my mouth and pull my cheeks apart with my fingers like I'm making a face at her, to show her that the medicine has truly been swallowed.

After she's gone, I go to the bathroom and fish the blue and white capsule from way back in my mouth, which I hid like a squirrel, high in the gum line. She would never have found it without running her fingers through every inch of my mouth. If you've been caught cheeking your meds, they actually do that. But I've been a good boy. Until today.

I know there's nothing I can do about the dissolving tablet, but maybe, with practice, I can squirrel away both the capsule and the green pill. Whatever Hal was feeling when he did what he did, at least he was *feeling*. Right now, even despair would seem like a victory. So I drop the pill into the toilet and pee on it for good measure, then flush, happy to medicate whatever foul creatures live in the sewers.

Then I go back to my bed, lie down, and wait for the world to end.

149 Half-life

I know more about psychoactive medication than is safe for any one human being to know. Kind of like the drug dealer who's done everything, and can speak with authority on the various forms of high.

Most antianxiety meds act quickly, do their business, and then are caught by the liver – the policemen of the body – which flushes them out in less than a day. Ativan can calm you down instantly if injected. In less than an hour if taken orally, but its effects wear off just a few hours later.

On the other hand, Geodon, Risperdal, Seroquel, and all the

other heavyweight antipsychotics have a much longer half-life, evading the liver for quite a while. What's more, the "therapeutic effect," as they call it, builds up over time. You gotta take the stuff for days, even weeks, before those meds start doing what they're paid to do.

Of course most of the side effects of those drugs are immediate, making you feel within an hour that you're something other than human. When you suddenly stop taking them, if you don't have seizures and die, those side effects go away within a day or two. It takes longer for the actual therapeutic effects to vanish, just as it took a longer time for them to begin.

In other words, for a few golden days, you remember what it feels like to be normal, before you plunge headlong into the bottomless pit.

150 Last Man Standing

Morning mist burns away, leaving a myriad of cotton-white clouds from horizon to horizon. They move quickly across the sky, the day strobing between sunlight and shadow. Below that dramatic vista, the sea is as glass – a perfectly reflective surface, mirroring the sky. Clouds above, clouds below. There seems to be no difference between the heavens and the depths.

Not even the relentless momentum of our ship – now carried by a steady wind – can stir these waters. It is as if we are skating upon the sea, rather than sailing through it. I know the Abyssal Serpent follows us somewhere beneath the glassy surface of the water, but like the ship, it travels in complete stealth, leaving no evidence of its passage.

Neither Carlyle's nor anyone else's head rolls about the crow's nest anymore. In fact, the place has entirely lost its magic. There is no bar, no chairs, no inebriated customers lost in neon cocktails. The crow's nest is now on the inside exactly what it appears to be on the outside: a barrel, three feet wide, just large enough for a lookout to stand and scan the horizon.

"Like any other appendage," the captain tells me, "it has atrophied from lack of use."

Without the cocktail to dull me, there's a clarity to my senses as sharp as a butcher's blade. It cleaves through flesh and bone, revealing places within that were never meant to be exposed to the light of day. It purifies me, leaving me scoured both inside and out.

It's just me and the captain now. The rest of the crew is gone. Perhaps they abandoned us during the night. Or perhaps creatures of the deep dragged them overboard. Or perhaps they were pulled down between the copper plates and digested by the living pitch that holds the ship together. I don't miss them. In a way it's as if they were never really there to begin with.

The captain stands behind me at the helm, and pontificates to his congregation of one.

"There is hell in both the day and the night," he says. "I have sat in the burning heat of day under a relentless sun, and under the stone gazes of a disinterested humanity." He

touches the copper railing, running a single finger across it as if checking for dust. "You long for the slightest copper, but resent it when it arrives. Do you follow?"

"I do."

He slaps me hard across the back of my head. "Never follow! Always lead."

I rub my smarting scalp. "How, when there's no one left?"

The captain looks around, seeming to notice for the first time that there is no one else on board. "Point taken. In that case, you should revel that you are the last man standing."

"What are we looking for, sir?" I ask, peering out at the

clouds both above and below the horizon. "How will we know when we arrive?"

"We'll know," is all he says on the matter.

I hold my position at the tiller. With no navigational charts, I turn the wheel on impulse and whim. The captain does not disapprove of any of my choices.

Then something up ahead comes into view. It's just a speck at first, but as we draw closer, it resolves into a post protruding from the water. I steer us toward it, and as we come closer still, I can see that it is more than a post. There is a crossbar, and a figure limply attached to it.

A scarecrow.

Its arms are stretched wide, its eyes are tilted toward the cloud-spotted sky in eternal supplication – and it occurs to me that all scarecrows look as if they've been crucified. Perhaps that's what frightens the crows away.

There are no crows to scare this far out to sea, however. No gulls or grackles, no birds at all, not even a parrot. Like so much else in the captain's world, the scarecrow is dedicated to a point-less task.

"The scarecrow is the final sign," the captain tells me with a solemnity to his voice. A hint of fear in a man who shows no fear. "Directly beneath him is the deepest place in the world."

As we near the scarecrow, the wind, which has been so steady that I had tuned it out, suddenly diminishes and disappears, leaving a silence so complete, I can hear my heart beating in the blood vessels of my ears. Above us, the sails lose their stiff convex tone, and sag limp and lifeless. We coast a bit more until the captain drops anchor, the chain rattling out until it pulls taut. The anchor's depth is nothing compared to the depth of the trench beneath us, but the mystery of an anchor is that it never needs to touch bottom, or even come close, to keep the largest of ships in place.

The scarecrow is still a hundred yards ahead, at about eleven o'clock to port. "This is as close as I dare get, boy," the captain tells me. "The rest of this journey is yours and yours alone."

Yet there is still not a bathyscaphe or diving bell. Nothing to get me to the bottom.

"But how…"

The captain puts up his hand, knowing what I'm about to say. "You would not have made it this far, were you not meant for this," he tells me. "A method will present itself."

I offer him a sly grin. "A method in the madness?"

He does not smile back. Instead he chastises me. "The parrot spoke of madness, but for men like you and me, it is as science."

"Science, sir?"

He nods. "Aye; the singular alchemy of transmuting that which mightn't be, into that which is. 'Madness,' the parrot called it, but to me, anything less is mediocrity." Then he looks to me with a hint of desperation that he tries to hide. "I envy you," the captain says. "All my life I've dreamed of the reward that lies in wait down there, out of my grasp until today. But you will call that treasure forth. You will fill our hold to the brim with booty beyond the imagining of the human soul."

I wonder how I could manage to bring such treasure up from the deep, but I know the answer will be the same as the nature of my descent. The method in the madness will make itself clear.

And then the captain asks, "Do you believe me, Caden?"

I can tell he's not asking this idly, or even asking for my good. He *needs* me to believe it, as if his own life depends upon it. It is in this moment that I realize that everything has shifted. He is no longer leading me – I am leading him. Not just him, but everything else in this world of his. I can even feel the Abyssal Serpent anxiously awaiting my next move. It is a heady and frightening prospect to be the king of all destinies.

"Do you believe me, Caden?" the captain asks again.

"Yes, I believe."

"Do you forsake the parrot and all his lies?"

"I do."

Finally he smiles. "Then it is time for you to be baptized by the deep."

I climb into the dinghy, a copper rowboat so small, it doesn't seem to be able to hold its own weight above the waterline, much less mine. The captain lowers it, and as it touches the sea, it makes not so much as a ripple. I peer over the side to find nothing but my own reflection in the mirrored surface of the sea. I know that face is mine, and yet I don't recognize myself.

Each time I peer overboard, I half expect the Abyssal Serpent to launch itself out of the water, clamp onto my head, and take me down. What does the serpent wait for? I wonder.

"Godspeed to your reward," the captain says. I free the dinghy from the pulleys, and take to the sea alone.

I row a steady pace toward the scarecrow, listening to the rhythmic squeak of the oar sockets that complain with each stroke. I face the ship as I row, for one must always row with one's back to one's destination. The ship seems to shrink quickly as I leave it. The green metallic vessel that felt so massive when I was on it appears little more than a toy boat now. I cannot see the captain.

At last I come up alongside the scarecrow. I expected it to be on a floating buoy, but the pole is actually a wooden post that drops into the depths, presumably all the way to the bottom almost seven miles below. No tree has ever grown long enough to birth such a pole. It is encrusted with mussels and barnacles growing a foot above the waterline, coming almost close enough to touch the scarecrow's work boots. His jeans and his plaid flannel shirt seem out of place in such a tropical environment, but what am I thinking? Everything about him is out of place here.

He wears my father's white straw fedora. His nose is the broken red heel of my mother's shoe. His eyes are the large blue buttons on Mackenzie's yellow fleece coat. If he were set free from his pole, I wonder, would he walk on water like Calliope did? Is there anything to his limbs besides fabric and stuffing? There is only one way to find out.

"Can you speak," I ask, "or are you just a scarecrow after all?" I wait, and when he doesn't respond I begin to feel that maybe I'm on a fool's errand. Perhaps I'm doomed to sit in this boat in the shadow of this splayed figure until nightfall and beyond. Then with a slight rasp of his canvas skin, he turns his head to me, and his blue button eyes rotate slightly, like binoculars seeking focus.

"So you're here," the scarecrow says, as if he knows me and has been waiting for me to arrive. His voice is subdued, yet loud, made of many tones, like the voice of a whispering chorus.

I tell my heart to cease its sudden pounding. "I'm here. Now what?"

"You quest to achieve the bottom," he says. "There are many ways to accomplish this. You could tie the ship's anchor to your leg and let it take you down, perhaps."

"That would kill me," I point out.

The scarecrow shrugs as well as a scarecrow can. "Yes, but you *would* reach the bottom."

"I'd like to get there alive."

"Ah," says the scarecrow. "That's a different story."

And then he's silent, looking out toward nowhere, as I had found him. The silence becomes uncomfortable. I wonder if he's already lost interest and has dispensed with me – but then I realize he's waiting for me to make a move, although I don't know what move I should make. Since I know I must do something, I maneuver the dinghy as close to him as I'm able, and I tie its leading rope around the pole, mooring it there, making it clear that I'm not leaving. I can wait as long as he can. I observe a small crab rising out of his shirt pocket. It looks at me, then it crawls back in.

The scarecrow turns his head slightly. The look on his canvas face is pensive. "Twister's a comin'," he says.

I look to the sky. The puffy clouds still move at a steady pace, but there's nothing to suggest a storm of any kind. "You sure about that?"

"Very," he says.

And that's when the sea that has been as still as glass begins to move.

I spot a slight rippling to my right and I follow its path. Something has come to the surface. I see only glimpses of it. Sharp metallic scales. An undulating, vermiform body. I know this beast intimately. The Abyssal Serpent circles us, and I am terrified. As it increases its pace, the sea itself seems to resonate with its movement, beginning to revolve in a slow eddy, but quickly picking up speed. The waters begin to spin around the scarecrow's pole, and the rope that holds the dinghy in place goes taut. Beneath the spinning waters I see the single glowing red eye of the dread serpent. It is as domineering as the eye of the captain. As invasive as the eye of the parrot. It is the culmination of every eye that has witnessed my life and passed judgment.

"Twister's a comin'," the scarecrow says again. "Better take cover."

But there is no place to take cover and he knows it. The serpent circles faster. The spinning water dips in the center, revealing more layers of sea life clinging to the scarecrow's pole, which has become its own vertical reef. And as the dinghy rocks in the growing current, I see the rope holding it to the pole begin to fray against a cluster of sharp mussel shells.

I leap from the dinghy as it is torn away from the pole, and I cling to the scarecrow's legs. The hapless rowboat circles the pole in the growing whirlpool and the pitch holding together its copper planks abandons it, spilling into the water like an oil slick. The dinghy falls to pieces. There are other things I see spinning in that water, too. I see bits of waterlogged parchment and bright feathers swirling with the malevolent black pitch. They stir round and round like the ingredients of a new cocktail.

As I cling tightly to the scarecrow's legs, I look down, and I am dizzied by vertigo. The whirlpool deepens at alarming speed, and the spiraling water pulls away from us, until I am looking down a funnel that has no visible bottom. The whirlpool roars in my ears like a freight train. The taste of salt spray nearly gags me.

And the scarecrow says, "If you're going, now's the time."

Until that moment, all I could think about was holding on. "Wait, you mean—"

"Unless you feel the anchor was a better idea after all."

The thought of dropping into the center of a whirlpool only makes me cling tighter and climb higher until I'm at his shoulders.

If I commit to this dive, there's no undoing it. There is no safety cable to slow my descent, no camera to document my fall. No one to catch me at the bottom and send me on my merry way. Yet I know I must do this. I must abandon myself to gravity. That's why I'm here. So I fill my head with all the thoughts that have propelled me to this moment. I think of my parents and the horror of their helplessness. I think of the navigator, and his choice to be the sacrifice. I think of my sister, who understands that cardboard forts can become all too real, and I think of the captain, who has tormented me yet has trained me for this moment. I *will* be baptized by the deep. The parrot would call this the grandest of failures, I'm sure. Well, if this is the culmination of all failure, then I shall make a glorious success of it.

"Mind the pole on the way down," says the scarecrow. "Bye now."

I let go, and plunge into the funnel, finally ready to know the unknowable depths of Challenger Deep.

There are books I will never finish reading, games I will never finish playing, movies that I've started and will never see the end of. Ever.

Sometimes there are moments when we objectively face the never, and it overwhelms us.

I tried to defy the overwhelming never once, when I realized there are songs in my own music library that I will probably never hear again. I went to my computer and created a playlist with every single song. There were 3,628 songs that would take 223.6 hours to play. I kept at it for a few days before my interest waned.

And so now I mourn. I mourn for the songs that will never reach my ears again. For the words and stories that lie on eternally unopened pages. And I mourn my fifteenth year. And how I will never, from now until the end of time, be able to complete it the way it should have been. Rewinding, and living it again, this time without the captain and the parrot and the pills and the shoelace-free bowels of the White Plastic Kitchen. The stars will go dark and the universe will end before I get this year back.

That is the weight chained to my ankle, and it is far heavier than any anchor. That is the overwhelming never that I must face. And I still don't know if I'll disappear into it, or find a way to push beyond.

I am falling into the eye of a whirlpool almost seven miles deep. I spread my arms like a skydiver, giving myself over to it. The ocean swirls around me, the spiraling force of the water keeping a vertical tunnel of air open like a wormhole.

Through the raging walls of the whirlpool, I can see the Abyssal Serpent spiraling down with me, matching the pace of my descent, the same way it matched the pace of the ship. I wait for it to leap through the water to devour me, but still it does not. With the sun and sky just a pinprick far above, the light around takes on a dimming azure shade. Will the blue fade to black, leaving me in total darkness?

It should take three and a half minutes to fall to the bottom of the trench, but I fall much longer than that. The minutes stretch until they feel like hours. There's no way to measure how long I fall, but for the popping of my ears as the air pressure increases. The weight of how many atmospheres is above me now? No barometer in the world could measure it.

"Those who speak of having seen the bottom lie," the captain had said. Now I know he spoke the truth.

Then below me I see a precarious sight, and I know I must be nearing the bottom. The jagged remains of shipwrecks poke through the walls of the whirlpool. I hit the tip of a mast and it breaks. I tumble through the tattered remains of an ancient sail, and then another and another, each one straining to catch me but failing, until at last I plunge into the silty gray ooze that lines the bottom of the world. Gray, not black. This is where the black pitch goes to die.

I ache, but I am not broken. The sails couldn't catch me but they did slow me down. I stand up, forcing my wobbly knees to hold my weight.

I have done it! I am here!

The whirlpool still rages, but here within its eye is a wet moonscape fifty yards across. And to my astonishment I see that this moonscape is punctuated by pile after pile of gold and jewels. All treasure seeks the world's lowest point. Here lie the riches of Challenger Deep!

Breathless and stunned, I wander the trove, struggling to walk within the muck that fills the space between treasure piles.

At a jangle of coins, I turn to see another creature with me. A small one. It clumsily tries to make its way over a pile. It's about the size of a small dog, but walks on two legs. Its flesh is a sickly shade of pink. It has awkward arms but no hands. I do not recognize it until I hear it say, "Just rewards, just rewards. Nothing just about them."

It's the parrot, or at least his ghost, or maybe his undead remains; I can't be sure. Without feathers, he looks malnourished and slight, like those little meatless game hens you get at the supermarket. His bullet wound oozes, but not with blood. It takes me a moment to recognize it as orange Jell-O. The kind with the little pineapple chunks in it.

I make my way over to him, ready to gloat. The captain was right; he was wrong. I chose wisely. Now I get to rub it in. Yet he looks at me mournfully with his unpatched eye as if I'm the one to pity.

"Saw this coming," he says. "We can lead a horse to water — we can even make him drink. But to keep drinking, well, that's up to the horse, the horse, of course, of course."

He pecks for a moment at the scarecrow's pole that rises in the center of the whirlpool eye, dislodging a tiny phosphorescent sea slug and devouring it. The tiny slugs I now see are everywhere, giving everything an eerie glow. Their light dances on the jewels and piles of gold, making the treasure that much more enticing.

"I took on the trench and conquered Challenger Deep," I tell him. "So you can go back to bird hell, or wherever it is you came from."

"Yes, you have achieved the bottom," he says. "But the bottom gets deeper with each trip; you know that, don't you?"

I feel queasy inside. A concussion from the fall, perhaps?

"Take your treasure, then," he says. "Take it, take it. I'm sure it will follow you wherever you want to go."

I reach out to the pile in front of me and pull out a single doubloon. It feels lighter than I expected. Far too insubstantial for a piece of gold. That queasy feeling begins to stray from my gut. Now I feel it stretching out to my fingertips that hold the coin. Something is about to dawn on me. I don't want it to. I want to remain blissfully ignorant, but I can't. I turn the doubloon over in my fingers. Then I reach for its edge with my other hand, grab it with my thumbnail, and peel back a gold foil cover, to reveal a dark-brown interior.

"It's chocolate…"

The parrot gives me his perpetual grin. "A lifetime supply."

And when I look around me – really look around me, I can see that the jewels are all attached to little plastic settings. They're not jewels at all. They're Ring Pops. I can see them already beginning to dissolve in the muck.

"April fool," says the parrot. "And May, and June, and July."

The sick feeling has taken hold of my spine now. It rises vertebra by vertebra up my neck. I feel my cheeks and ears flush with it. I try to forge a mental wall to keep it from entering my brain, but I know the wall will not hold.

"Take a closer look at that doubloon," the parrot says. "Dare you, dare you!"

I look at the foil of the chocolate coin again, and then I see it. The face on the coin is the captain's but not the way I know it. This face is far more horrible. Far more real. I hear the parrot squawking, but he's getting farther and farther away. I'm falling again. Even though I'm already at the bottom of the world, I'm falling.

Doubloon to festoon. Festoon to festival. Festival to vegetable. And vegetable to—

The vestibule of a crumbling building.

We're on vacation in New York. I am ten. There was a street festival snarling traffic, so we took the subway again. My parents and my sister and I have, once more, come up from under the city in the wrong place. A bad place. A place I know we probably should not be.

Our hotel is in Queens. This is not Queens. It may be the Bronx. That's what Mom thinks. I don't say so, but I secretly think that maybe we're in a borough that doesn't exist on any map. I am jittery, and a little sick to my stomach. We were just in Times Square, and visited the massive Hershey's store there, where we got far too many edible souvenirs. Both Mackenzie and I have been gorging ourselves during our subterranean journey of mystery.

Mom and Dad argue. Dad insists the subway is still the best way to get us where we need to go. Mom insists we hail a taxi.

I look around. We are on a corner near a grocery, but its doors and windows are shuttered with graffiti-covered steel. At the curb are overstuffed cardboard vegetable crates waiting for a trash pickup that may be days away. Cabbage and potatoes and carrots and broccoli. The stench of rotten produce is so strong it doesn't help my Hershified stomach.

That's when I turn and see a man sitting in the arched entrance to the old building next door. The vestibule. It's a word Dad taught me when we passed through Grand Central

Station. "When a building is so grand," Dad had told me, "its entry needs its own special name." I said the word over and over because I liked the way it felt on my tongue.

This vestibule is an archway that leads into a dark building that has every indication of being abandoned. The man's clothes are tattered and so dirty there's no telling what color they were originally. His heavy beard is tangled. The man sits where the full sunlight hits him harshly. A foot more and he could be away from it, in the shade, but he seems to avoid the shade like it's toxic. But he does have something to shield him from the sun.

He has a Cap'n Crunch box on his head.

Mackenzie laughs when she sees him. "Do you think it's full, or did he eat it all before he put it on?"

But I don't find it funny. I'm not sure what I find it, but I *don't* find it funny.

I look to see that Dad has caved, and is by the curb trying to hail a taxi, while Mom instructs him that he needs to be more aggressive about it.

I am terrified of the man in the doorway with the cereal box on his head, yet there is something so compelling about him that I feel I must have a closer look.

I'm a few feet away from him when he sees me. He squints one eye in the sun, then I realize he's not squinting. One of his eyes is bruised and swollen shut. I wonder how it happened. I wonder if maybe somebody who didn't like him camping in the vestibule beat him up. He looks at me with his one seeing eye, as wary of me as I am of him. His eye is bright and alert. More than alert, it seems to peer deeper than eyes usually do. I know that means he's "off." Maybe worse than "off." But I can't help but also notice that the color of his eye isn't all that different from my own.

"Is it true, then?" he asks.

"Is what true?" My voice is shaky and weak.

"The birds," he says. "They don't have heartbeats. The rats neither. You know that, doncha?"

And when I don't answer he holds up his hand.

"Spare something?"

I reach into my pocket to pull something out. All I have are chocolate coins from the Hershey's store, a little soft from being in my pocket. I put the whole handful into his palm.

He looks at them and begins laughing.

Just then my arm is almost wrenched out of its socket by my mother.

"Caden! What are you doing?"

I stammer for a moment, for I have no real explanation.

"Leave the boy alone!" the Cap'n says. "He's a good boy, ain'cha, son?"

Mom pulls me behind her, then regards the man festooned in the cereal box uneasily. And then my mom – who insists bums on the street just use money to get drunk, who believes giving handouts to beggars allows them to stay beggars, who will only donate to charity by credit card – pulls out her purse, and hands him a dollar. Clearly something about this particular man has motivated her to open her purse, just as it had motivated me.

Dad, who has finally snagged a taxi, calls from the curb, a bit mystified by his family's sudden attention to a homeless man.

"Good yer takin' a taxi, 'stead a' the subway," the Cap'n says to us, but it's me he's looking at with his one good eye. "Subway's bad this time a day," he says. "It's forever down there."

156 No Miracles Here

Vestibule, vegetable, festival, festoon, doubloon.

I'm holding the doubloon so tightly it begins to melt in my fingers.

"The answer was right there in your pocket," the parrot says. "Funny how that works."

Then he looks past me, and I follow his gaze. The space around us is rapidly shrinking. Piles of false riches are swept up in the raging waters. The whirlpool is collapsing.

The parrot whistles. "Such a thing, such a thing. Epiphanies are never convenient, and often arrive too late." He doesn't seem so much pleased with himself as simply resigned.

"Wait! You've got to help me!"

He shrugs. "I have. I am. I will. But there are no miracles here. Just momentum. We can only hope it's upward."

He turns and hops from one pile of false gold to another, then right into the swirling wall of water and disappears, leaving me alone at the bottom of the world.

As the space around me diminishes, the piles of "treasure" are ripped away, becoming debris spinning in the contracting circle of water. There's no one to call out to, no one to help me. The only presence I can feel beyond my own is that of the serpent, its anticipation building to a fever pitch. The waters will close in around me, it will finally have me, and no one, not even the damnable captain, will ever find me again.

I cling on to the scarecrow's pole in the center of the tightening circle. I try to climb it, but it's covered in slippery algae. I can't even get a grip on it.

If I brought myself to this place, then there must be a way to bring myself out, but how? What am I missing?

The only answer I get comes from the serpent. It speaks to me. Not in words, for it knows no language. It speaks to me in feelings, and it projects into me hopelessness of such immense weight, it could crush the very spirit of God.

Your fate is inescapable, that feeling says. *You were doomed from the moment you chose to make this dive. I will open my jaws and take you — but I will not consume you. No, that would be too easy. I will chew you like a piece of gum, until anything resembling Caden Bosch is gone, and you are nothing but black pitch between my teeth. And there you will remain, trapped in the maw of madness for all eternity.*

It would be so easy to give in. Seven miles of ocean about to come down on my head and a doomsday demon just a few feet away: Why not just leap into its mouth right now? At least David had a slingshot to battle Goliath. What have I got?

What *have* I got?

In those final moments, as the eye of the vortex contracts toward me on all sides, the parrot's words come back to me. *"The answer was right there in your pocket."*

I look at the doubloon still gripped in my right hand. I had thought he meant the chocolate coins in my memory – but the parrot wasn't in that memory. He knows many things, but that's something he couldn't know!

I shove my other hand into my pocket. At first I think there's nothing there – but then I do find something. It's oddly shaped, and I can't quite figure out what it is until I pull it out.

It's a blue puzzle piece.

A piece the exact shade of blue as the tiny spot of sky miles and miles above my head.

And suddenly I can feel the serpent cringe.

Because all that remains to complete the sky is this one single piece …

… and the sky wants its completion even more than the serpent wants me.

I look to my right hand that holds the coin, and my left hand that holds the promise of sky. I know I have been a victim of many things beyond my control – but in this moment, in this place, here is something I have the power to choose. *There are no miracles here*, the parrot had said – but neither is there hopelessness, no matter what the serpent wants me to believe. Nothing is inevitable.

With the whirlpool barely a yard wide and closing, I drop the doubloon, close my fingers around the puzzle piece, and thrust my fist upward, offering completion to the distant sky.

And suddenly I'm rising.

As if a hand has grabbed my wrist, I am slingshotting upward as the whirlpool collapses around me.

Churning white water surges at my feet. I feel the furious wail of the serpent. I sense the burning of its fiery eye. It snaps at my heels but is always an inch away.

I feel like my arm will be torn loose. I can feel the acceleration in every joint of my body, so much faster than when I had fallen. Faster than the paltry pull of gravity. Faster than the serpent, still trying to flood my mind with its requiem of hopelessness.

The blue circle of sky above me grows and grows until I shoot past the scarecrow and away from the deep.

I see nothing but blue as I soar upward into the embrace of sky.

157 Kind of Like Religion

There are many things I don't understand, but here's one thing that I know: There is no such thing as a "correct" diagnosis. There are only symptoms and catchphrases for various collections of symptoms.

Schizophrenia, schizoaffective, bipolar I, bipolar II, major depression, psychotic depression, obsessive/compulsive, and on and on. The labels mean nothing, because no two cases are ever exactly alike. Everyone presents differently, and responds to meds differently, and no prognosis can truly be predicted.

We are, however, creatures of containment. We want all things in life packed into boxes that we can label. But just because we have the ability to label it, doesn't mean we really know what's in the box.

It's kind of like religion. It gives us comfort to believe we have defined something that is, by its very nature, indefinable. As to whether or not we've gotten it right, well, it's all a matter of faith.

158 Morons in High Places

My trip to the sky takes me many places I can't remember, across many days that I can't count, before I arrive back where I started. A fluorescently lit white room, encased in invisible Jell-O. I can feel my body trembling, but I'm not cold. I know it's the meds – whatever I'm on, or whatever I'm coming off of.

A pastel persona peers down at me. She asks me a question in Cirque-ish, and I respond in Klingon. I close my eyes for a moment, night turns to day, and suddenly it's Dr. Poirot in front of me instead of the pastel. I'm not shaking anymore, and he's actually speaking English, although his voice isn't quite synced to his lips.

"Do you know where you are?" he asks.

Yes, I want to say, *the White Plastic Kitchen* – but I know that's not the answer he wants to hear. More importantly, it's not the answer I want to believe.

"Seaview Memorial Hospital," I tell him. "Juvenile Psychiatric Unit." Hearing the words come out of my mouth brings me one step closer to trusting that they're true.

"You've had a bit of a setback," Poirot says.

"No duh."

"Yes, but you're on the other side of it now. I'm pleased to say that for the past few days I've seen nothing but upward momentum. Your awareness of your surroundings is a good sign, a very good sign."

He shines a penlight in each of my eyes and checks my chart. I expect him to leave, or perhaps transform into one of the nurses again, but instead he pulls up a chair and sits down.

"Your blood work showed a sudden drop in your medication levels about a week ago. Any idea why that might be?"

I consider serving him up a nice big platter of dumb, but what's the use? "Yeah," I tell him, without mincing words, "I was cheeking my meds."

And then he gets a little smug, and says something I'm not expecting at all.

"Good."

I look at him for a moment, trying to determine whether he actually said that, or if I just heard it in my head.

"How is that good?" I ask.

"Well, it wasn't good at the time – not at all – but it's good now. Because now you can see the result. Cause and effect, cause and effect. Now you know."

I want to be annoyed at him, or at least mildly irritated, but

I can't. Maybe because for once I don't mind that he might be right. Or maybe it's the meds.

There's something odd about Poirot. It was on the edge of my perception, but now he moves close enough for me to realize what it is. His colorful wardrobe is gone. Instead he wears a beige button-down shirt, with an equally uninteresting tie.

"No Hawaiian shirt?" I ask.

He sighs. "Yes, well, hospital management felt it didn't project sufficient professionalism."

"They're morons," I tell him.

That actually makes him squawk out a guffaw. "You'll find in life, Caden, that many decisions are made by morons in high places."

"I've been a moron in a high place," I say. "I think I do better on the ground."

He smiles at me. It's a little different from his therapeutically fixed grin. It's warmer. "Your parents are in the waiting area. It's not visiting hours, but I gave them special permission to be here. That is, if you want to see them."

I consider the prospect. "Well ... is my father wearing a straw fedora, and is my mother walking with a broken heel?"

Poirot turns his head slightly to better regard me with his working eye. "I don't believe so, no."

"Okay, that means they're real, so yes, I want to see them."

Anyone else might look at me strangely for saying that, but not Poirot. The fact that I'm developing "reality criteria" is a good thing as far as he's concerned. He stands up. "I'll send them in." Then he hesitates, regards me for a moment more, and says, "Welcome back, Caden."

As he leaves, I resolve that, if and when I get out of here, I'm going to buy him an expensive silk tie covered with brightly colored birds.

159 10:03.

I want to give Skye back her puzzle piece, but I can't find it. The puzzle remains finished except for that one piece. No one is allowed to touch it, lest they face Skye's significant wrath. Then one day she's discharged, and the pastels take it apart, and put it back in the box for other patients. I think it's outrageously cruel to keep a puzzle that they know is missing a single piece.

Hal never comes back, and no one ever tells me convincingly whether he lived or died. I do receive a letter, though, that is covered with lines and scribbles and symbols that I can't read. It could have come from him, or it could be a practical joke from one of the more unpleasant patients who has since gone home, or it could be from someone who cares about me and is trying to placate me – kind of the way my parents used to write responses to the letters I sent to Santa when I was little. On this matter, I weigh all theories equally.

I never hear from Callie. It's okay. I never expected to. I hope her life takes her far away from anything that reminds her of this place, and if that means taking her far away from me, I can accept that. She walked on water, rather than drowned. That's enough for me.

Then one day it is finally determined that I have become one with the real world once more – or at least am within striking distance – and I'm released into the loving arms of my family.

On that final day of my "mental cast," I wait in my room with all my things packed in sturdy yellow plastic bags provided by the hospital. There's nothing in there but clothes. I decided to leave my art supplies for other patients. The colored pencils were taken away by the staff when I wasn't looking one day, leaving just plastic markers and soft pastels – things that don't need to be sharpened.

My parents arrive at 10:03 in the morning, and even bring Mackenzie. My mom and dad sign about as much paperwork as they had to sign when I was admitted, and just like that the deed is done.

I ask for a few minutes to say good-bye, but it doesn't take as long as I thought. The nurses and various pastels wish me well. Angry Arms of Death gives me a knuckle-tap and says "stay real," which is ironic in ways that neither him nor his skulls can grasp. GLaDOS is having her group, and although I poke my head in to say good-bye, it's awkward for everyone. Now I know how Callie felt the day that she left. You're on the other side of the glass even before you step outside.

My dad gently puts his hand on my shoulder and checks in with me before we move toward the canal-lock exit doors. "You okay, Caden?" Now he reads me in ways he never did before. Like Sherlock Holmes with a magnifying glass.

"Yeah, fine," I tell him.

He smiles. "Then let's get the hell out of here."

Mom tells me we're going to Cold Stone on the way home, which she knows is my favorite. It will be good to have ice cream that you don't eat with a wooden spoon.

"I hope you haven't made a big deal about this at home," I tell them, "like balloons and 'welcome home' banners and stuff."

The uncomfortable silence tells me that there is, indeed, a big deal awaiting me.

"It's just one balloon," Mom says.

Mackenzie looks down. "I got you a balloon. So?"

Now I feel bad. "Well ... is it big, like a refugee from the Thanksgiving Day Parade?" I ask.

"No, not really," she says.

"Then I'm sure it's fine."

We stand before the exit. The inner door opens, and we step into the little security air lock. My mom puts her arm around me, and I realize she's doing it as much for herself as for me. She needs the comfort of finally being able to comfort me; something she hasn't been able to do for a long time.

My illness has dragged us all through the trenches, and although my trench was, well, the Marianas, I won't discount what my family has been through. I will never forget that my parents came to the hospital every single day, even when I was clearly in other places. I will never forget that my little sister held my hand, and tried to understand what it's like to be in those other places.

Behind us, the inner doors swing closed. I hold my breath. Then the outer doors open, and once more I am a proud member of the rational world.

An hour later, after an insanely decadent ice-cream fest, we arrive home and I see Mackenzie's balloon right away as we pull onto the street. It's attached to our mailbox in the front yard, bobbing lazily with the breeze. I laugh out loud when I see what it is.

"Where on earth did you find a Mylar brain?" I ask Mackenzie.

"Online," she says with a shrug. "They've got livers and kidneys, too."

I give her a hug. "Best balloon ever."

We get out of the car, and, with Mackenzie's permission, I untie the helium-filled brain, and release it, watching it rise up and up until it disappears.

160 The Way It Works

Nine weeks. That's how long I was hospitalized. I check the calendar hanging in the kitchen to confirm it, because it felt like so much longer.

School is already out for the summer, but even if it wasn't, I'm not in any condition to sit in a classroom and focus. My attention span and my motivation rank up there with that of a sea cucumber. Part of it's the illness, part of it's the medication. I am told it will slowly get better. I reluctantly believe it. This, too, shall pass.

It's up in the air what will happen when school starts again. I may not go back until January, and then repeat the second half of sophomore year. Or I may go to a new school for a fresh start. I may be homeschooled until I catch up. I may just go in as a junior in September, business as usual, and eventually make up what I missed in summer school next year. Advanced calculus has fewer variables than my education.

My doctor says not to worry about it. My *new* doctor – not Poirot. Once you leave the hospital, you gotta get a new doctor. That's the way it works. The new guy's okay. He takes more time with me than I thought he would. He prescribes my meds. I take them. I hate them, but I take them. I'm numb, but not as numb as I was. The Jell-O seems to be of the whipped variety now.

My new doctor's name is Dr. Fischel, which is appropriate, because he kind of does have a face like a trout. We'll see where that goes.

161 Points Exotic

I have this dream. I'm walking on a boardwalk somewhere with my family. Maybe Atlantic City, or Santa Monica. Mackenzie drags my parents onto an entertainment pier – roller coasters, bumper cars – and although I try to go with them, I lag behind and can't catch up. Pretty soon I've lost them in the crowd. And then I hear this voice.

"You, there! Been waitin' for you!"

I turn to see a yacht. Not just your run-of-the-mill yacht but one of Bond-villain proportions. Gleaming gold, with pitch-black windows. There's a Jacuzzi, and lounge chairs, and a crew that seems to be made exclusively of beautiful girls in string bikinis. And standing at the gangway is a familiar figure. His beard is trimmed to a goatee, and his uniform is a white double-breasted suit with gold trim. Even so, I know who he is.

"We can't sail without a first mate. And that would be you."

I find myself halfway down the gangway, just a few feet from the yacht. I don't remember moving there.

"It will be my pleasure to have you aboard," the captain says.

"What's the mission?" I ask, much more curious than I want to be.

"Caribbean reef," he tells me. "One that no human has yet laid eyes on. You're certified in scuba, aren't you?"

"No," I tell him.

"Well, then, it's up to me to certify you, isn't it?"

He smiles at me. His good eye stares at me with familiar intensity that almost feels comfortable. Almost feels like home. His other eye has no eye patch, and the peach pit has been replaced by a diamond that glitters in the midday sun.

"All aboard!" he says.

I linger on the gangway.

I linger.

I linger some more.

And then I tell him, "I don't think so."

He doesn't try to convince me. He just smiles and nods.

Then he says in a low voice that is somehow louder than the crowd on the pier behind me, "You'll be going back down there eventually. You know that, don't you? The serpent and I won't have it any other way."

I think about that, and although the thought chills me, I can't deny the very real nature of that possibility.

"Maybe," I tell the captain. "Probably," I admit. "But not today."

I turn and walk back up the gangway to the pier. It's narrow and precarious, but I've done precarious before, so it's nothing new. When I'm safe on the pier once more, I glance back, thinking that maybe the yacht might have vanished, as such apparitions do – but no, it's still there, and the captain is still waiting, his eye fixed on me.

He will always be waiting, I realize. He will never go away. And in time, I may find myself his first mate whether I want to or not, journeying to points exotic so that I might make another dive, and another, and another. And maybe one day I'll dive so deep that the Abyssal Serpent will catch me, and I'll never find my way back. No sense in denying that such things happen.

But it's not going to happen today – and there is a deep, abiding comfort in that. Deep enough to carry me through till tomorrow.

Challenger Deep is by no means a work of fiction. The places that Caden goes are all too real. One in three U.S. families is affected by the specter of mental illness. I know, because our family is one of them. We faced many of the same things Caden and his family did. I watched as someone I loved journeyed to the deep, and I felt powerless to stop the descent.

With the help of my son, I've tried to capture what that descent was like. The impressions of the hospital, and the sense of fear, paranoia, mania, and depression are real, as well as the "Jell-O" feeling and numbness the meds can give you (something I experienced firsthand when I accidentally took two Seroquel, confusing them with Excedrin). But the healing is also real. Mental illness doesn't go away entirely, but it can, in a sense, be sent into remission. As Dr. Poirot says, it's not an exact science, but it's all we have – and it gets better every day as we learn more about the brain, and the mind, and as we develop better, more targeted medication.

Twenty years ago, my closest friend, who suffered from schizophrenia, took his own life. But my son, on the other hand, found his piece of sky, and escaped gloriously from the deep, in time becoming more like Carlyle than Caden. The sketches and drawings in this book are his, all drawn in the depths. To me, there is no greater artwork in the world. In addition, some of Hal's observations on life are derived from his poetry.

Our hope is that *Challenger Deep* will comfort those who have been there, letting them know that they are not alone. We also hope that it will help others to empathize, and to understand what it's like to sail the dark, unpredictable waters of mental illness.

And when the abyss looks into you – and it will – may you look back unflinching.

Neal Shusterman

If you need help dealing with mental illness, or you know someone who needs help, here are some resources for you:

UK

Young Minds (www.youngminds.org.uk)

Talklife (www.talklife.co)

Mind (www.mind.org.uk)

Time to Change (www.time-to change.org.uk/gct-involved/
get-involved-schools/school-resources)

CALM (https://www.thecalmzone.net)

US

National Alliance on Mental Illness (www.nami.org) features the
latest information on mental health illnesses, medication,
and treatment and resources for support and advocacy.
The NAMI helpline is (800) 950-NAMI (6264).

Strength of Us (http://strengthofus.org) is an online community
for teens and young adults living with mental illness.

American Psychiatric Association (www.psychiatry.org/ mental-health/people/teens)

Ok2Talk (ok2talk.org) is Tumblr posts by real teens living with mental illness.

American Academy of Child and Adolescent Psychiatry (www.aacap.org) provides comprehensive descriptions of mental illnesses, as well as resources for families and a psychiatric locator.

Bring Change 2 Mind (bringchange2mind.org) is a nonprofit that seeks to change the stigma surrounding mental health issues. Provides personal stories and ways to get involved. Also, they have a helpline: (800) 273-TALK (8255).

Active Minds (http://activeminds.org) is a group that focuses on mental health issues on college campuses.

Child Mind Institute (www.childmind.org) provides clinical care and research for the mental health of children.

Healthy Minds. Healthy Lives. (apahealthyminds.blogspot.com) features blog posts for teens offering resources and information about mental health.

National Federation of Families for Children's Mental Health (www. ffcmh.org) provides support to families living with mental health issues.

Teen Mental Health (teenmentalhealth.org) provides resources for teens.

Teens Health (teenshealth.org/teen/your_mind/) has articles on dealing with mental health issues.

Cope. Care. Deal. (www.copecaredeal.org) is a collection of research on the treatment and prevention of adolescent mental disorders.

Families for Depression Awareness (www.familyaware.org)

World Health Organisation (www.who.int/mental_health/ resources/child/en)

Jack.org (www.jack.org) is a Canadian organization for teens and parents.

Acknowledgments

Challenger Deep has been a labor of love, the creation of which spanned many years. First and foremost, I'd like to thank my son Brendan for his contributions; my son Jarrod for his amazing book trailers; and my daughters, Joelle and Erin, for their many insights and for being the wonderful human beings they are. My deepest gratitude to my editor, Rosemary Brosnan; associate editor, Jessica MacLeish; and everyone at HarperCollins for the amazing amount of support they have given this book. Thanks also to my assistants Barb Sobel and Jessica Widmer for keeping my life and speaking schedule on track. I'd like to thank the Orange County Fictionaires for their support and critiques through the years; NAMI, the National Alliance on Mental Illness, for being such a great resource; and finally my friends for always being there through the best and worst of times.

Thank you all! My love for you is bottomless.

NEAL SHUSTERMAN is the *New York Times* bestselling author of more than thirty award-winning books for children, teens and adults, including the Arc of a Scythe trilogy, the Unwind dystology, the Skinjacker trilogy, *Downsiders*, *Dry* and *Challenger Deep*, which won the National Book Award in America. He also writes screenplays for motion pictures and television. Neal has four children and lives in Florida.

Follow him online at www.storyman.com
or on Twitter: @NealShusterman

Arc of a Scythe 1

SCYTHE

"A true successor to The Hunger Games" Maggie Stiefvater

SCYTHE

NEAL SHUSTERMAN

What if death was the only thing left to control?

In a perfect world, the only way to die is to be gleaned by a professional scythe. When Citra and Rowan are chosen to be apprentice scythes, they know they have no option but to learn the art of killing. But the terrifying responsibility of choosing their victims is just the start...

THUNDER HEAD

It's been a year since Rowan went off-grid. Hunted
by the Scythedom, he has become an urban
legend, sniffing out corrupt scythes.

Citra, meanwhile, is forging her path as Scythe Anastasia. But
conflict amongst the scythes is growing, and when her life is
threatened, it's clear that there is a truly terrifying plot afoot.

The Thunderhead observes everything, and it does
not like what it sees. Will it intervene? Or will it simply
watch as this perfect world begins to unravel?

Arc of a Scythe 3

THE TOLL

Everything has changed in the world of the scythes. Citra and
Rowan have disappeared. The floating city of Endura is gone.
It looks like nothing else stands between Scythe Goddard
and absolute power. Now that the Thunderhead is silent, the
question remains: Is there anyone left who can stop him?

The answer lies in the Tone, the Toll
and the Thunder.